DEATH'S FACE!

Something compelled Jimmy O'Rourke to look up. He froze with fear at the sight of a Japanese soldier aiming an Arisaka rifle at him, about to pull the trigger. The Japanese soldier was too far away for Jimmy to attack, and Jimmy couldn't run from a bullet. All he could do was remain on his knees, straddling the dead Japanese soldier underneath him, and wait for the bullet to come.

The Japanese soldier tightened his finger on the trigger...

Nightmare Alley

by
John Mackie

A JOVE BOOK

Excepting basic historical events, places, and personages, this series of books is fictional, and anything that appears otherwise is coincidental and unintentional.

The principal characters are imaginary, although they might remind veterans of specific men whom they knew. The Twenty-third Infantry Regiment, in which the characters serve, is used fictitiously—it doesn't represent the real historical Twenty-third Infantry, which has distinguished itself in so many battles from the Civil War to Vietnam—but it could have been any American line regiment that fought and bled during World War II.

These novels are dedicated to the men who were there. May their deeds and gallantry never be forgotten.

NIGHTMARE ALLEY

A Jove Book/published by arrangement with
the author

PRINTING HISTORY
Jove edition/March 1985

ISBN: 0-515-08041-1

Jove books are published by The Berkley Publishing Group,
200 Madison Avenue, New York, N.Y. 10016. The words
"A JOVE BOOK" and the "J" with sunburst are trademarks
belonging to Jove Publications, Inc.

PRINTED IN THE UNITED STATES OF AMERICA

ONE . . .

Pfc. Frankie La Barbara found out about the new orders long before anyone in the Twenty-third Infantry Regiment received official notification. Frankie happened to be at division headquarters one afternoon, dozing on a bench in a corridor, when he heard a scrap of conversation between a brigadier general and a colonel who were walking by.

"They say New Guinea's got the worst health conditions in the world," the brigadier said, grim resignation in his voice.

"If we can handle Bougainville, we can handle anything," the colonel replied. "Let's go to the officers' club for a drink."

Frankie opened his eyes and recognized the officers. They were on the staff of Major General Clyde Hawkins, commanding officer of the Eighty-first Division, parent unit of the Twenty-third Regiment. The two officers might have thought Frankie wasn't paying attention, but Frankie wasn't as dumb as he looked. Frankie knew how to put two and two together, and it sounded to him as if he'd be going to New Guinea before long.

Frankie took out a package of Chesterfield cigarettes and fired one up with his Zippo lighter. He looked at the backs of

1

the officers silhouetted against the bright Hawaiian sunlight shining through the windows at the end of the corridor. Farther down he could see other officers and enlisted men coming and going. Frankie felt a sinking sensation in his stomach, because he didn't want to leave Hawaii and all those pretty girls in downtown Honolulu. He didn't want to return to the hell of the front lines.

It was May twentieth, 1944. The Eighty-first Division had been evacuated from bloody Bougainville on April fifth, after beating the shit out of the Japs there, although the Eighty-first had taken nearly sixty-five percent casualties. The survivors had been transported to Hawaii for R&R, and Frankie hoped they'd spend the rest of the war there, playing soldier in the hills of Oahu and fucking whores. Frankie thought the Eighty-first had done enough fighting. They'd been among the first Army troops to go ashore on Guadalcanal, and they'd assaulted New Georgia, in addition to goddamn Bougainville. Let somebody else do the fighting for a change.

"What's the matter with you?" asked a voice nearby.

Frankie looked up and saw First Lieutenant Dale Breckenridge, platoon leader of the Twenty-third Regiment's reconnaissance platoon, of which Frankie was a member. Frankie was so stricken by the thought of going to New Guinea that he hadn't noticed the approach of Lieutenant Breckenridge, whom he'd driven to division headquarters.

Frankie stood up, his face pale, He was from New York City, stood six feet tall, and weighed 195 pounds. "I just heard something," he said. "I heard we're going to New Guinea before long."

Lieutenant Breckenridge wrinkled his brow. He was four inches taller than Frankie, with broader shoulders and a bulky, muscular physique. People said he controlled the maniacs and ex-criminals in the recon platoon through sheer physical menace and intimidation. "Where'd you hear that?"

"General Sully and Colonel Jessup just walked by and they said it."

Lieutenant Breckenridge looked down the corridor. "I don't see them."

"They're gone now, but they were just here. Why is it that

2

nobody ever believes me? Why is it that everybody thinks I'm a fucking liar?"

"Because you *are* a fucking liar."

"Well, I'm not lying about this."

Lieutenant Breckenridge narrowed his eyes and looked at Frankie, trying to figure out what Frankie's angle was, because Frankie always was playing one angle or another. Frankie was from New York City, after all.

"Don't believe me," Frankie said with a shrug. "See if I care."

Lieutenant Breckenridge couldn't imagine what Frankie's angle might be, so he thought maybe Frankie was telling the truth. "What exactly did they say?"

"General Sully said something about New Guinea, and Colonel Jessup said we'd move out soon."

"Are you sure?"

"Yes I'm sure."

"You didn't dream it?"

"No."

Lieutenant Breckenridge wondered if the division really was going to New Guinea. He glanced at his watch. It was three o'clock in the afternoon, and he didn't have anything else to do except pick up some correspondence and bring it to Colonel Hutchins. He had time to snoop around and confirm what Frankie had told him, but it was top-secret information and nobody would tell him even if they knew. He'd have to use more subtle methods, but couldn't think of any off the top of his head.

"Did General Sully and Colonel Jessup say anything else?" Lieutenant Breckenridge asked.

"That was it," Frankie replied, "except something about going to the officers' club and getting drunk."

"Now I know you're lying. They'd never say out loud in Headquarters that they were going to get drunk."

Frankie shrugged. "They said they were gonna go to the officers' club and have a drink, but you know it won't be just one. Officers never drink just one. They'll have six or seven, and somebody'll have to carry them home afterward."

Lieutenant Breckenridge knew that Frankie La Barbara was

3

right. The two officers would probably get smashed. Lieutenant Breckenridge thought that maybe he should go to the officers' club and have a drink himself. Perhaps he would overhear something. He had plenty of time, and he wanted to know where the division would be going next, partially out of curiosity and partially because he wanted to get himself psyched up as soon as he could.

"Drive me to the officers' club, Frankie."

"I had a funny feeling that was where you'd want to go, Lieutenant."

"Shut up and move out."

"Yes, sir."

Lieutenant Breckenridge strolled toward the door, rolling his massive shoulders. He was much taller than everyone else in the corridor and reception area. He had a big head covered with light-brown hair cut short and parted on the side, and his face was scarred slightly by the acne attacks of his youth. He pushed open the door, and Frankie La Barbara followed him outside into the bright sunshine.

A lawn extended down a gentle incline from the headquarters building; then came a sidewalk and the street. Soldiers and WACs walked back and forth on the sidewalk, and military vehicles rumbled past on the street. On the other side of the street were wooden buildings painted pale yellow and flying the American flag and individual unit flags.

Frankie La Barbara sat behind the wheel of the jeep, and Lieutenant Breckenridge climbed in beside him. Frankie started the engine and backed out of the parking spot, turning the wheel and spotting a blond WAC on the sidewalk.

"Wow—looka there!"

"Keep your eyes on the road and let's go, La Barbara."

"Yes, sir."

Frankie cut the wheel and stomped on the gas pedal. The jeep accelerated down the road, and Lieutenant Breckenridge ducked behind the windshield so he could light a cigarette. He puffed until the end of the cigarette was cherry red and then leaned back in the seat, wondering if the division really would be in New Guinea in a month.

Lieutenant Breckenridge wasn't anxious to return to the front. He'd been wounded on New Georgia and again on Bou-

4

gainville, and had only recently returned to duty. He still felt dull pain in his left leg, especially when it rained. Life was easy far from the war, and he'd grown accustomed to it. He wished he didn't have to go back and fight.

He didn't even like to think about war. It was just too awful, bloody, and gruesome. So many of his men had become casualties. Even his platoon sergeant was in the hospital, recovering from wounds. The food was awful. The constant tension made you crazy. You had to shit in holes in the ground instead of nice comfortable toilets.

"Oh, fuck," Lieutenant Breckenridge said.

"What's the matter, sir?" Frankie asked.

"Shut up and keep driving."

They passed rows of barracks and saw men marching in close-order drill on parade grounds or returning from the boonies, carrying full field packs, their uniforms filthy and sweaty, their faces sagging with fatigue.

Lieutenant Breckenridge, like Frankie, had hoped the division wouldn't have to fight anymore. New divisions were arriving from the States all the time, and Lieutenant Breckenridge wanted to believe that they'd do the fighting. The Eighty-first Division had become part of the Oahu Defense Force, but that was a joke. The Hawaiian Islands were in no danger of a Japanese invasion. The Japanese were being pushed back all over the South Pacific. They'd been kicked off the Solomon Islands, and their big base at Rabaul was being starved out. The American Navy had won major victories in the Coral Sea and at Midway, and the Army had recently taken Hollandia and Aitape on New Guinea in brilliant attacks masterminded by General MacArthur himself. General MacArthur was working his way across New Guinea toward the Philippines, his ultimate goal, where he'd vowed to return someday.

Two soldiers wearing fatigue pants, combat boots, and khaki T-shirts ran into the intersection ahead, turning to face the traffic and standing at parade rest, with their feet apart and their hands clasped behind their backs. Frankie hit the brakes, which slowed down the jeep. It came to a stop in front of one of the soldiers.

The soldiers were road guards for a larger unit that approached the intersection from the right, at double-time. They all were dressed like the road guards, and they ran in step with each other, the hair on their heads shorn short and their T-shirts soaked with sweat.

Beside them ran an older man, evidently a sergeant, with thinning hair and gnarled features on his face.

"Run a mile!" he shouted.

"Run a mile!" they replied.

"Every day!"

"Every day!"

"All the way!"

"All the way!"

"One-two!"

"One-two!"

"All the way!"

"All the way!"

Lieutenant Breckenridge puffed his cigarette as he watched them pass. They were a company of infantry evidently, because other types of soldiers didn't run around like that in the middle of the day. Other soldiers were busy typing letters, fixing trucks, and doing the other things that support troops do, but the infantry was out there training all the time, getting ready for war.

The infantry company double-timed through the intersection and the road guards pulled back. Frankie shifted the jeep into first gear and drove toward the officers' club. Lieutenant Breckenridge realized he'd have to start training his recon platoon real hard if they were going back to the war. He'd double-time their asses into the ground so they'd be ready when they hit the beach on New Guinea. And he'd have to stop smoking, because cigarettes cut your wind. He took his Chesterfield out of his mouth and looked at it, telling himself that he ought to throw it away. But he decided to finish it: It would be his last one.

Frankie shifted up to third gear and then hit the brakes to make a right turn. He shifted down to second, let up the clutch, and whacked the gas pedal. The wheels of the jeep screeched as it zipped around the corner, and Lieutenant Breckenridge held the dashboard grips so he wouldn't fall into Frankie's lap.

"Slow down, you crazy bastard!" Lieutenant Breckenridge said.

6

"I'm only going thirty miles an hour."

"Take those corners slower! Where's the fire?"

Frankie sniffed and grumbled something. A fire constantly raged inside him. Frankie was high-strung; he was always chewing gum and smoking cigarettes, pacing back and forth, looking for deals, listening for news, and trying to screw anything in a skirt.

He saw a skirt on the sidewalk to his right. It was another of those blondes, and Frankie really liked blondes. She wore the white uniform of a nurse, and he really liked nurses. He hit the horn of the jeep and she turned to look. He winked and waved. Lieutenant Breckenridge wanted to punch Frankie in the mouth.

"Keep your eyes on the road, La Barbara!"

"They *are* on the road!"

Lieutenant Breckenridge blew smoke out the side of his mouth. He wondered why he'd chosen Frankie to drive him to division headquarters. He should have known he'd have trouble with Frankie La Barbara. Everybody had trouble with Frankie La Barbara, but Frankie had been nearby when Lieutenant Breckenridge had to go to division headquarters, so he'd picked Frankie absentmindedly.

My mind's going soft too, Lieutenant Breckenridge thought. *If I don't start waking up, I'm going to get my ass shot off on New Guinea.*

The officers' club, a large, manorial structure with low sloping roofs, loomed up ahead, military and civilian vehicles parked all around it. Officers could be seen swarming toward its doors, because it was approaching five o'clock in the afternoon and officers all over the post were going off duty.

A Chevrolet painted OD green backed out of a parking spot in front of the building, and Frankie slowed down so he could pull in next. The Chevrolet drove away and Frankie aimed the nose of the jeep into the spot. He shifted into neutral, hit the brakes, and turned off the engine.

"Here we are, Lieutenant."

"Wait here for me, and you'd better be here when I come out."

"You can trust me, sir. What time you think you'll be out?"

7

"I'll ask the questions, La Barbara. You just wait for me and stay out of trouble, got it?"

"I got it."

"Good."

Lieutenant Breckenridge swung his long, thick legs out of the jeep and planted his big feet on the pavement. He stood and walked toward the officers' club, pulling up his belt and tucking in his shirt, so he'd look neat. He wore green fatigues, combat boots, and a fatigue hat styled something like a baseball hat. Other officers swaggered up the sidewalk that led to the front door of the officers' club. Lieutenant Breckenridge stood out, because he was so much bigger than they.

Frankie watched him enter the officers' club and wished he could go in there, too, because that's where the nurses hung out. If he were an officer, he wouldn't even bother going into Honolulu to pick up girls. He'd just hustle the nurses in the officers' club. There were so many of them on the post. But other than the nurses, Frankie didn't suppose there was much interesting going on in the officers' club. Officers were all assholes, so what did they know about having fun? They probably just sat around and tried to act like General MacArthur while they got blind drunk.

Frankie leaned back in his seat and looked at his watch. It was quarter to five in the afternoon. He hoped Lieutenant Breckenridge wouldn't be in there too long, because Frankie didn't like to sit in one place for long. He lit another cigarette and watched the officers walk by, heading for the club. They joked and guffawed with each other, relaxing after a day of work. Some were extremely serious, as if they'd had a hard day's work, but Frankie couldn't imagine what they'd done that was so hard, because what did officers do? Just give orders and lay around. Even Lieutenant Breckenridge had become a lazy son of a bitch since the division came to Oahu. He'd gained twenty pounds, and sometimes you wouldn't see him for days at a time.

Frankie spotted a blonde to his right on the sidewalk. He straightened up and focused on her. She was alone, wearing a white uniform, and he realized she was the nurse he had passed a little while ago. Frankie wished he could pin the bars of a lieutenant to his lapels, because nurses normally wouldn't go out with ordinary enlisted men; but Frankie didn't consider himself an ordinary enlisted man. He knew he was good-looking, because he'd always had lots of girl friends back in the States. Women often told him that he resembled the popular actor Victor Mature. He'd never had trouble getting laid in his life until he wound up in the Army and was sent to places where there were few women. He had supreme confidence in his masculine attractiveness, and had learned long ago that even the ragpicker who sleeps underneath the bridge can fuck the queen in the castle if he just has confidence.

Frankie looked in the rearview mirror and adjusted his fatigue hat at a rakish angle. Then he climbed out of the jeep and walked to its front, then leaned against the grill. No officers were headed in his direction; only the nurse. She glanced at him as she approached, then looked away.

Frankie snapped to attention and threw her a smart salute. "Hi," he said.

She looked at him, looked away, looked at him again, and then looked away again. Frankie wanted to chase after her, but didn't dare do that in front of the officers' club. He had to play it cool; otherwise he might get court-martialed for some weird offense.

He put his hands in his pockets and watched her back as she walked toward the door of the officers' club. She had a real nice figure and an especially nice ass. Frankie thought a woman's ass was the most important part of a woman's anatomy, aesthetically speaking.

"Take your hands out of your pockets, soldier! Where in hell do you think you are!"

Frankie pulled his hands out of his pockets and saw a major approaching on his left. The major had a five o'clock shadow on his face and a nose like a button.

"What are you doing here, soldier!"

Frankie snapped to attention. "I just drove my platoon leader here, sir! I'm waiting for him, sir! He should be right back, sir!"

The major looked Frankie up and down. "If you're waiting for him, you'd better wait like a soldier! And leave those nurses alone—understand?"

"Yes, sir!"

"As you were!"

The officer turned around and walked toward the front door of the officers' club. Frankie returned to the front seat of the jeep, sat, and leaned back. "Fucking officers," Frankie muttered. "If I ever bump into that son of a bitch on a dark night in Honolulu, I'll beat the piss out of him."

TWO . . .

Officers were lined up four deep around the bar. Inside the jukebox, Benny Goodman was playing his clarinet. Other officers sat around tables. A big picture window overlooked the tennis courts, where men and women banged balls around. Three bartenders rushed back and forth behind the bar, and Lieutenant Breckenridge waited his turn while glancing around, seeing who was there, finally spotting General Sully and Colonel Jessup sitting at a table against one of the walls. They looked awfully glum, which tended to substantiate Frankie La Barbara's story. New Guinea was supposed to be the shithole of the war.

"What'll you have?" asked the bartender.

"A whiskey and soda," Lieutenant Breckenridge replied.

The bartender scooped ice cubes into a glass and then poured the whiskey, sending up a thin trail of condensation smoke. Lieutenant Breckenridge wondered how he could get close to General Sully and Colonel Jessup so he could overhear what they were saying. All the tables near them were full. But there had to be a way. Maybe he could walk past real slow, even say hello to them, inviting himself to sit down. He knew them

11

somewhat because he was a minor celebrity in the division. Before the war he'd been first-string fullback at the University of Virginia.

The bartender placed the glass of whiskey and soda in front of Lieutenant Breckenridge, who paid him and then stepped back from the bar so somebody else could order. He sipped the drink; it tasted just right. Licking his lips, he gazed over the heads of the other officers at General Sully and Colonel Jessup. *I might as well just walk over there,* he said to himself. *What the fuck.*

"Hi, Dale."

Lieutenant Breckenridge turned around and saw Lieutenant Utsler, who was on the staff of General Sharkey, the operations officer at division headquarters.

"Hi, Jack. How're you doing?"

"Not bad. How about you?"

"Can't complain."

Lieutenant Breckenridge looked down at Lieutenant Utsler, because Lieutenant Utsler was only five feet eight inches tall. Lieutenant Utsler had graduated from Yale summa cum laude, which was why he had a soft staff job, whereas Lieutenant Breckenridge had barely squeaked through the University of Virginia, earmarking him for the good old infantry.

"Say, Jack," Lieutenant Breckenridge said, "I heard a rumor today and I wonder if you know anything about it."

"I don't know anything about anything," Lieutenant Utsler said, taking a step backward and frowning.

Lieutenant Breckenridge grabbed him by the arm. "Let's go someplace quiet where we can talk."

"I'm waiting for somebody!"

"It won't take long."

Lieutenant Breckenridge pulled Lieutenant Utsler away from the bar and manhandled him gently toward a vacant stretch of wood-paneled wall.

"You're hurting me!" Lieutenant Utsler said, trying to wriggle out of Lieutenant Breckenridge's grasp.

"Calm down."

They reached the wall and Lieutenant Breckenridge turned Lieutenant Utsler loose.

"Listen," said Lieutenant Breckenridge, bringing his face

close to Lieutenant Utsler. "I heard today that we're going to New Guinea. Is that so?"

Lieutenant Utsler's eyes bounced around like Ping-Pong balls. "I told you that I don't know anything about anything!"

"Oh, yes you do. You're on the operations staff, which means you know everything about everything. We're going, aren't we?"

"I don't know anything about anything, I told you!"

Lieutenant Breckenridge examined Lieutenant Utsler's face for those telltale twitches and grimaces that indicate a lie, and he saw them. Lieutenant Breckenridge groaned. "It's true. We're going to New Guinea."

"I didn't say we're going to New Guinea!" Then Utsler glanced around nervously, because he was afraid somebody might have heard him. He raised his face and whispered: *"I didn't say we're going to New Guinea."*

"But you didn't say we're not going, either."

"I don't know anything about anything!"

"C'mon, Jack, you can tell me. Everybody's gonna know pretty soon anyway, so what's the difference?"

"Loose lips sink ships."

"Hey, Jack," Lieutenant Breckenridge said, "do I look like a Jap spy? I'm only Lieutenant Breckenridge from the fighting Twenty-third, and you're talking to me as if I were Tojo."

"You might tell the wrong person. Loose lips sink ships."

Lieutenant Breckenridge now was certain that the division was going to New Guinea. The next objective was to find out when. A blond nurse came into his field of vision. She was just arriving, and her name was Diane Latham. Lieutenant Breckenridge knew her slightly because she worked on the ward where Sergeant Butsko, his former platoon sergeant, was laid up.

"Hey, Jack," Lieutenant Breckenridge said, "you wanna get laid?"

The change of subject was too quick for Lieutenant Utsler. "Huh?"

"I asked you if you wanna get laid."

"I always wanna get laid."

"Turn around casually and look at that blond nurse over there."

13

Lieutenant Utsler took his time about it, shifting his feet and glancing in the direction Lieutenant Breckenridge had indicated.

"Like her?" Lieutenant Breckenridge asked.

"She's quite attractive."

"She's a great fuck too," Lieutenant Breckenridge lied. He didn't know anything about Nurse Latham, but he was trying to con Lieutenant Utsler.

"You're such a crude bastard," Utsler said.

"She's a great fuck anyway."

"How would you know?"

"How do you think I know? Would you like to meet her?"

"I wouldn't mind."

Lieutenant Breckenridge leaned closer. "When are we going to New Guinea?"

"You son of a bitch, you're blackmailing me!"

"She's real good in bed, Jack. And she's easy."

"She's probably waiting for her boyfriend."

"She's waiting for *you,* Jack. You can be her boyfriend—if you want. You're just her type. Believe me, I know what I'm talking about."

Lieutenant Utsler looked at the blonde and wondered what it would be like to bury his head in her lovely breasts.

"When are we going to New Guinea?" Lieutenant Breckenridge asked.

"You sure you're not going to tell anybody?"

"I'm sure. Besides, we're all going to know pretty soon anyway, so what does it matter?"

"That's true."

"When are we going to New Guinea, Jack?"

"You say she's a real easy fuck?"

"She'll be real easy for you, because you're her type."

"How do you know I'm her type?"

"Trust me, I know. How soon are we moving out?"

"About a month, but for Chrissakes, don't tell anybody."

"You can trust me. Where are we going in New Guinea?"

"We don't know yet. Probably somewhere west of Hollandia."

"Thanks, Jack. You're a pal. I'll never forget this."

"Now you can introduce me to the blonde. Jesus, she's

14

surrounded by guys already. We'll never get through them."

"Don't worry about it. You just stay here and I'll bring her over."

"She's a real easy fuck, you say?"

"All you got to do is get her alone someplace and put her hand on it. That gets her real hot and bothered. She'll take it from there."

"You're sure?"

"I wouldn't lie to you, Jack. Why are you suspicious, for crying out loud?"

"Because you're a shady character, Dale."

"Me? A shady character? Why am I a shady character?"

"Because of the enlisted men you hang around with. They're all a bunch of criminals and wise guys, and you must be just like them, since you get along with them so well."

"Hey, I don't hang around with them," Lieutenant Breckenridge said. "They're not my buddies. They're my *men*. I'm their *platoon leader*. You know what it's like, Jack. You're in the same Army I'm in—I think. You should understand, but anyway, you just stand right where you're standing and try to appear to be a nice guy while I go get Diane. That's her name—Diane. Be calm and don't come in your pants or anything like that when I bring her over, because she likes guys who're relaxed and sure of themselves. Got it?"

"Got it."

"Good. I'll be right back. And smile, for Chrissakes. Nobody wants to meet a sourpuss."

Jack smiled, revealing straight white teeth, but he was nervous and felt awkward, and his lips did funny things. Lieutenant Breckenridge walked toward Diane Latham, who was standing in the middle of a bunch of officers, because male officers outnumbered nurses and WAC officers by forty to one in the officers' club. Lieutenant Breckenridge pushed his way through the throng and put himself into her line of vision.

"Hi, Lieutenant Latham," he said. "Remember me?"

She smiled. "Sure. You're the one who visits Sergeant Butsko every day."

He placed his arm around her shoulder and pulled her away from the others. "I have to talk to you about something important," he said, a note of urgency in his voice.

15

"What is it?" she asked, surprised, because she hardly knew Lieutenant Breckenridge.

"It'll only take a moment."

The other officers said "Wait a minute!" and "Where are you going?" but Lieutenant Breckenridge maneuvered Diane Latham away from them and stood with her next to one of the three-foot-square wood-paneled pillars that held up the roof.

Diane Latham was amazed by the ease with which he was manipulating her, and knew she was being manipulated, but was curious about what he had to say.

"Listen," he said, "do you see that officer leaning against the wall over there?"

"What officer?" she asked.

"The one behind me."

"You mean the one grinning like a hyena?"

"That one."

"What about him?"

"He's in trouble."

"He doesn't look like he's in trouble."

"Well, he is. The smile is his last desperate stab at sanity."

"What's wrong with him?"

"He needs to talk to a female. He's very lonely, and he'll be shipping out pretty soon. He might be dead this time next week. Will you talk to him for me?"

"Why doesn't he find somebody to talk to on his own?"

"He's a little shy."

"He doesn't look shy."

"Well, he is."

"Why doesn't he go to one of the whorehouses in Honolulu?"

"Because he's from a fine old Massachusetts family, and people like him don't do things like that. Besides, he wants to talk to a decent girl, like you, not one of those raunchy old whores."

She was drinking a whiskey sour and sipped some of the foam. "I've heard that some of those whores are as beautiful as movie stars."

"But they've got raunchy hearts. They're not nice girls, like you."

"What makes you think I'm so nice?"

16

"Because Sergeant Butsko says so, and I can tell just by looking at you."

"Well, you look nice too."

"I do?"

"Yes."

"Well...ah...I...listen, please talk to that poor officer over there for a while, will you? Just a few minutes. He'd really appreciate it, and so would I."

"You would?"

"Of course I would."

"He looks awfully strange."

"You'd look awfully strange too if they were going to ship you to the front lines in about a week. Will you do it?"

"Okay, but only for a little while."

"Good. Thank you. I really appreciate it."

She stood as if waiting for him to say something else, and he realized she wanted him to ask her out. *She likes me!* he realized. He thought it amazing how some women fell for you when you least expected it, and other women wouldn't give you the right time of day.

"Listen," he said, "what are you doing later?"

"Nothing."

"Let's have a drink together."

"What time?"

"I'll meet you here at eight o'clock."

"I don't want to stay here that long. Meet me at the nurses' residence."

"Fine. Let me have your address and phone number."

She told him the information, and he wrote it in the little note pad he always carried in his shirt pocket.

"I'll see you later," he said with a wink. "Be gentle with that officer over there."

"What did you say his name was?"

"Jack Utsler. Lieutenant Jack Utsler. I've got to be going. Be good and stay sweet. 'Bye."

"'Bye."

Lieutenant Breckenridge walked swiftly toward the door and didn't look back over his shoulder to find out what was going on. He didn't want to know what was going on. Hordes of officers were in the anteroom and he sidestepped them, feeling guilty for lying to the nice nurse, but he'd had to find out if they were going to New Guinea and when they were going. Colonel Hutchins would want to know as soon as possible. So would everybody else.

He stepped outside. The sun was a big red ball dropping toward the horizon. He wondered what Jack was saying to the nurse and what the nurse was saying to Jack. What a mess that was going to be. He decided he shouldn't see her later at eight o'clock as he'd promised, because she'd probably shoot him dead. On the other hand, if he didn't keep his date with her tonight, he'd see her tomorrow in the hospital when he went to see Butsko, his good old platoon sergeant, whom he visited every day. Maybe he'd have to go to the hospital when she wasn't on duty. He'd call and find out what the schedule was for that ward. Yes, that was the way to go about it. And he wouldn't see her tonight, because he didn't want to get shot.

He approached the jeep and saw Frankie dozing behind the wheel.

"Wake up, La Barbara!"

Frankie jumped three inches into the air. "Huh! What!"

"It's me." Lieutenant Breckenridge climbed into the jeep. "Let's go."

"Go where?"

"Back to regiment. Hurry up."

"Yes, sir."

Frankie backed the jeep out of its parking spot and drove off, heading toward the headquarters of the Twenty-third Infantry Regiment.

They arrived fifteen minutes later. Lieutenant Breckenridge got out of the jeep; Frankie kept going, to check the jeep in at the motor pool.

Lieutenant Breckenridge looked at his watch as he approached the wooden building, which was painted pale yellow, like everything else on the post. It was six-thirty, and the molten sun had not yet set behind the horizon. The sun cast long shadows from the palm trees planted in front of the headquarters building, and a dog yapped in the distance.

Lieutenant Breckenridge entered the orderly room, and Lieutenant Weslowska sat behind the sergeant major's desk.

18

Lieutenant Weslowska was the officer of the day, which meant he had to sit at the desk all night and handle any problems that might come up. The sergeant major and his various aides had gone home for the night.

"Hi, Bob," Lieutenant Breckenridge said. "The old man still in?"

"Yep."

"Tell him I want to talk to him about something important."

"I think he's drunk back there."

"He's always drunk back there. So what?"

Lieutenant Weslowska picked up the phone, pressed a button, waited a few moments, and then mumbled into the mouthpiece. He waited a few moments more, then hung up the phone.

"He said he'll see you now, and he sounded like he just woke up."

Lieutenant Breckenridge pushed open the door, walked down the corridor, and knocked softly on the door at the end of the corridor.

"Come in!" said the voice inside.

Lieutenant Breckenridge entered the office. The bamboo curtains were drawn, and in the dimness he saw Colonel Bob Hutchins lying on his leather-covered sofa, his telephone on the floor beside him. The faint odor of whiskey was in the air.

"What's on your mind, son?" Colonel Hutchins asked, not bothering to get up. His voice was slurred and his belt had been loosened to provide some breathing space for his big potbelly.

Lieutenant Breckenridge held up the pack of mail and correspondence he'd picked up at division headquarters. "I'm just getting back from Division, and while I was there I heard a rumor that we'll be shipping out to New Guinea in about a month."

"Who told you that?"

"One of my friends who works there."

"Do you believe him?"

"I think so. Also, Frankie La Barbara heard General Sully and Colonel Jessup talking about it."

Colonel Hutchins yawned. "I figured they'd be sending us back into the war pretty soon. Turn on that light on my desk, will you?"

"Yes, sir."

Lieutenant Breckenridge walked to the desk and flicked the switch on the lamp. Colonel Hutchins stood, tied up his belt, and shuffled across the room, his graying hair mussed and his features puffy. His desk was piled high with documents and maps, and he sat on his chair, shuffling through the papers. Finally he pulled out a map of the southwest Pacific and looked down at New Guinea.

"Your friend say where we're going on New Guinea?" Colonel Hutchins asked.

"He figured it would be somewhere west of Hollandia."

"That makes sense." Colonel Hutchins sniffed, then wiped his nose with the back of his hand. "We'll be shipping out in about a month, you said?"

"Yes, sir."

"That's not much time." He looked down at the map and placed his forefinger on Hollandia. "It's hard to say exactly where General MacArthur would want us to go next. I imagine he's looking for the best possible places to jump off from when the time comes to invade the Philippines. We could go in anywhere along the north coast from Hollandia to the Vogelkop Peninsula."

"I imagine he's looking for good airfields."

"If the Hollandia operation is any indication of what's to come, he'll try to take areas that are weakly defended." Colonel Hutchins sighed and dropped onto his chair. "We don't know what he knows, so we can't figure out what he's going to do. Want a drink?"

"Don't mind if I do."

Colonel Hutchins opened a drawer in his desk and took out a bottle of one-hundred-proof Old Taylor and two glasses. He poured three fingers of bourbon into a glass, then pushed the bottle and other glass toward Lieutenant Breckenridge, who poured himself a tall drink and sat down. Colonel Hutchins gazed at the deep-amber fluid he swished around in his glass. The office was silent and the sun was setting outside. Lieutenant Breckenridge sipped some bourbon, and it was very fine, a far cry from the white lightning brewed on Bougainville by the Headquarters Company mess sergeant.

Both men thought about New Guinea, and everything they'd

heard about it was bad. It was supposed to be the asshole of the war. The colonel and the lieutenant drank in silence, because there was nothing to say. They were going to war again, and each of them wondered if he'd be alive when the last shot was fired.

Frankie La Barbara charged into the barracks and saw the guys getting ready to go to town. Pfc. Morris Shilansky, the former bank robber from Boston, combed his curly black hair in front of the full-length mirror near the door. The Reverend Billie Jones, an itinerant preacher from Georgia before the war, buttoned up his colorful Hawaiian shirt emblazoned with dancing girls, suns, and palm trees. Corporal Lupe Gomez, the ex-pachuco from Los Angeles, shined his shoes. Pfc. Jimmy O'Rourke, the former movie stuntman from Hollywood, admired his smile in the small circular mirror he kept in his footlocker. Craig Delane, the rich guy from New York, dressed himself in the spotless white linen suit that he always wore to town.

Everybody looked at Frankie, who burst into their midst.

"Guess what!" Frankie screamed. "We're going back to the front!"

Craig Delane's hand froze on his genuine silk necktie. "Oh, God—no!"

Morris Shilansky pulled himself away from the mirror. "How do you know that?" he asked Frankie.

"I heard it at Division!"

"Are you sure?"

"I'm sure."

"When are we going?"

"About a month."

Craig Delane collapsed onto his bunk, closed his eyes, and groaned: "I don't want to go back to the war. I hate the war."

Corporal Gomez jumped into the air and stretched out his arms. "Why us? We done enough fighting, for Chrissakes!"

Morris Shilansky pulled out his pack of Camels and thrust one in his mouth. "I'm goin' AWOL right fucking now!" he said. "Anybody wanna come with me?"

"I'll go with you!" said Frankie La Barbara. "Just wait a minute until I get out of this uniform!"

21

The Reverend Billie Jones pulled out his handy pocket Bible. "I think we oughta all get down on our knees and say a few words to the Lord."

Frankie La Barbara turned on him. "Fuck you in your ass, you crazy holy-roller bastard! This ain't no time for horseshit!"

"Horseshit! You call the Lord horseshit?"

The Reverend Billie Jones stuffed his Bible into his back pocket and advanced toward Frankie La Barbara with the clear intention of doing him bodily harm. Frankie La Barbara felt better instantly, because the prospect of punching somebody in the chops always raised his spirits. Jimmy O'Rourke, the movie stuntman, jumped in between them, because that's what Clark Gable would have done.

"Settle down, you two!" he said. "Do you wanna get Sergeant Cameron out here?" The mouth of the Reverend Billie Jones was a grim line, and Frankie La Barbara's eyes glittered with excitement as both men raised their fists and prepared to go to war even before they arrived in New Guinea.

The door to Sergeant Cameron's private room off the corridor banged open, and Sergeant Cameron, attired in his khaki shorts, charged into the main room of the barracks. "What the fuck is going on here now!"

The Reverend Billie Jones and Frankie La Barbara stopped in their tracks and lowered their hands.

"Nothing's going on here, Sarge," the Reverend Billie Jones said, trying to smile.

"That's right," Frankie said, "we're just going back to the front in about a month, that's all."

Sergeant Cameron blinked. He was tall and lanky, with red hair, large ears, and a nose like a potato. "We're going back to the front?"

"That's right."

"Says who?"

"Says me."

"Who the fuck are you?"

"I'm the guy who just got the straight dope at Division. Lieutenant Breckenridge knows it too. He's telling Colonel Hutchins all about it right now."

Sergeant Cameron staggered backward, as if someone had punched him in the stomach. "Oh, shit." He sat on the nearest footlocker and wheezed.

The barracks fell silent. Outside, there were shouts of laughter as other soldiers headed for town, but the men from the recon platoon had fallen into a deep depression. They remembered buddies who'd died on Guadalcanal, New Georgia, and Bougainville, and also remembered wounds they'd sustained themselves. Every one of them had been wounded somewhere along the line, and some of the most illustrious members of the recon platoon were still in the hospital, recovering from bullets, shrapnel, and bayonet stabs received on Bougainville.

"Them fucking Japs!" Sergeant Cameron said.

"Pagan bastards!" added the Reverend Billie Jones, whose closest friend, Private Homer Gladley from Kansas, had been shot to death on Bougainville.

"Slant-eyed cocksuckers!" said Frankie La Barbara, sitting on his bunk and reaching for his pack of Chesterfield cigarettes.

Corporal Gomez pulled out his switchblade knife and pressed the button. The blade flashed out and he whipped it through the air. "I cut their fucking throats."

Morris Shilansky wondered where to run and hide after he went AWOL. Craig Delane felt certain that he would die on New Guinea, because he believed in the law of averages, and the law of averages said that front-line infantry soldiers didn't last long. Jimmy O'Rourke, who had black hair and wore a Clark Gable–style mustache, wondered if he should shoot himself in the foot.

"I need a drink," said Sergeant Cameron.

"Me, too," said Frankie La Barbara, moving to his footlocker and taking out a fifth of Jim Beam. He unscrewed the top, drank some down, and tossed the bottle to Sergeant Cameron.

Nobody felt like going to town anymore. The men could hear the rattle of Japanese machine guns and the dull cough of Japanese knee mortars. The men passed the bottle of Jim Beam around, and when they were finished, Craig Delane broke out a bottle of Black & White Scotch.

The men from the recon platoon proceeded to get rip-roaring drunk.

THREE . . .

It was evening in the post hospital, and Colonel Hutchins burped as he made his way down the dark corridor. It was after nine o'clock, and the lights had been dimmed so the sick and wounded could catch up on their sleep. Colonel Hutchins had dressed himself in his tan class A uniform, complete with necktie tucked in under the third button of his shirt. He carried his cunt cap in his left hand and approached the nurses' station.

"Hello, ladies," he said with a cheery smile.

"Hello, Colonel Hutchins," they replied, because he was a daily visitor and they knew him well.

"Sergeant Butsko is in the solarium, I assume?"

"Yes, he is," said one of the nurses, "and he's been a real problem today. He wants to get out of the hospital, but he's not well enough yet."

"I'll reprimand him, if you like."

"Oh, no!" said another nurse. "Don't do that!"

"No!" agreed another nurse. "Don't tell him we said anything!"

Colonel Hutchins grinned; evidently Butsko was terrorizing the nurses. "I'll take care of everything," he said. "Don't worry about a thing."

Colonel Hutchins turned away and walked down the corridor to the brightly lit solarium at the end. It was there that soldiers who weren't too sick stayed up late, playing cards and listening to the radio. Butsko could usually be found in the biggest poker game, gambling for the highest stakes, with chips showing on the table because gambling for real money was prohibited in Army hospitals.

Colonel Hutchins entered the solarium and headed for the biggest card game, expecting to find Butsko there, but instead saw Butsko sitting in his wheelchair, smoking a cigar and looking out the window, his back to Colonel Hutchins. Stars twinkled in the sky outside the window, and lights in buildings glowed brightly.

Colonel Hutchins picked up a chair, carried it to Sergeant Butsko, and placed it beside him. Butsko turned toward the sound. He was a big, bulky man with straight black hair and a face etched with scars, thirty-five years old, but appearing ten years older.

"Hi, Colonel," he said.

"How're you feeling today, Butsko?" Colonel Hutchins asked, sitting beside him.

"I can't take it here anymore. I got to get out before I go completely psycho."

"How's your leg?"

"I can walk on it, kind of."

"What the hell is *that* supposed to mean?"

"It means I'm not completely crippled and I can get around."

"But you're not ready for duty yet, are you?"

"Light duty, maybe."

"What do the doctors say?"

Butsko *harumph*ed. "They say I'm not ready to be released, but what do they know? They wanted to cut this leg off once, the fucking pill-rollers. I hate their guts."

"Calm down. Save it for the Japs."

"What Japs? I don't see any Japs."

"The regiment's going back to the war," Colonel Hutchins said.

Butsko turned to look at Colonel Hutchins. "We are?"

"Yes."

"It official?"

26

"Not yet, but it will be soon."

"Where are we going?"

"To New Guinea, and don't say *we*. It looks like you won't have to go. Consider yourself lucky."

Butsko thought for a few seconds and smiled as the realization dawned on him. "That's right," he said. "I won't have to go."

"Thank your lucky stars."

Butsko looked out the window at the stars. "I didn't know I had some lucky ones, but I guess I do. Thank you, lucky stars."

Colonel Hutchins chuckled as he lit a cigarette. He blew smoke into the air and shook his head. "I must be crazy, but you know, Butsko, in a way I'll be glad to go back to the war. Garrison life can get a man down. If we have one more of those silly chickenshit inspections, I think I'm gonna shoot a general."

"Shoot one for me," Butsko said. "Shoot two."

"Those fucking pompous bastards, sniffing around for dust on windowsills and piss stains on toilet bowls. Is this supposed to be a janitor Army, or is it supposed to be a fighting Army?"

"Don't talk to me about it," Butsko said. "I get sick to my stomach."

Colonel Hutchins stopped talking and puffed his cigarette. At the big poker table a soldier with an arm in a sling raised the dealer twenty dollars and called his hand. A nurse entered the solarium, carrying a tray of pills and syrups. Butsko looked out the window and wondered what his wife was doing just then. She hadn't visited him for three days. *I know what she's doing*, Butsko thought darkly. *She's fucking some other son of a bitch.*

"You know, Butsko," Colonel Hutchins said, "ever since I heard the news about going back to the war, I haven't known whether to be pissed off or happy. I guess I actually feel a little bit on both sides. In a peculiar way I'm looking forward to going back to the war. Although I hate war, I also like war. Have you ever felt that way, Butsko?"

"Sure," Butsko replied. "War sure as hell relieves the boredom, don't it?"

"Sure as hell does."

"The main problem is that it can also relieve you of your life."

"That's true."

Butsko shrugged. "There's no point in worrying about it, because you don't have no choice. If we don't stop the Japs out here, we'll have to stop them in San Francisco and Los Angeles. Somebody's got to do the dirty work, and it's us— or I should say *you*, because I'm gonna sit this one out."

Colonel Hutchins puffed his cigarette and thought about what Butsko had said. A chubby little brunette nurse approached them, carrying her tray of pills and stuff.

"Time for your medication, Sergeant Butsko," she said.

"Shove it up your ass," Butsko replied.

"Come on, now, Sergeant," she said cheerily. "Take your pills like a man."

"Fuck you."

Colonel Hutchins felt embarrassed, because he was an officer and so was the nurse, but Butsko was only an enlisted man.

"Take the pills, Butsko," he said firmly. "That's an order."

Butsko grinned. "Pulling rank on me, huh?"

"That's right."

"Gimme the pills," Butsko said to the nurse.

She handed him the little cup of pills, and he tossed them into his mouth, then accepted the cup of water and washed them down.

"I think there's saltpeter in these pills," Butsko complained, "so's I can't get a hard-on and screw any of these nurses."

The nurse smiled and stepped away. "Don't flatter yourself, Sergeant. What nurse would want you?"

Butsko smiled and turned to Colonel Hutchins. "Spunky little bitch, ain't she?"

The nurse walked away. Butsko burped as the pills went down. He wondered why they kept giving him pills, because the pain wasn't so bad anymore. He didn't trust doctors. He thought they were all assholes. "Say, you didn't bring your flask with you today, did you, Colonel?"

"Sure did, Sergeant."

"Pass it over here, will you, sir?"

Colonel Hutchins glanced around to make sure no nurses were watching him, then reached into his hip pocket for his trusty old flask.

The street lamps shone on Lieutenant Breckenridge as he walked toward the nurses' residence. He didn't put his hands in his pockets because he couldn't be sure he wouldn't run into one of those officers who had conniption fits whenever they saw a soldier with his hands in his pockets.

He was on his way to see Nurse Latham, and he knew he was making a mistake, but she had a gorgeous face and a figure that would make a pastor burn down his church. She'd be fancy as a movie star if she wore the right makeup and styled her hair like Veronica Lake.

She was going to be mad at him; he knew that. Jack Utsler would have tried to get into her pants, and she wouldn't be happy about it. Or maybe she would be. Maybe she was naked in the grass with him right now, bouncing up and down on his dork.

Lieutenant Breckenridge didn't think she was bouncing up and down on Jack's dork. She was probably sharpening a knife up in her room, waiting for Lieutenant Breckenridge to show up. Actually she probably thought he'd never show up, after what he had done. But he was going to show up. It was a challenge to him. He considered himself an intelligent fellow and thought he could talk his way through anything.

He walked up the sidewalk to the nurses' residence, and he was wearing his class A uniform with necktie knotted flawlessly and cunt cap low over his eyes and tilted slightly to the side. On the right front of his cunt cap his first lieutenant's silver bar gleamed; he looked like one sharp young officer, ready to take on the world.

He entered the lobby of the residence and walked toward the curved mahogany reception desk.

"Hello," he said to the elderly gray-haired lady sitting behind the desk. "I'm here to see Lieutenant Diane Latham."

"Your name?"

"Lieutenant Dale Breckenridge."

"One moment, please."

The woman plugged a line into the switchboard, waited, said something. Lieutenant Breckenridge took off his cunt cap, because he'd remembered that men are supposed to remove their hats indoors. *I used to have good manners once,* he said to himself. *The Army is ruining me.*

"She'll be right down," the gray-haired lady said. "Have a seat."

"Thank you, ma'am."

Lieutenant Breckenridge sauntered away from the desk and sat on one of the sofas in the lobby. A young naval officer sat on a chair on the other side of the room, and a middle-aged Army officer puffed a pipe on another sofa.

Lieutenant Breckenridge took out a cigarette, although he'd sworn not to smoke anymore. Tomorrow he'd stop, first thing in the morning, but you couldn't expect a man to stop smoking cigarettes after he'd been smoking all day. He lit up the cigarette. He wasn't nervous at all. When a woman has you dead to rights, the only thing to do is deny everything and tough it out. That tactic had worked for him in the past, usually, and he was certain it would work again. Lieutenant Breckenridge may have had many faults, but lack of confidence was not one of them.

A young brunette nurse entered the lobby from the back of the building and walked toward the young naval officer, who snapped to attention, his face blushing. They muttered to each other and he took her arm, leading her toward the front door. Lieutenant Breckenridge could see the young naval officer's face twitching slightly, because he was nervous. Lieutenant Breckenridge wanted to tell him that women were only people, like men, and they like to fuck just as much once you get them going.

The problem was getting them going. Lieutenant Breckenridge didn't think that was so hard. If the average woman would agree to go out with you, she'd probably fuck you if you played your cards right. It might take awhile, but sooner or later she'd give in.

An older nurse entered the lobby, and the Army major smoking the pipe rose to meet her. He had a big nose and a suave manner as he took the nurse's arm. *Now that guy's gonna get laid tonight,* Lieutenant Breckenridge thought. *I bet he'll have her pants off within the hour.*

He heard footsteps approaching and turned around. It was Lieutenant Diane Latham, wearing her khaki skirt and shirt and her khaki cunt cap. As he stood, Lieutenant Breckenridge wondered if women in the military called their cunt caps *cunt caps* too. The thought amused him and he smiled.

"Hi," he said. "Nice to see you."

"Nice to see you too."

"Let's take a walk."

"I have a car," she said. "Want to go for a ride?"

"Sure."

Lieutenant Breckenridge didn't take her arm, because he didn't know her that well yet and didn't want to scare her, although she didn't appear to be the type who was easily scared. He indicated the door with his right hand and she joined him as he headed for it. He opened the door for her and they stepped outside.

"Lovely night," she said.

"Yes, it's very beautiful."

"I didn't think you'd come," she told him as they walked down the sidewalk.

"What made you think that?" he asked, lighting a fresh cigarette with the butt of his old one.

"Some men make promises they don't intend to keep."

"When I say something, you can build a house on it." Lieutenant Breckenridge thought of Sergeant Butsko at that moment, because he'd learned that bullshit line from him.

"Really?" she asked.

"Yes, ma'am."

"I thought so," she replied, smiling sweetly. "There appears to be something decent about you."

"Well, I'm not that decent."

She laughed. "I hope not."

They walked around the residence building and headed for the parking lot in back. *There's something wrong here*, Lieutenant Breckenridge thought. *She's being so nice. Why isn't she saying anything about Jack Utsler? What happened with her and him?* He decided to elicit the information in the coolest possible way.

"You look lovely tonight," he said.

31

"Thank you very much. So do you."

"Your uniform becomes you."

She turned to him and smiled. "Yours becomes you too."

"It was very kind of you to talk to that friend of mine at the officers' club . . . Lieutenant Utsler?"

"It was the least I could do for the poor guy, since he was going back to the front and all."

"There were no problems, I hope."

"Not really. He got a little fresh, but we have to expect that sort of thing, don't we?"

He chortled. "Well, *I* don't expect that sort of thing."

She glanced at him coyly. "Girls never get fresh with you?"

"Not yet."

"Well, you never know what might happen to you one of these days."

"Life is full of surprises, I suppose."

They entered the parking lot. Cars gleamed in the light of the street lamps, and he said to himself: *Evidently, Utsler didn't make as much of an idiot of himself as I'd thought.*

"It's this car over here," she said, walking toward a yellow 1936 Packard convertible in immaculate condition.

"That's your car?" he asked.

"That's it. Help me take the top down, or does wind in your face bother you?"

"I love convertibles."

She unlocked the door and he helped her unfasten the canvas roof from the top of the windshield, folding the roof backward. The chromium on the instrument panel shone in the dim light, and he saw the big letter *A* affixed to the windshield, which indicated that she could get the maximum allotment of gasoline for the car.

"Where'd you get the car?" he asked.

"My father gave it to me."

Gee, thought Lieutenant Breckenridge, opening the door on the driver's side for her. *Her father must be rich.*

"Would you like to drive?" she asked.

"Could I?"

"Of course."

She handed him the keys, then sat behind the wheel and slid across the front seat to the passenger side. He dropped into the driver's position and found the lever underneath the seat, pushing back so he'd have enough room for his long legs.

"I haven't driven a car like this for a long time," he said.

"Have fun."

He inserted the key into its slot. "Where shall we go?"

"I know a real pretty place that overlooks the ocean near here. That sound okay?"

"Sounds fine."

"Drive out of the parking lot and take a left."

He started up the Packard, and the straight-eight engine purred softly. He backed out of the parking spot and headed toward the exit. Overhead the full moon shone on him; the man in the moon seemed to be smiling. *I'm going to fuck this girl*, he said to himself, *and I just know it's going to be a great experience. She is obviously crazy about me. This is my lucky day.*

He drove out of the parking lot and took a left, accelerating down the road. Soldiers turned to stare at the beautiful yellow car, and Lieutenant Breckenridge felt like he was on top of the world.

"It's really nice to drive a car again," he said.

"I'm glad you like it." She opened her purse and took out a package of Old Golds. "Want a cigarette?"

"Yes, please."

"I'll light it for you."

She placed two cigarettes in her mouth, bent low behind the dashboard, lit both with the flame of her Zippo lighter, and placed one of the cigarettes between his lips.

He could taste her saliva on the cigarette, and it made him feel intimate with her, arousing him sexually. He thought that her sweet little ass usually sat where his ass was sitting just then, and that turned him on even more. *I'm going to fuck the jelly out of her beans*, he thought. *She'll never forget me for the rest of her life.*

"Take a right at the next corner," she said.

He slowed down the Packard and eased the wheel to the right. The sleek convertible sailed around the corner like a yacht.

"This is a wonderful car," he said. He glanced at her, and her blond hair floated in the windstream. "I don't want to appear

33

too forward," he said, "but I think you're very beautiful."

"Well," she replied, "you never seemed to notice before."

"I did notice, but I was in the hospital to see my old platoon sergeant, and I guess I was paying more attention to him than you."

"You and he appear to be very close."

"He's the greatest soldier in the Army."

"I think he's a nasty son of a bitch."

"He's that too."

They came to a gate, and a little guardhouse was in the center of the road. An MP came out of the guardhouse, and Lieutenant Breckenridge hit the brakes. The MP looked at the post sticker on the windshield, checked out Lieutenant Breckenridge and Nurse Latham, came to attention, and saluted. Then the MP waved them through.

Lieutenant Breckenridge returned the salute and drove out of the military post.

"Bear left at the light," she said.

"Yes, ma'am."

He shifted into top gear and pressed down the gas pedal. The Packard zoomed down the road, and stars glittered in the sky. The air was laden with the perfumelike fragrance of tropical flowers; Lieutenant Breckenridge eased the yellow Packard to the left.

Few cars were on the road, and no civilian homes were near the military post. Lieutenant Breckenridge felt that somehow he had escaped from the Army, and here he was, in a car with a beautiful girl, just like in civilian life.

"I really hate the goddamned Army," Lieutenant Breckenridge said. "I wish this goddamned war would end so I could go home."

"Where are you from?" she asked.

"Virginia."

"What did you do before the war?"

"I was in college—the University of Virginia." He hoped she'd put two and two together and realize he was the Dale Breckenridge who'd been the star fullback for the team, and its captain too. His picture had appeared in newspapers and magazines from coast to coast.

34

"I was in college too," she replied. "The University of Wisconsin at Madison."

He frowned: She didn't know who he was. A lot of women had screwed him on the basis of his past history, because women love to fuck stars, but this would not be true of Diane Latham.

"Take a left at the next crossroads."

Stars glittered in the sky like diamonds, and he could smell the salt air of the sea in the air. The night was warm but not too warm. He was sure she had a blanket somewhere in the trunk of the Packard. He'd lay it on the beach, or wherever she was taking him, and then they'd fuck like animals all night long.

He glanced at her. Her golden hair flowed behind her. She smiled, and her teeth were white and perfectly even. She wore her cunt cap at a jaunty angle, and Lieutenant Breckenridge wanted to steer to the side of the road, stop the engine, and put it to her then and there.

"Take a left at the next intersection," she said. "Keep your eyes on the road."

"Yes, ma'am."

He peered ahead into the night. A car approached from the opposite direction, its two headlights gleaming like the eyes of a monster. The car came closer and then swooshed by, making the Packard tremble slightly; then the road was deserted again, and Lieutenant Breckenridge saw the intersection in his head-lights.

There were no traffic lights or signs. Lieutenant Brecken-ridge tapped the brakes, shifted to second, let the engine slow the car further, and then stomped on the gas pedal. The car accelerated around the corner, its wheels screeching on the pavement. Lieutenant Breckenridge held the wheel tightly and kept the car in line. It gathered speed and passed a colonnade of palm trees lining the road.

"You say your father gave you this car?" he asked.

"Yes," she replied.

Lieutenant Breckenridge couldn't contain his curiosity any-more. "What does he do?"

"He's a general."

"A general?"

"Uh-huh."

Lieutenant Breckenridge swallowed hard. "Where is he a general?"

"On the post."

"On our post?"

"Uh-huh."

Lieutenant Breckenridge was taken by surprise. He'd never dreamed that she was the daughter of a general. He'd have to be careful how he treated her, and was glad she'd had no major problems with Lieutenant Utsley. He'd never heard of General Latham before.

"What does your father do on post?"

"He's in the Quartermaster Corps."

That was why Lieutenant Breckenridge never heard of him before. Her father was one of those faceless officers who ran the Army behind the scenes. But a general in the Quartermaster Corps had a lot of influence. A general in the Quartermaster Corps could make a lot of trouble.

She laughed gaily. "What's wrong with you?"

"Nothing."

"You act like you've just eaten something that disagrees with you."

"I'm all right."

She laughed again. "I know what's bothering you. You're afraid of my father, and that makes you afraid of me."

"Nonsense."

"You're even afraid to admit it, but don't worry: I don't run to Daddy whenever something goes wrong. I handle my problems myself."

"I'm glad to hear that." He turned for a moment and gazed at her breasts, which were round, firm, and jiggling slightly with the motion of the car.

"Keep your eyes on the road."

A hill loomed ahead, and Lieutenant Breckenridge increased the pressure on the gas pedal to maintain the Packard's speed. The vehicle zoomed up the hill; at its top the Pacific Ocean was straight ahead, moonlight shining on the waves.

"Hey," he said, "that's really beautiful."

"Slow down and bear right."

The paved road became a dirt road that wound through trees and bushes. Lieutenant Breckenridge steered to the right, his view of the ocean cut off. The Packard rocked from side to side as it drove over boulders and depressions in the road. No other cars were about, and it reminded Lieutenant Breckenridge of the jungles in which he'd fought the Japs at night. A shiver passed through him as he remembered those nighttime banzai attacks, when the Japs had screamed and hollered and tried to overrun the American positions, and sometimes got away with it.

"Bear left," she said.

He eased the wheel in that direction and the ocean came into view again. He passed some scattered vegetation and then rolled onto an open grassy spot on top of a cliff that overlooked the ocean.

"What a view!" he said.

"You can stop anywhere around here."

He hit the brakes and the Packard slowed to a stop. Pulling up the emergency brake, he stepped on the gas and turned off the ignition. The engine roared and died. Wind from the ocean blew the exhaust fumes away. Waves crashed to the shore below, and Lieutenant Breckenridge could see the coastline dotted with the lights of towns. All those lights would go off in seconds if the warning of a Japanese air-attack warning was sounded, but the Japs hadn't attacked the Hawaiian Islands since Pearl Harbor, and everyone felt that Hawaii was a relatively safe place. Still, a person could never relax completely, because the Japs were sneaky and no one could be sure of what the bastards would do next.

He turned to her. The breeze rustled her hair, and her eyes sparkled in the moonlight. He leaned toward her to take her in his arms.

She held up her hands and pressed them against his shirt. "Not so fast."

He became flustered and blushed, because if not then, when?

"Let's get out of the car," she said. She pointed to the edge of the cliff. "Let's stand over there and see the view."

"I can see it from here."

"It's better over there."

"Okay," he said, because he knew men had to humor women.

37

He'd have to give in to all her whims and play the game her way so he could take her pants off, and then the tables would turn.

He opened the door on his side and got out of the Packard. He walked around the front of the car to the passenger side in order to open her door, but she opened the door herself and stepped out.

The moonlight made a sheen on her cheek and spangles in her hair. He wanted to press his lips against hers and squeeze one of her magnificent boobs, but that would have to wait for later. They had to look at the moonlight first.

He took her hand, and together they walked to the edge of the cliff. Before them stretched the Pacific Ocean. The lights of ships could be seen heading toward Honolulu or sailing into the open sea. Stars glittered overhead and the waves crashed into the shore below.

Lieutenant Breckenridge looked down and saw the waves advancing in rows toward huge boulders piled on top of each other. The cliff he stood on fell off to a sandy slope dotted with bushes and rocks, and then came another plateau. Below that plateau was the rocky shoreline.

"This is really nice," he said.

"It's my favorite spot on the island, and maybe even in the world," she replied, crossing her arms underneath her sumptuous breasts.

He wondered who she'd brought here before. Probably countless young men like him whom she let seduce her. Lieutenant Breckenridge felt a pang of despair when he realized he was just another guy to her, because beautiful women always have all the men they want, and even more than they want.

"What's wrong?" she asked.

"Nothing."

"You certainly are a moody one."

"Am I?"

"You are. Take my word for it."

He turned to her and placed his hands on her shoulders, gazing into her eyes. "I'm crazy about you," he said.

A peculiar Mona Lisa smile played on her lips, and for a moment Lieutenant Breckenridge thought he saw contempt in her eyes, but decided it was only the strange combination of moonlight and shadow. He leaned forward to kiss her lips, but she stopped him again.

"No," she whispered, wagging her forefinger in front of his face.

"Why not?"

"Make a wish first."

"I have nothing to wish for, because I have everything I want here with me now."

She looked at him slyly. "Are you trying to sweet-talk me, Lieutenant?"

"I'm telling you the truth, Lieutenant."

"You wouldn't lie to a woman to have your way with her?"

"Not me."

"Face the ocean, close your eyes, and make a wish. It's a tradition here on the islands, you know. The natives often come to spots like this, overlooking the ocean when the moon is full, and make wishes."

"Really?" he asked. "I never heard of that custom before."

"You haven't been here that long."

"Ah, that must be it."

"Go ahead. You wish first, and then I'll make my wish."

"Right here?"

"You can move a little closer to the edge. The natives say the closer you are to the water the better."

He pointed toward the rocks. "We can go down there and really get closer."

"This will be fine. We don't have to overdo it."

"Okay."

He stepped toward the edge of the cliff and looked down at the partly sandy, partly rocky slope. Closing his eyes, he wished: *Please have this girl fuck me without too much trouble.*

"You son of a bitch!" she screamed.

She kicked him square in the ass with all her strength, and Lieutenant Breckenridge went flying over the edge of the cliff. He landed on his stomach, and the stones tore his shirt and flesh as he tried to grab on to something to stop him. His hand closed around a small thorny bush, ripping his fingers to shreds, and he cried in pain, letting go of the bush and tumbling over onto his back at the same time.

The incline was steep, and Lieutenant Breckenridge couldn't

slow his momentum. He kicked out his leg as a brake, and his shin slammed into a boulder, making him shout in pain again. The rocks on the ground rent his shirt, and his face scraped against dirt, removing a layer of skin. He clutched wildly at another bush and shredded both his hands. He tumbled over and around as he plummeted down the incline. He thought for sure he was going to die.

"Haaaalllpppp!" he screamed.

But there was no one to save him, and the sand and rocks scraped his hide off his body as he continued his downward descent, rolling, flipping. flailing wildly with his hands, bumping his head, skinning his knees and elbows.

He rolled into a pile of boulders at the bottom of the hill and came to a sudden stop, half unconscious and lying on his back. Blinking his eyes, he looked up the hill and saw Diane Latham drawing back her arm. She threw a rock at him and it sailed down the hill. He was too weak and disoriented to get out of the way, but her aim was off and the rock thudded into the ground several feet to his right.

"What was that for!" he screamed at the top of his lungs.

"You know very well what it was for, you rotten bastard!"

She turned and walked out of his line of sight. A few seconds later he heard the engine of the Packard start up, and then shafts of light from the headlights projected over the edge of the cliff. The shafts of light angled to the side, and he realized she was backing up and turning around. He rolled over and got to his hands and knees, shaking his head, trying to figure out what had happened to him.

What have I ever done to that bitch? he asked himself, and then he remembered Lieutenant Utsley. Lieutenant Utsley must have got real nasty with her, he realized. Probably tried to make her blow him right off the bat.

Lieutenant Breckenridge got to his feet and leaned against a pile of boulders as the ocean crashed against the shoreline only twenty feet away. He ached all over and checked himself out, but didn't think anything was broken. He looked up the hill; it was a long, steep way to the top. It was also a long way back to the post, and few cars were on this remote part of the island, so he probably wouldn't be able to hitch a ride.

He leaned forward and moved his left leg in his effort to climb the hill, but his ankle gave out and he collapsed onto his face. Cursing softly, he lay on the ground and took deep breaths, wondering how women could be so cruel.

The Singapore Lounge was a filthy, grungy bar near the docks of Honolulu. Soldiers, sailors, and Marines in uniform and civilian clothes were lined up three deep at the bar or seated around tables. Dim lighting was provided by electric bulbs inside Japanese lanterns of red, white, and blue, suspended from the ceiling. Frankie La Barbara and Morris Shilansky were seated at a tiny table in the corner, drinking shots and beers. They both wore civilian slacks and brightly colored Hawaiian shirts covered with designs of flowers, canoes, hula-hula girls, and the bright, blazing sun.

Shilansky had crafty eyes and a nose like a hawk. "I don't know," he said. "It's dangerous."

A cigarette dangled out of the corner of Frankie La Barbara's mouth. "You think it's as dangerous as going to New Guinea?"

"Yeah, because we can get the firing squad."

"Bullshit," Frankie said. "First of all, they ain't gonna catch us, and second of all, if they do catch us, they'll just send us to the stockade for a little while."

"I don't wanna go to the stockade here. They say it's a real hellhole."

"You think it's a worse hellhole than New Guinea?"

Shilansky thought for a few seconds. "No."

"Then what the fuck are you worried about?"

"I dunno. Going AWOL is a big step."

"Going to New Guinea is a bigger step. On New Guinea we won't have much of a chance. If the Japs don't get us, the snakes will, or the scorpions, or fucking malaria, or you name it."

"Desertion in the face of the enemy might be worse."

Frankie waved his arms wildly through the air. "What fucking enemy? Where do you see the enemy? There ain't no enemy on Oahu, you asshole. And they ain't gonna catch us anyway, because we're smarter than they are."

"We are?"

"Maybe you're not, but I am."

"Then why don't you go AWOL yourself? What do you want me to go with you for?"

Frankie narrowed his eyes and glared coldly at Morris Shilansky for a few moments. Then Frankie leaned back in his chair and hung his arm over the back. "As a matter of fucking fact, I don't need you for anything. I just thought I'd do you a favor and let you come with me, but if you wanna die on New Guinea, that's okay by me. If you wanna be an asshole, be an asshole. It don't make a shit to me either way."

A waitress with a big ass walked by, and Frankie lunged toward her, grabbing her apron and making her stop.

"Hands off the merchandise, big boy," she said, looking down at him with her eyebrows raised.

"Two more shots and two more beers," Frankie said.

Frankie let go of her apron and turned around to face Morris Shilansky again. Shilansky was deep in thought, staring at his half-full glass of beer.

"Now what's your problem?" Frankie asked.

"I don't know what to do," Shilansky replied.

"About what?"

"About going AWOL with you."

Frankie raised his forefinger to his lips and glanced around furtively. "The walls got ears," he said. "Keep your voice down."

"Sorry."

Frankie threw up his arms. "Make up your mind, asshole, because after this round, I'm going over the hill."

"Where you going?"

"None of your fucking business."

"You'll get caught."

"No I won't."

"Other guys get caught."

"Other guys ain't Frankie La Barbara."

Morris Shilansky raised his glass of beer to his lips and threw back his head, emptying the glass down his throat. Then he brought the bottom of the glass down hard on the table. He wiped his mouth with the back of his hand and wondered what to do. He knew that he definitely didn't want to go back to the war, but on the other hand, he was afraid of going AWOL.

42

He'd heard numerous stories about how prisoners were beaten to death by sadistic sergeants in the stockade and nobody gave a fuck.

The waitress returned with the drink orders, placing the two shot glasses and the two bottles of beer on the table.

"Anything else?" she asked.

"Yeah," Frankie replied with a smirk. "Sit on my face."

"Why, you dirty pig," she told him, disdain and contempt in her voice.

"You got a great ass, kid," Frankie said.

"You got a big mouth."

"The better to eat your pussy with."

"Oh, my God," she said, rolling her eyes. "What next? That'll be a dollar and a half for the drinks, please, and don't give me any more crap or I'll hit you over the head with this tray."

Frankie pulled a massive roll of bills out of his pocket, and her eyes bugged out of her head. He peeled off two one-dollar bills and tossed them onto the table. "Keep the change, sweetheart."

"Thank you, sir."

She scooped up the money and walked away quickly, but she didn't get far. A sailor with his white hat on the back of his head grabbed her arm and pulled her toward his table.

Morris Shilansky shook his head. "What a rotten job she's got."

"The bitch is in love with me," Frankie La Barbara said.

"In love with you? She hates your fucking guts."

"What makes you think that?"

"Because of the way you were talking to her."

"You're a bigger asshole than I thought. The worse you treat 'em, the better they like it. You oughtta know that by now."

"I still think she hates your guts."

"I could fuck her tonight if I wanted to."

"Bullshit."

"You wanna bet?"

Shilansky reached into his pocket. "You're on."

Frankie reached into his pocket, too, then stopped. "I can't fuck her tonight because I'm going AWOL." He pointed his

43

forefinger at Morris Shilansky. "And you'd better not rat on me, you big asshole."

"I ain't no stool pigeon, Frankie. You should know that by now."

Frankie La Barbara looked down at his shot and beer. "Yeah. Okay. Well, I guess this is gonna be our last drink together. You're going to New Guinea to get your ass shot off, and I'm going over the hill." He raised the shot glass into the air. "Good luck to you, buddy. You're gonna need it when you hit that New Guinea beach."

Morris Shilansky raised his own glass. "Good luck to you, Frankie. I hope they don't catch your ass."

"They won't—don't worry about it."

Both men touched the rims of their shot glasses to their lips, then tilted their heads back and poured the whiskey down their throats. It was cheap whiskey and burned all the way down, so they reached for their bottles of beer to put out the fire.

It was their sixth shot and beer apiece, and the sudden onslaught of more alcohol into their systems made them dizzy. Frankie took out a cigarette and lit it up, inhaling deeply. Morris Shilansky peered through the smoke at the crowd of servicemen laughing, shouting at each other, and getting drunk as quickly as they could. Waitresses threaded their way through the mob, and the jukebox blasted a Glenn Miller tune.

"Hey, Frankie," Morris Shilansky said, "when you go AWOL, where are you gonna hide?"

"That's for me to know and for you to find out."

"Come on, Frankie, tell me."

"What you wanna know for?"

"I just wanna know."

"Well, I don't wanna tell you. If you wanna know, you gotta come with me."

"Why d'ya want me to come with you?"

"Because two is better than one. If you went with me, we could look out for each other. But that's okay; I'll do fine all by my lonesome."

"Maybe I'll go with you if you tell me where you're going."

"No deal. But I can promise you it'll be safer than New Guinea, you dumb asshole."

"I ain't no dumb asshole."

44

"No?" Frankie was half in the bag now, and he reached forward, pulling open the buttons on the front of Shilansky's Hawaiian shirt. "What's that?" Frankie asked, pointing to a scar on Morris Shilansky's stomach.

"You know what it is."

"Tell me."

"It's a bayonet wound."

"And what's that one?"

"Another bayonet wound."

"What about that cut on your forehead?"

"Jap rifle butt."

"Where'd you get that big scar on your shoulder that I can't see but I know is there?"

"Jap bullet."

Frankie shook his head scornfully. "You're gonna die on New Guinea, you stupid asshole, but you're too dumb to realize it. What's even worse than that, you're too dumb even to save your life. Do you really think you're gonna survive another trip to the front?

Morris Shilansky furrowed his brow and thought about that for a few minutes. He knew damn well that the odds were against him. He'd seen too many die already. The booze was twisting his mind, and he didn't want to get shot at anymore. "No," he said, "I don't think I will."

"Then what the fuck you gonna go for?"

"It's my duty."

Frankie snorted and looked at Shilansky as if he were a pile of shit. "Duty?" he asked. "Are you kidding me? You think it's your duty to die for a fucking jungle that you never even heard of before?"

"You heard what Sergeant Cameron said. If we don't fight them here, we'll have to fight them in San Francisco."

"We won't have to fight them anywhere if we go AWOL, asshole. Other guys who think like Sergeant Cameron will fight them and stop them because they believe all that happy horse-shit, but I don't and neither do you. Am I right?"

"Yeah."

Frankie looked at his watch. "I gotta get going. If you wanna die, that's your business. They're gonna bury you in some swamp someplace while I'm sticking my dick into that fat waitress back there. See you around, chump. Keep your head down."

Frankie stood and held out his hand. Shilansky dragged himself to his feet and shook it. Frankie winked, pulled his hand away, and turned around, swaggering toward the door. A serviceman in a Hawaiian shirt stumbled in front of him and Frankie pushed him out of the way. He patted a waitress on the ass, stole a bottle of beer off another waitress's tray, and was swallowed up by the smoke and tumult of the Singapore Lounge.

Shilansky was still on his feet, but his knees wobbled and he leaned back against the wall. He felt peculiarly alone and desolate, although he was surrounded by other men and the crew of waitresses. *I should go back to the post*, he said to himself, but he didn't want to go back. They were going to send him to New Guinea, and he knew he was going to die there. You can't keep going to the front and expect not to get killed. *I don't want to die. I'm too young to die.* Shilansky had been a crook before the war, and crooks always think they can beat the system. He didn't think he could beat the war, but he might be able to go AWOL successfully, especially if he was with Frankie La Barbara, who was a very sharp guy.

Shilansky closed his eyes and saw himself lying on the ground in a jungle, bleeding from ten different places, dead as a doornail. He blinked and saw himself fighting knife to knife with a Jap soldier twice as big as he. Blinking again, he saw himself being blown to bits by Japanese hand grenades.

He lurched after Frankie La Barbara, but bumped into the table and fell to his hands and knees on the floor. The white arm of a sailor blouse appeared and helped him to his feet. Shilansky staggered into the crowd, waving his hands over his head.

"Wait for me!" he shouted. "I wanna go with you!"

Craig Delane, the rich ex-socialite from New York City, sat at a table in the post library, reading the entry on New Guinea in an encyclopedia:

New Guinea is the world's largest island after Green-land. Its total area is 344,158 square miles and is located

46

only one hundred miles from the Australian mainland. Political control of the island is divided between Australia and the Netherlands. The island is dominated by a complex mountain system and has many active volcanoes. It experiences the hot and humid climate common to equatorial regions, but the highlands have much cooler temperatures.

Rainfall is heavy. The north coast receives one hundred inches annually, and some spots receive even more. November to April is the monsoon season, and May to October brings torrential rains to the main parts of the island that stand athwart the southeast trade winds. There are numerous large swampy areas. Rivers frequently overflow their banks. The average temperature is eighty-two degrees Fahrenheit, fluctuating no more than seven degrees up or down the scale throughout the year.

New Guinea encompasses a huge variety of vegetation, and much of the island is botanically unexplored. More than two-thirds of the island consists of rain forests, and areas of poor drainage have swamp forests. Many highland areas are covered with hardy variations of kunai grass, also known as spear grass. The forest floor consists of moss and decayed vegetation many feet thick. Lichens and moss can be found on most trees.

Fauna is remarkably similar to that of Australia. There are more than one hundred species of marsupials, and the tree kangaroo is the largest indigenous animal. New Guinea is famous for its birds of paradise, whose beautiful and distinctive plumage causes them to be hunted by natives, who sell the feathers to traders.

New Guinea is home to many races and cultures. Natives share similar traits with African Negroes, Indonesians, Polynesians, Mongolians, and Caucasians. Links with Australian aborigines are not considered likely. Most natives are short, around five feet tall. Those living in the highlands are somewhat taller. Pygmies, known as Negritos locally, can be found in random villages all over the island. The local native population arrived by migration, but anthropologists have been unable to determine where they came from.

47

Tribal leadership is usually based on age and achievement. Villages have populations ranging from fifty to three hundred persons. There is widespread belief in spirits, especially spirits of the dead. The practice of sorcery and magic is widespread. There is frequent inter-village hostility, sometimes leading to war. Sacrifices are commonly made to spirits, and incidents involving human sacrifices have been reported. Headhunting is common among some native tribes.

Chinese, Japanese, and Western traders also live on the island in small numbers, despite an environment that is extremely inhospitable to those not born to it.

Health conditions on New Guinea rank among the worst in the world. The anopheles mosquito is a dangerous and deadly carrier of malaria, and can be found in great abundance all over the island, particularly in damp areas. Dengue fever is a constant menace, and the quickly fatal blackwater fever exacts a heavy toll of human life every year. Amoebic and bacillary dysentery are constant hazards. Tropic ulcers can develop from a scratch. Other threats are hookworm, ringworm, scrub typhus, and the dread yaws. In addition to the above-mentioned terrible anopheles mosquito, there are millions of other insects on the island, including countless species of flies, leeches, chiggers, ants, and fleas. Numerous poisonous snakes make their home on New Guinea. It is believed that certain of the more remote native tribes still practice cannibalism.

Craig Delane looked up, his jaw hanging open. *Cannibalism?* he thought. *Malaria? What in the hell are the "dread yaws"?* Groaning, he closed the encyclopedia, because he couldn't bear to read any more. It was too awful. He didn't want to go to New Guinea.

Somehow I've got to get out of this, Delane said to himself. He had a rich father back in New York, and he thought he'd better call him and ask for help. His father was a banker and had a lot of connections in Washington. Maybe the right bribe to the right politician would pull Craig Delane out of the war.

Delane stood and carried the book past ranks of tables where other soldiers read and tried to forget their troubles. He dropped the encyclopedia on the desk of the librarian, a WAC who smiled sweetly at him, but he didn't even notice. Somehow he had to make a call to New York.

I wonder what time it is in New York right now, he said to himself as he headed for the nearest door.

A fog rolled in from the ocean, covering the Honolulu waterfront. Morris Shilansky staggered through the swirling mists, trying to catch up with Frankie La Barbara. Servicemen in uniform and civilian clothes crowded the sidewalks, while whores beckoned from alleys. Eerie halos of light surrounded street lamps, and music filtered into the street from innumerable bars.

"Frankie!" Shilansky shouted. *"Wait for me!"*

On the street corner ahead, a tall man lit a cigarette, cupping his hands around the flame of his lighter. The man turned and looked toward Shilansky. *"Change your mind?"* the man asked; his voice was the voice of Frankie La Barbara.

"Yeah!" replied Shilansky.

"Hurry the fuck up!"

Shilansky hunched up his shoulders and ran toward Frankie La Barbara, but he was fairly drunk and bumped into a Marine in uniform.

"Watch your fucking step!" said the Marine.

"Fuck you!" replied Morris Shilansky.

"Fuck me?" asked the Marine.

He spun around and grabbed Shilansky's shirt, which was made of cheap material, and it ripped.

"You ripped my shirt!" Shilansky said.

"I'm gonna rip your fucking head off," the Marine replied.

The Marine drew his fist back, his teeth bared in anger, and then suddenly his mouth and eyes closed, his knees sagged, and he dropped to the ground, revealing Frankie La Barbara standing behind him, wearing brass knucks on his left hand.

"Let's get out of here!" Frankie said.

Morris Shilansky looked down at the Marine, who lay on his stomach, blood oozing from a dent in the back of his head.

"I think you killed him," Shilansky said.

"He started it."

Frankie grabbed Shilansky's shirt and pulled him into the first alley they saw. They made their way past the garbage cans, and a black cat screeched as it ran in front of them. They emerged from the other end of the alley, looked both ways, and then turned left on the sidewalk.

"Where we going?" Shilansky asked.

"AWOL," Frankie replied.

"I know we're going AWOL, but where we going AWOL?"

"Where you think'd be the best place to hide?"

"I dunno."

"Where is the one place they'd never find us?"

Shilansky wrinkled his big nose and thought about it for a few seconds. "On a submarine?"

"You dope—where'd we get a submarine?"

"I dunno."

Frankie pulled Shilansky closer and whispered into his ear as they moved swiftly across the foggy street. "When you're on the lam, the best possible place you can hide is a whorehouse!"

A smile spread over Shilansky's face. "A whorehouse?"

"Fucking A," said Frankie La Barbara.

On a desolate country road ten miles from the post, Lieutenant Dale Breckenridge limped along, his uniform torn to shreds, bruises all over his body, and a big knot on top of his head. He was sure that his left ankle was sprained, and his right ankle didn't feel so good either. His left shoulder was wrenched loose. Both his kneecaps were bereft of skin. He was a big fucking mess.

I guess Utsler tried some real rotten shit on her, he thought, holding his ribs because he was certain at least one of them was broken. *The bitch damn near killed me.*

He wanted to see a doctor immediately, but there were no hospitals nearby. No cars had passed him since he began his long trek back to the post, and he hoped to arrive at Headquarters Company before reveille, otherwise he'd be AWOL on top of everything else. Somehow he didn't think he could make it. He felt too worn out and crippled.

Boy, that bitch must really hate me, he thought. *She sure had me fooled. I thought she wanted to fuck me, and instead she pushed me off a goddamned cliff.*

He thought of how beautiful she'd been, how her blond hair had glinted in the moonlight, how her fabulous boobs had strained against her blouse. *I think I'm gonna stay away from women for a while. They can't be trusted.*

He heard the faint sound of an engine behind him, and spun around. Sure enough, far in the distance he saw two headlights flickering. *Oh, my God, I hope they stop for me,* he thought, holding out his thumb.

The vehicle came closer, and Lieutenant Breckenridge moved toward the middle of the road so they wouldn't miss him. He raised his hand high in the air and pointed his thumb back toward the post. "Please stop for me," he muttered. "I don't think I can go much farther on my own."

He thought he must look like a raggedy-ass bum with his clothes all torn and his face covered with bruises and scabs. Maybe it'd be an old farmer who was afraid to pick him up. Or an old lady who'd think he was an escaped rapist. The vehicle came closer and Lieutenant Breckenridge jumped into the air, waving his hands. *"Stop!"* he shouted, blinded by the headlights of the vehicle. *"Please stop!"*

The vehicle slowed, and he could see that it was a jeep! *The Army has saved me,* he thought, stumbling forward. The jeep stopped and an MP wearing a white helmet and carrying an M1 carbine stepped down.

"What's the problem here?" the MP said. He had the three stripes of a buck sergeant on his sleeve.

"Don't you salute officers, soldier?" Lieutenant Breckenridge snarled.

"You're an officer?"

"You're damned right I'm an officer."

The sergeant didn't know what to do, because Lieutenant Breckenridge was a mess; but then he spotted the silver bars on Lieutenant Breckenridge's collar and realized that he was indeed an officer. Snapping to attention, the MP saluted.

Lieutenant Breckenridge returned the salute, although he felt as though his arm were going to fall off. "Take me to the post hospital right away!" he said.

"What happened to you, sir?"

Lieutenant Breckenridge hadn't been able to think up a plausible story, because what could he say? He certainly didn't dare to tell the truth. "It's none of your business what happened to me."

"I'm afraid it is, sir. I'll have to put this down on my report."

"I'll tell you while we're on our way to the hospital. Help me into the jeep, will you, Sergeant?"

"Yes, sir."

The sergeant grabbed Lieutenant Breckenridge's arm.

"Easy, there," Lieutenant Breckenridge told him.

The MP sergeant eased Lieutenant Breckenridge toward the jeep and helped him into the front seat beside the driver, who looked at Lieutenant Breckenridge peculiarly.

"What're you looking at, soldier?"

"Nothing, sir."

"Keep your eyes on the road!"

"Yes, sir."

The sergeant climbed into the backseat and stared at the big knot on top of Lieutenant Breckenridge's head. "Back to the base," he said to the driver.

"Hup, Sarge," replied the driver, shifting into first gear.

The transmission made a *clunk* sound and the jeep drove off into the night. Lieutenant Breckenridge slouched in the front seat and tried to dream up a plausible story for the MP's report.

Pfc. Craig Delane stood in one of the phone booths in the telephone exchange, waiting for his call to go through to New York City. He'd been in the phone booth for ten minutes already, talking to a variety of operators and hearing buzzes, squeaks, and chirps in his ear while around him, in other booths, soldiers in uniform and civilian clothes also tried to make telephone contact with the outside world.

Delane leaned against the wall of the phone booth and pushed his fatigue cap to the back of his head. He reached into his shirt pocket, took out a cigarette, and lit it up. *Dengue fever,* he thought. *The dread yaws. Numerous poisonous snakes. Certain of the more remote native tribes still practice cannibalism.*

He heard a few clucks and clicks in his ear, and then a

woman's voice said: "The First Manhattan Savings and Trust Company."

Delane's heart leaped in his chest. He'd gotten through! "Mr. Oswald Delane, please?" he said in a quavering voice.

"One moment, please."

He heard another click and looked at his watch. It was ten-thirty in the evening on Honolulu, and a telephone operator had told him there was a six-hour time difference between Honolulu and New York City. That meant it was four-thirty in the afternoon there, and his father should still be at his desk.

Another woman's voice spoke into his ear: "Mr. Delane's office."

"I'd like to speak with him, please. I'm his son Craig, and I'm calling from Honolulu."

"One moment, please."

Craig puffed his cigarette nervously as he waited. He could picture his father sitting behind his big oak desk, puffing a pipe probably, looking distinguished in his Brooks Brothers suit, with his neatly trimmed salt-and-pepper mustache beneath his aquiline nose.

The phone clicked again and then his father's voice boomed into his ear: *"Craig!"*

"Dad!"

"How are you, son?"

"Not so good!"

There was silence on the other end for a moment. "What's wrong, my boy?"

"Dad, you've got to get me out of the Army!" Craig Delane said earnestly. "I can't take it any more!"

There was more silence on the other end, then: "What in the name of Sam Hill are you talking about, son?"

"Listen to me Dad: I can't tell you exactly where I'm going, but I'm going back to the front again, and I've had enough of the war. Can't you do something to get me transferred back to the States?"

"Craig," his father said sternly, "I can't believe you're saying what you're saying. Why, we've all been so proud of you. Your mother and I tell everyone we meet about how you're fighting the Japs and how you were in the middle of the big

53

campaigns on Guadalcanal, New Georgia, and Bougainville. How can you quit just when the going is getting a little tough?"

"Because I'll probably get killed if I go back to the front. I've had enough of this goddamned war, Dad. You know people in Washington. Can't you have me pulled back to the States, for crying out loud?"

"No son of mine is a quitter," his father said with a firm edge on his voice. "You're letting your mother and me down."

"Dad, I'm going to get killed out there!"

"I'll say to you what the Roman fathers used to say to their sons: Return from the war carrying your shield, or being carried upon it."

"Dad, are you crazy? This is no time for baloney! I don't want to die! I'm too young to die! Get me the fuck out of here!"

"How dare you talk to your father this way! You're spoiling everything, Craig! We've all been so proud of you, and now you're spoiling everything! I can see that the Army hasn't changed you at all. You flunked out of college and now you're trying to flunk out of the Army, but I'm not going to let you. You're going to do your duty like any other soldier. No Delane has ever been a quitter. I'm not going to tell your mother about this call. I'm going to forget about it. Maybe you're drunk— I don't know. You're certainly not in your right mind, but then, I don't suppose you've ever been in your right mind. You've given your mother and me a lot of grief, young man, and we don't want any more. Do your duty to your God, your family, and your country. Good luck to you. Do you need any money?"

"Yes."

"How much?"

"As much as you can send."

"I'll send you a check for one hundred dollars in the morning mail."

"Only a hundred dollars?"

"You're greedy. All you ever cared about was money, whiskey, and loose women. I'm ashamed of you, but you can redeem yourself by being a good soldier."

"You son of a bitch!" Craig screamed. "You want me to get killed so you can say you lost a son in the war! You don't care about me! All you care about is your fucking reputation!

Maybe if I get killed, your bosses will feel sorry for you and give you another promotion!"

"I do believe you've lost your mind, Craig. I'll speak with you some other time when you've found it."

Click!

The connection went dead in Craig Delane's ear. Craig was so mad, he wanted to tear the telephone machine off the wall and smash it over somebody's head. His face flushed with anger, he pushed open the door to the telephone booth and walked through the corridor, passing rows of telephone booths full of soldiers. His hands were in his pockets and his cigarette dangled out of the corner of his mouth. *That fucking hypocrite,* he said to himself. *That money-grubbing, phoney-baloney son of a bitch!*

Delane stepped outside and saw two MPs approaching the telephone exchange.

"Take your hands out of your pockets, soldier!" one of them said.

"Fuck you," Delane replied.

"What was that?"

"I said yes, Sergeant."

"It'd better be yes, Sergeant."

"Yes, Sergeant."

"And take that cigarette out of your mouth when you talk to me."

"Yes, Sergeant."

The two MPs passed Delane and opened the door to the telephone exchange, going inside. Delane put his cigarette back into his mouth and thrust his hands into his pockets again, heading for his barracks, thinking about his father and mother and how much he hated them.

Diane Latham stood in front of her mirror, brushing her hair before going to bed. She wore only her US Army–issue underpants.

Her room was tiny, furnished with a double bunk, two dressers, a chair, and a desk. Her roommate wasn't in yet, and Diane was glad to have some time alone for a change, because she was feeling guilty about what she'd done to Lieutenant Breckenridge.

She thought she was justified but was afraid she'd gone a little too far. He might be seriously injured, lying at the bottom of the cliff, and maybe a mountain cat or a poisonous snake would kill him. But she'd been so angry. Lieutenant Utsler had treated her very crudely. He'd tried to put his hand up her dress as soon as they were in a dark corner, and she'd slapped his face. Lieutenant Utsler told her that Lieutenant Breckenridge had told him that she was an easy fuck, and that made her madder than she'd ever been in her life.

Lieutenant Breckenridge may be a rat, she thought as she brushed her hair, but that wasn't sufficient cause to injure him physically. Several times she'd thought of going back to see how he was, but she wasn't feeling *that* sorry for him. He'd treated her worse than any other man she'd ever met in her life, and that was saying something, because lots of guys had tried to force her to fuck them, and many had told terrible lies, and the ones she'd given in to had come in her mouth, come in her hair, and treated her like shit the morning after.

She really didn't like men very much, and Lieutenant Breckenridge had been the last straw. All the anger and resentment of her short lifetime (she was twenty-three years old) had boiled up in her heart and she'd pushed the son of a bitch off the cliff. It would be terrible if he died there, but in a way he deserved it. No man had a right to treat a woman the way he'd treated her.

He'd been awfully nice when they'd been together in the car. It was hard to believe he was the same man who'd told that horrid Lieutenant Utsler that she was an easy fuck. There was something sexy about Lieutenant Breckenridge, too, although he wasn't a particularly handsome man. He was powerfully built and much taller than she, and that had turned her on a little. She was a tall woman herself, and she seldom met men who were much taller than she was. She thought it would be exciting to make love with a man that much taller and with such huge muscles but she'd have to wait until another came along, because she despised Lieutenant Breckenridge, whom she considered the lowest of the low.

The lampshade filtered the light that illuminated her curvaceous body, and her legs were shapely and smooth, with none of the dimples and flab some women have on their thighs.

Her ass was perfectly round and didn't hang the way some women's asses hang. Her boobs pointed up and out instead of lying flat on her stomach like two deflated balloons. She admired her figure in the mirror and hoped someday a man would come along who would be worthy of it.

She finished with her hair and laid the brush on the dresser. Strapping her watch on her wrist, she saw that it was eleven o'clock in the evening. She clicked off the light and climbed into the top bunk, because she had to be on her ward at six o'clock in the morning and wanted to be well rested, unlike her roommate, who stayed out all night with men and showed up on the ward the next day looking worse than soldiers who'd been wounded in combat.

Nurse Latham didn't cover herself with a sheet, because it was warm in the room. She lay on the bunk in the darkened room and the warm night breeze blew in through the windows, wafting over her supple body. She thought of Lieutenant Breckenridge lying at the bottom of the cliff, and a faint smile came to her lips. *I'll bet that son of a bitch never lies to a woman again*, she thought.

Frankie La Barbara and Morris Shilansky came to an intersection, and Frankie La Barbara stopped and looked around.

"Whatsa matter?" asked Shilansky.

"I wanna see if anybody's following us."

"Nobody's following us."

"How the fuck would you know?"

"Because I can see."

"You're drunk out of your mind, you cocksucker. Follow me."

Frankie turned right onto a narrow street paved with cobblestones. A street lamp shone on two sailors walking toward them in a crooked line. One sailor wore his hat low over his eyes; the other sailor had lost his hat somewhere along the line. They mumbled as they stumbled past Frankie and Morris Shilansky, and straight ahead, glowing in the fog, was a red light in front of a three-story wooden building in need of a paint job.

"That's the place," Frankie said.

"I never been here before," Shilansky replied, looking around.

"What's the name of the joint?"

"The Buckingham. It's not a bad whorehouse, as whorehouses go. The madam is an old friend of mine from New York."

They climbed the steps to the front door of the house. Frankie La Barbara looked to his left and right on the street, then pressed the doorbell. A small window was cut into the door, and two eyes heavily made up with mascara and false eyelashes appeared. The eyes widened, and then the door opened, revealing an attractive woman in her thirties, with black hair and sultry Latin features, wearing a low-cut red cocktail dress.

"Well, look who's here," she said with a big smile full of teeth stained pale yellow by too much coffee and too many cigarettes.

Frankie glanced around furtively. "I don't want nobody to see me. Can I talk to you alone?"

The smile vanished from her face, because she knew something was wrong. "Come with me."

They entered the vestibule, where a big Chinese bouncer stood behind the door, his hand on the switchblade knife in his pocket. The woman led Frankie and Shilansky down a corridor where lamps hung from the ceiling, filtering light through beaded shades. The woman opened a door, walked down another corridor, passed through two more doorways; finally they entered a kitchen where two whores sat at the table, drinking coffee and eating doughnuts.

"Get lost," the woman in the red dress said.

The two whores picked up their coffee and doughnuts, scrutinized Frankie and Shilansky, and departed via another door.

"Have a seat," the lady in red said. "Who's your friend, Frankie?"

"His name's Morris Shilansky, and he's from Boston."

"I been in Boston once," she said. "It's a real nice town."

"You been everywhere," Frankie said. "That's your problem."

She smiled at Shilansky. "My name's Rita," she said, "and I don't pay any attention to what that son of a bitch says"—she indicated Frankie with a motion of her chin—"because if I did, I would've killed myself long ago."

"Hi, Rita," Shilansky said.

"Want some coffee?"

"Sure."

"Me too," Frankie said.

"I knew you wanted some, Frankie. You want everything that's not nailed down."

"Why the fuck not?"

She sashayed to the stove and touched her fingers to the pot of coffee sitting on one of the unlit burners. "This is still hot," she said, taking two mugs down from the cupboard. "What's going on, Frankie?"

"Me and Shilansky just went AWOL."

"Yeah?" she said.

"Yeah."

"Just like that?"

"Why the fuck not?"

"You're a real pistol, Frankie. When the MPs catch you, they'll hang you from the highest pole they can find."

"The MPs ain't gonna find me."

She picked up the two mugs of coffee and carried them toward the table. "Why won't they?"

"Because you're gonna hide us, Rita."

"I am?"

"That's right."

"What if I don't?"

"I'll break your fucking legs."

She sat down and sighed. "So that's the way it is, huh?"

"That's the way it is, sweetheart."

"You know I can have one of my bouncers break your fucking head right now, don't you?"

Frankie reached underneath his shirt and pulled out an Army-issue Colt .45 that he'd stolen from the Headquarters Company armorer. "Where are they?"

"Put the heat away, will you?"

"I think I'll put it right here on the table, here, where I can get to it fast."

He dropped it onto the table and reached for his mug of coffee, taking a swig. She looked at his Colt .45 and knew he'd use it. Frankie was a tough hoodlum from Little Italy in New York City. He'd been in the Mob, and his father and all his uncles still were. Rita had worked for one of his uncles.

That's how she'd got her start "in the life." If you didn't play ball with people like Frankie, they killed you if you were lucky, or made you suffer for a long time if you weren't.

Rita smiled her most cordial smile. "Frankie," she said, "my home is your home. Whataya need?"

"A room for me and Shilansky, here. Three squares a day. A little pussy now and then. And nobody knows we're here."

"Come off it, Frankie," she replied. "Everybody already knows you're here."

"I mean nobody on the outside."

"I suppose you want all this for nothing?"

"Whataya mean, for nothing? Frankie La Barbara don't want nothing for nothing. Frankie La Barbara always pays his way." He reached into his pocket and took out his big fat roll of bills. "I got fifteen hundred bananas here. That oughtta cover everything."

"For how long?"

"About a month."

"And then what?"

"Shilansky and I leave."

"Shilansky and you leave for where?"

"That's for me to know and for you to find out."

"If that's the way you want it, that's the way it'll be."

"That's the way I want it."

"I can get in trouble for this, you know."

"That's your problem."

There's not much I can do about this, she thought, looking into Frankie's eyes and seeing the raw desperation. *I'll just have to play along and hope for the best.*

"You wanna see your room now?" she asked "Or do you wanna finish your coffee first?"

"We wanna finish the coffee first."

"What're you gonna pay me, or shouldn't I ask?"

"Twenty dollars a day room and board for the both of us."

"What about the female companionship?"

"We'll pay the going rates, as always."

She thought that wasn't such a bad deal financially, but if the MPs caught Frankie and his drunken friend, she'd probably wind up in the clink for aiding and abetting fugitives, although she could always say she didn't know they were fugitives.

"I got some work to do," she said. "Call me when you need me."

"Okay," Frankie replied. "You got any food in that refrigerator?"

"Help yourself."

She stood and walked toward the doorway, then paused and looked back. "Put that gun away before somebody sees it and gets nervous."

"Right," Frankie said, picking up the Colt .45 and jamming it into his belt, covering it with his shirt.

She left the kitchen and Frankie sipped his coffee. Everything was going okay. He looked at Shilansky. "See?" he asked. "I toldja it'd be easy."

"So far, so good," Shilansky replied, "but tell me one thing, Frankie: Where are we going when we leave here?"

"I ain't figured out that part yet," Frankie replied, reaching for his package of cigarettes. "But I will. We gotta take this one step at a time, understand?"

"Yeah, I guess so."

"You worry too much. We ain't going to New Guinea no matter what happens, so cheer the fuck up, willya?"

"I'm trying to," Shilansky said.

FOUR . . .

It was quarter to six in the morning, and a glimmer of dawn was on the horizon. All the lights in the barracks were ablaze, and the voices of men could be heard as Lieutenant Breckenridge limped over the sidewalk toward the orderly room.

He wasn't limping badly, like a cripple, but his normally smooth gait had a discernible stutter whenever his left leg came down. He wore clean starched fatigues and the brim of his cap low over his eyes, a large, muscular man with his pants bloused around the tops of his combat boots.

The first formation and roll call were at six o'clock, and chow was six-fifteen. Lieutenant Breckenridge hadn't thought he'd make the first formation, but he'd done it. He approached the orderly room, a small wooden building painted yellow, and climbed the three steps, opening the door and going inside.

"What happened to you?" asked Gerald Kurkin, the first sergeant of Headquarters Company.

"Had a little accident in a car," Lieutenant Breckenridge replied.

Kurkin had thinning light-brown hair and lumpy features. He lifted a piece of correspondence off his desk, while next to him Pfc. Lawrence Nagle, the Headquarters Company clerk, banged on his typewriter. Lieutenant Breckenridge found a chair and sat down, taking out a cigarette and lighting it up.

He still was sleepy, because he hadn't got to bed until two o'clock in the morning, after he'd filled out his report at the provost marshal's office and been treated at the post hospital.

He'd told the MPs he'd been hitchhiking and had been picked up by a drunk who subsequently drove off the road and hit a tree. Lieutenant Breckenridge said the car and driver were gone when he woke up. He tried to make it back to the post and was picked up by the MPs.

The MPs were suspicious of his story, but what could they do? No crime had been committed, so they drove him to the hospital, where he was patched up and sent home.

Now it was another day. Somewhere on his medical records it would state that he'd been found battered and cut on a lonely country road one night, but no one would pay any special attention to it. It was all over except for the healing of cuts and bruises. He tried not to think about Nurse Latham, because when he remembered her his cuts and bruises felt worse.

He puffed his cigarette as other young lieutenants showed up at the orderly room. Sergeants passed through, and then Captain Irwin Spode, the CO, arrived.

"*Atten*-hut!" shouted Sergeant Kurkin.

Everyone leaped to his feet and stood at attention.

"As you were," said Captain Spode, walking toward his office and opening the door.

Lieutenant Breckenridge sat down and looked at his watch. It was five minutes before the first formation. The door to the orderly room opened and Sergeant Cameron walked inside and looked around, finally letting his eyes come to rest on Lieutenant Breckenridge.

He walked toward Lieutenant Breckenridge and bent low, murmuring: "Sir, can I speak with you alone for a moment?"

Something in Sergeant Cameron's voice said it was urgent. "Of course, Sergeant," Lieutenant Breckenridge said. "Let's go outside."

He arose and followed Sergeant Cameron to the door. Together they stepped out into the pale dawn light.

"What's wrong?" asked Lieutenant Breckenridge.

"Let's go someplace where nobody can hear us."

They walked to the side of the orderly room. Opposite them was the big open parade ground surrounded by the barracks of the regiment. Smoke curled into the sky from the chimneys of mess halls.

"Sir," said Sergeant Cameron, his eyes darting about nervously, "six men from the recon platoon weren't in their bunks this morning. Should I count them as AWOL, or what?"

"What six?"

"Corporal Gomez, Pfc. O'Rourke, Pfc. Delane, Pfc. La Barbara, Pfc. Shilansky, and Pfc. Billie Jones."

"Shit," said Lieutenant Breckenridge.

"I don't know what to do, sir."

"I don't either."

"We gotta do something." Sergeant Cameron looked at his watch. "First formation is in five minutes."

"Those stupid sons of bitches," Lieutenant Breckenridge said. "They drive me crazy."

"Should I report them AWOL or shouldn't I?"

"Let me think for a moment."

Lieutenant Breckenridge lit another cigarette and puffed it nervously. He knew the men should be reported as AWOL, but he didn't want that to happen. Then they'd be fugitives, and when they were caught they'd be thrown into the stockade. Maybe he should give them a chance, another twenty-four hours or so. Maybe they all had gotten drunk and couldn't make it back to the post.

"Don't report them AWOL," Lieutenant Breckenridge said. "We'll cover for them for twenty-four hours. Maybe they'll drag their asses back by then."

"If you say so, sir."

"I didn't say anything, Sergeant. We never had this conversation. I'm not giving you any orders of any kind about this matter. What you do you'll do on your own. If anything goes wrong, it'll be your ass."

"It'll be your ass, too, sir, and they'll be harder on you than they will be on me, because you're an officer."

"I know that. We'll both be in trouble, but I'm willing to take the chance."

"Me too."

"Okay. If the men return, let me know." Lieutenant Breck-

65

enridge took off his cap and ran his fingers through his short brown hair. "I wish I knew where they were. I'd go get the bastards myself."

"You might ask Sergeant Butsko, sir. He might have an idea."

Lieutenant Breckenridge put his cap back on and lowered the visor over his eyes. "That's a good idea. I'll go see him after formation."

Breeeeeeeeeeeeeeettttttt! Whistles blew all across the parade ground, and seconds later, men charged out of the doors of their barracks. They lined up platoon by platoon in their company areas, dressed right and covered down. Sergeants and officers barked orders, and the men tried to steel themselves for the day that lay ahead. Sergeant Cameron took his position in front of the recon platoon, and Lieutenant Breckenridge stood with the other lieutenants beside the orderly room. There were four platoons in Headquarters Company, and in front of all of them stood First Sergeant Gerald Kurkin.

The company stood at attention stiffly. Captain Spode marched out of the orderly room and proceeded to a position in front of Sergeant Kurkin, who saluted Captain Spode. Captain Spode saluted back. Sergeant Kurkin about-faced and looked at the company.

"Report!" shouted Sergeant Kurkin.

"First Platoon all present and accounted for, Sergeant!"

"Second Platoon all present and accounted for, Sergeant!"

"Third Platoon all present and accounted for, Sergeant!"

Now it was Sergeant Cameron's turn, and without hesitation he raised his stiffened fingers to his right eyebrow and shouted: *"Reconnaissance Platoon all present and accounted for, Sergeant!"*

Sergeant Kurkin executed another slick about-face. Captain Spode stood in front of him, also at attention. Sergeant Kurkin saluted and yelled: *"Headquarters Company all present and accounted for, sir!"*

Captain Spode returned the salute, while back in formation Lieutenant Breckenridge took a deep breath and closed his eyes. *The deed is done,* he thought. He wondered why he was sticking his neck out for the men who'd gone AWOL, but deep down he knew the answer. He'd been in combat with them, and he

66

had to help them just as they'd helped him when the bombs were falling and the bullets were flying and the Japs were charging and screaming *banzai* at the tops of their lungs.

It was a small white Baptist church with a white steeple and a bell in the belfry. Its doors were locked at that early hour of the morning, and no one was supposed to be inside, but one man, in a garish Hawaiian shirt, knelt in front of the altar, his hands clasped together in prayer, an expression of misery on his face.

He was Pfc. Billie Jones, the former itinerant preacher from Georgia, who'd snuck into the church the night before, hidden in a closet, and been praying ever since, because he didn't want to go to New Guinea and die.

Billie had been in the original recon platoon that had gone ashore on Guadalcanal and fought innumerable battles since then. He'd seen many of his close friends die, and had been wounded several times. His closest friend, Private Homer Gladley, had been killed during the final days of fighting on Bougainville, and Billie Jones hadn't been right since.

He had become afraid, and didn't want to die. He was praying for the Lord to save him somehow, but no great miracle had occurred, and he was becoming more AWOL with every passing moment, and more worried. He didn't know what to do or where to go. Why wasn't God helping him?

He heard the snap of a lock in a door and realized the church was being opened for the day. Panicked, he ran back and dived into one of the pews, ducking his head and lying on the floor. He knew he'd be in trouble if someone found him. The MPs would be called and they'd toss him into the stockade, where the guards would beat him to death.

He heard a door squeak open, and the voice of a woman humming "Faith of Our Fathers" drifted into the church. The interior became lighter as the doors were opened wide and the sunlight shone inside. The footsteps and hum of the woman came closer; she was walking down the main aisle of the church. Billie Jones bit his lower lips and hoped she wouldn't see him, but he knew she would. How could she miss him?

"My goodness!" said the woman. "What in the name of heaven are you doing in there?"

Billie Jones raised his head and smiled. "Hello."

She was a slender woman wearing a long skirt and glasses, around forty years old with graying hair. "I said what are you doing in there?" she asked again, not unkindly.

"Praying, ma'am."

"Praying on your stomach? I never heard of that before. Are you a Christian?"

"Yes, ma'am."

"Have you been here all night?"

"Yes, ma'am."

She looked him over as he picked himself up off the floor and stood in front of her. Although he wore civilian clothes, she surmised that he was a soldier. Nearly all the young, healthy-looking American males on the Hawaiian Islands were soldiers.

"Are you AWOL?" she asked.

"Yes, ma'am."

"Hmmm. I think we'd better have a little talk. Come with me, please?"

"Yes, ma'am."

All over Honolulu, teams of MPs prowled the streets, looking for AWOLs. Each team consisted of two men, and one of these teams, wearing tan dress uniforms with black and white MP bands around their right arms, entered an alley in a particularly tough neighborhood.

The alley stank of piss and garbage cans. A dog slept in front of a doorway, and halfway down the alley the two MPs saw the figure of a man wearing dirty white civilian pants and a colorful Hawaiian shirt.

"That looks like one over there," said one of the MPs, a corporal.

The other MP, a pfc., followed him. Both men held their clubs ready to batter the man to a pulp if he started any shit with them, but the man in the colorful shirt lay still as if dead, his face cradled on his arms, surrounded by a pool of dried vomit.

"He looks Hawaiian," said the pfc. "Maybe he's a civilian."

"Maybe," said the sergeant. "See if he's wearing dog tags."

The pfc. didn't want to touch the vomit, but he'd have to if he wanted to check for dogtags. The smell got worse the closer he got, and he kicked the man onto his back, then reached into his collar and found the silver-colored chain made of tiny metal balls.

"He's got dog tags," the pfc. said.

"What's the fucker's name?"

The pfc. leaned closer, nearly choking on the smell of vomit and booze. "Gomez," he said, reading the dog tags. "Lupe Gomez."

"He ain't no Hawaiian," said the Corporal. "He's a spick. You watch him here while I go call the wagon."

Morris Shilansky, barefoot and wearing his civilian pants, stood beside the window and held the window shade open a crack with his forefinger, peering down into the street.

He saw two MPs on the opposite side walking along, swinging their billy clubs. Shilansky let the shade hang back into its usual position and pressed his back against the wall, his heart pounding, but in his haste he bumped against a night table and knocked over a lamp, which fell to the rug.

Frankie La Barbara, sleeping on a bed, opened his eyes, grabbed his Colt .45 from underneath his pillow, and sat up, pointing the pistol at Morris Shilansky.

"Don't shoot!" said Shilansky, holding up his hands as if to stop the bullet.

Frankie wore only his khaki skivvie shorts, and his wavy hair was mussed on his head. He lowered the pistol and jutted his lower jaw forward like a bulldog. "What do you think you're doing?"

"Nothing."

"What're you making such a racket for?"

"I bumped into the lamp by mistake."

"I think when your father fucked your mother it was a mistake."

Shilansky narrowed his eyes. "Hey, Frankie, watch what you say about my mother and father."

"Fuck you," Frankie said, reaching for his package of cigarettes. "You'd better watch where you're walking in the morning. I need my sleep because I got things to think about."

"Fuck what you got to think about."

Both men looked at each other, wondering whether a little

violence was called for. They were strong men, both around six feet tall, and each knew one of them would be in the hospital when it was all over, but neither could be certain he'd be the one to survive.

They decided what had occurred wasn't enough to provoke a major confrontation. Frankie put a cigarette in his mouth and lit it up. Shilansky sat in a upholstered chair nearby and stared at a picture of apples and oranges in a bowl, hanging from the wall.

"What're we gonna do today?" Shilansky asked.

"What d'ya think we're gonna do?" Frankie blew smoke out the side of his mouth. "We're gonna sit tight and stay out of sight; that's what we're gonna do. Maybe we'll get some girls up here for a little fucking."

"Now you're talking," Shilansky said.

Jimmy O'Rourke, the former stuntman from Hollywood, looked up the banana tree and saw a gigantic bunch of bananas. He figured there must be at least forty or fifty bananas in the bunch, sufficient for breakfast, and he was glad he'd stumbled unwittingly onto the banana plantation.

He was wearing fatigues and carrying a full field pack that contained bedding and two shelter halves, so he could pitch a tent someplace in a remote wooded area and wait for the war to end while living off the land.

He took off his full field pack and leaned it against the base of the tree. Then he grabbed the trunk and began to climb, one hand over the other, pushing up with his feet, until he reached the branch where the big bunch of ripe yellow bananas hung. Taking out his Ka-bar knife, he cut the bunch of bananas loose, and they dropped away, falling to the ground, landing with a thud. Jimmy jumped down, tore off five bananas, and sat with his back against the trunk of the tree. He peeled a banana and stuck the end into his mouth, biting it off.

It was ripe and delicious. A new plan formed in his mind. He thought maybe he should pitch his tent someplace in the surrounding countryside and live on bananas until the war was over. He'd read someplace bananas were very nutritious, and in a survival course at Fort Ord they'd told him a man could live off coconuts for the rest of his life and remain fairly healthy.

He was certain he could find some coconuts someplace to supplement his diet. He could trap rabbits, if there were any rabbits on Hawaii; and if there were no rabbits, he'd trap something else. Somehow he'd make it. Anything was better than going back to the war.

He stuffed the rest of the first banana into his mouth and peeled the second banana. *What a smart son of a bitch I am, he thought. The other guys are going to New Guinea, but not me. I'm gonna be alive when this goddamn war is over. I'll go back to Hollywood and become a fucking star, and nobody'll know the difference. They'll never catch me, because I'm one smart son of a bitch.*

He finished the second banana and tossed the peel over his shoulder. Then he froze suddenly, because he realized he shouldn't throw banana peels all over the place like that. He should take them with him and hide them in the forest, so no one would know he'd been around. *Leave no tracks or anything else around when you're in enemy territory.* That's what Sergeant Butsko used to say. *They'll never catch me,* Jimmy O'Rourke said to himself. *I'll outsmart them at every turn.*

The bushes rustled in front of him, and all of a sudden, like a bad dream, a Hawaiian man appeared, wearing a wide straw hat and carrying a machete in his right hand!

Jimmy dropped his banana and reached for his Ka-bar knife. The Hawaiian man screamed and ran away. Jimmy lunged for his full field pack, put it on, grabbed a handful of bananas, and sped off in the opposite direction.

This is going to be a little harder than I thought, he told himself. I'll have to be more careful in the future, but anyway, they'll never catch me because I'm a whole lot smarter than they are.

Lieutenant Breckenridge walked swiftly down the corridor of the hospital, heading toward the solarium. He passed nurses and orderlies, and patients limping on crutches and canes. Other patients lay on tables that had wheels and were pushed through the corridor. Lieutenant Breckenridge stepped to the side to get out of the way of one of these tables, and that placed him in front of a door to a room off the corridor. The door opened and Lieutenant Diane Latham stepped out, turning and finding herself face-to-face with Lieutenant Breckenridge.

"Yipes!" she said in alarm, and took a step backward.

"Uh-oh," he muttered, taking two steps back.

They stood and looked at each other. He couldn't help noticing how symmetrical and lovely the features of her face were, and she couldn't help noticing how beaten and bruised he was, with his left hand bandaged and the big knot on top of his head.

"Are you all right?" she asked.

"I'm not dead," he replied, "but I'm not going to hang around so you can finish the job."

He walked around her and continued on his way to the solarium, limping slightly. She turned around and watched him, the light from the solarium making a halo around his head. He looked a mess, and she felt sorry for what she'd done, now that she'd had a good night's sleep and wasn't mad anymore. *I've really got to do something about my temper,* she said to herself. *I might have killed the poor son of a bitch.*

Lieutenant Breckenridge entered the solarium and saw Butsko near the window, reading the Honolulu *Daily News*. Butsko looked up as Lieutenant Breckenridge approached.

"That was fast," Butsko said.

Lieutenant Breckenridge stopped in front of Butsko and pulled up a chair. "What was fast?" he asked.

"I just called you fifteen minutes ago. You didn't get the message?"

"No, but I don't have time to talk about that. Something terrible has happened."

Butsko grinned mischievously. "Bet I know what it is."

"Bet you don't."

"Bet I do."

"How much you wanna bet?"

"How about ten bucks?"

"You're on," Butsko said.

"Okay," Lieutenant Breckenridge replied, "why am I here?"

"Because Frankie La Barbara and Morris Shilansky have gone AWOL."

Lieutenant Breckenridge blinked his eyes in surprise. "How did you know?"

"A little bird told me."

"What's his name?"

"He's a she, and she owns a whorehouse. She's an old friend of mine and she told me Frankie and Shilansky are holed up on the top floor of her whorehouse. She called me because she didn't know what to do, and I called you because I think you should take a few men and go down there and get the stupid fuckers before the MPs do." Butsko held out his hand. "Pay up."

"What for?"

"I just told you why you're here."

"But you don't have the whole story."

"What's the whole story?" Butsko's jaw dropped open in alarm. "Did they *kill* somebody?"

"No, but they're not the only ones gone AWOL. Craig Delane, Billie Jones, Corporal Gomez, and Jimmy O'Rourke have gone over the hill too."

Butsko held the palm of his hand to his face. "Uh-oh."

"That's not all," Lieutenant Breckenridge said. "They were reported present and accounted for at formation this morning."

"How the hell did that happen?"

"I told Sergeant Cameron to report them present and accounted for."

Butsko wheezed and shook his head. "Looks like you're on the way to a court-martial, my friend."

"I thought I should give the men a chance to return of their own free will, without any serious consequences."

"That was dumb. You put your ass in a sling for a bunch of guys who are no fucking good, who never were any good, and who never will be any good."

"Well, we've all been together for a long time, and it seemed right to give them the opportunity to do the right thing."

"That bunch'll never do the right thing," Butsko said, "because they don't know what the right thing is. They only know how to do the wrong thing. They're the fucking scum of the earth. Don't you know that yet?"

"They're good men underneath it all."

"What a crock of shit that is. That kind of thinking is gonna get you into a whole world of trouble, if it hasn't got you into trouble already."

"What are you talking about?"

Butsko leaned forward and pointed his finger at Lieutenant Breckenridge's nose. "There's one important thing you haven't thought about."

"What's that?"

"They're all gonna get caught, probably today. And you know what's gonna happen when they get caught?"

Lieutenant Breckenridge moaned pathetically. "I think I'm getting the picture."

"I think you are too. It's gonna go something like this: After they're caught, somebody's gonna realize they were carried on the morning report as present and accounted for. The next step is the MPs are gonna come looking for *you*."

Lieutenant Breckenridge covered his face with both hands. "Oh, my God!"

"If I were you," Butsko said, "I'd have a talk with Colonel Hutchins right away. Spill your guts out to him. Cry and beg and promise you'll never do it again. Maybe he can stop the morning report before it gets to Division, because once it gets to Division, your ass is grass and the provost marshal will have the lawnmower."

Lieutenant Breckenridge jumped to his feet. "I'd better get going right now!"

"You mean you're still here?"

Lieutenant Breckenridge spun around and ran out of the solarium. He trotted down the hall past the nurses' station, and Lieutenant Diane Latham looked up to see him narrowly avoid collision with a patient in a wheelchair by dodging around the wheelchair at the last moment and continue through the corridor at top speed.

Lieutenant Latham returned to her paperwork but couldn't concentrate. She was curious about why he'd run like a maniac through the corridor. An expression of total panic had been on his face. What had transpired between him and Sergeant Butsko?

Her curiosity got the best of her, and she arose, laying her pen on the pile of paperwork. Adjusting the little nurse's cap on her head, she walked out of the nurses' station and down the corridor to the solarium, where she saw Butsko in the same place, the newspaper folded on his lap as he stared out the

74

window. He appeared to be deep in thought.

"Are you all right, Sergeant?" she asked.

He craned his neck so he could see her. "What makes you think I'm not all right?"

"Because I just saw Lieutenant Breckenridge run through the corridor as if somebody were chasing him with a gun, and here you are, staring out the window as if something serious is on your mind."

Butsko knitted his eyebrows together. "How well do you know Lieutenant Breckenridge?"

She became flustered. "I really don't know him *that* well."

"That's good, because he's in a whole world of trouble."

"What's he done?"

"He stuck out his neck for some of his men, and now he's gonna get his head chopped off."

"It's really that bad?"

"He might be in the stockade before the sun goes down today."

"Oh, my goodness!"

"He left so fast, I didn't have a chance to ask him how come he's all beat up. He looked like somebody chewed him over and spit him out, didn't he?"

"He certainly did."

"I don't know who beat him up, but it must've been one big, mean son of a bitch."

Lieutenant Latham didn't know what to say.

"I wish I could get out of this hospital," Butsko said. "All hell's breaking loose out there, and I can't do anything about it."

Craig Delane walked across the lobby of the Royal Hawaiian Hotel, wearing the silver bars of a first lieutenant on his collar and his Combat Infantryman's Badge above his left shirt pocket. He was masquerading as an officer because he knew no MP would dare ask an officer for his pass. His tan class A uniform was neatly pressed, and he had the bearing of an officer, plus the education of an officer. He was certain he could get away with the masquerade for a little while, and all he needed was a little while.

He approached the desk, carrying a beautiful expensive piece of leather luggage, the type that a gentleman traveler would carry.

"Can I help you, Lieutenant?" asked the clerk behind the desk.

"A room for the night, please."

"You're alone, Lieutenant?"

"I am."

"Sign in here, please."

Craig Delane wrote a phony name on the hotel register, and the clerk told him the room would cost twenty dollars a night. The clerk called the bellhop, who led Craig to the elevator.

The elevator rose up through the Royal Hawaiian Hotel, and a young woman gave Craig Delane the eye. He thought she was probably a high-priced prostitute, and at another time he might have given her a tumble, but not today.

The bellhop led him down the corridor to a door, opened it, and went inside, opening windows, showing Craig where everything was. The Royal Hawaiian was a fancy, expensive hotel, and everything was in order. Craig tipped the bellhop and waited for him to leave, then double-latched the door. Returning to his suitcase, he laid it on the bed and opened it up.

It was filled with newspapers so it would be heavy and the bellboy wouldn't get suspicious. He lifted a few newspapers, and underneath was a Colt .45 that he'd stolen from the armorer, along with a clip of bullets. Holding the pistol in his hand, he smiled grimly. His plan was to shoot himself in the head and die in style in the famous Royal Hawaiian Hotel.

He wondered exactly how to do it, because he'd like to make a dramatic presentation. He thought he should kill himself in the chair near the window, so the sunlight would illuminate his body as he lay slumped over, bleeding from a hole in the head.

A hole in the head? he wondered as he walked toward the mirror over the dresser and looked at himself. No, he didn't want a hole in his head, because a .45 caliber slug wouldn't make a little hole. It would blow his whole head apart. He'd shot Japs at close range with Colt .45s and had seen it happen with his own eyes. Blowing his head off would make more of a dramatic presentation than he wanted.

He looked at the chair and had an idea. He'd turn the pistol around and shoot himself in the heart, right below his Combat Infantryman's Badge. When he was found, everyone's eyes would be drawn to the wound and then to the badge. They would know he was a hero. And he imagined he would look rather romantic, his tan shirt stained with his ruby blood.

But somehow that wouldn't be enough of a dramatic presentation. Something more was needed, something elegant and dashing. Perhaps a suicide note, in which he would bid farewell to his comrades-in-arms. That would be nice, but somehow it wasn't enough.

Then he hit on it. A bottle of champagne in a silver bucket, a half-full glass of champagne on the table beside him, the suicide note next to the glass, and him in his class A uniform (he'd have to remove the lieutenant's bars first), slumped over in the chair, dead by his own hand, in the prime of his life.

He liked that. Walking to the bed, he sat and lifted up the telephone on the night table, dialed for the operator, and asked her to connect him with room service. When room service answered, he ordered a bottle of the finest champagne in the house.

He walked into the bathroom and looked at himself in the mirror, frowning because he was tanned and too healthy-looking. He'd rather be pale and poetic-looking on this, the most significant day of his life. He smiled; his teeth were white and straight. Smoothing down his light-brown hair with his hands, he admired his fine aristocratic features, or at least he thought he had fine aristocratic features. Butsko had told him once that he looked like a drowned rat, and that had injured him deeply.

There was a knock on the door. Delane closed the suitcase and hid the pistol in the top drawer of the dresser. Then he opened the door. The room-service waiter entered, carrying a bucket fulled with ice and the bottle of champagne. In his other hand the room service waiter carried a tray and two champagne glasses. He was an elderly gentleman wearing a toupee and a dyed mustache.

"Where would you like these, sir?"

"Over there by the window."

"Shall I open the bottle for you?"

"I'll do it myself."

"Yes, sir. Of course, sir. Certainly, sir."

The room-service waiter set the champagne bucket and its stand on the floor, and placed the tray with the glasses on the little table next to the big upholstered chair beside the window. Delane signed the tab and added a fat tip, which he wouldn't have to pay because you can't collect from a dead man.

"Thank you, sir. Very good, sir. Good day, sir."

The waiter waltzed out of the room, and Delane twisted the wires that held the cork in place. Removing the wires and tossing them over his shoulder, he worked the cork with his thumbs until it came loose; then it rocketed out of the bottle with a loud pop, bouncing off the ceiling and a wall, finally landing on the bed.

Delane looked at the label. It was a California champagne, because not much French champagne was available since the German occupation of France. But champane was champagne. It was the sentiment that counted, not the label.

He poured champagne into the glass, misty fumes exuding from the mouth of the bottle as he did so. Raising the glass, he watched the bubbles rise in tiny swirls. He sipped the liquid. It tasted wonderful. Ordering the champagne had been an inspired idea. He was proud of himself.

He moved to the dresser, retrieved the Colt .45, and carried it with him to the chair, where he sat down. He ejected the clip, jammed it back in again, and worked the slide mechanism so that a round would go into the chamber. Now the pistol was ready to fire. He clicked off the safety and placed the pistol on the little table next to his glass of champagne.

He raised the glass to his lips and took another sip. It reminded him of when he used to drink champagne with beautiful debutantes at the Plaza and St. Regis hotels in New York City, not to mention the Pierre and the Sherry Netherland. Those had been the good old days, the best days of his life. Then the war had broken out and he'd enlisted in the Army out of warped patriotism, or at least that's what he thought now.

He drained the glass and filled it up again. The champagne was smooth and pleasantly tart. It made him feel better. He believed that he was a gentleman and should be able to relax and drink champagne every morning, instead of running around in the jungles of the southwest Pacific, shooting at Japs who were shooting at him.

No more of that for me, he thought, gulping down his second glass of champagne. *I'm getting out of this goddamned war once and for all.* He filled the glass with champagne again and proceeded to pour the tingly liquid down his throat. He'd forgotten how much he'd liked champagne back in New York, and couldn't understand why he didn't drink it more often instead of the cheap whiskey he always ordered when he was out with his buddies.

He slurped down two more glasses of champagne and got a little tipsy. He loosened his necktie and his face became flushed. Lighting up a cigarette, he leaned back in the chair, the glass half full of champagne in one hand, the lit cigarette in the other.

After I finish this cigarette I'll do it, he thought. *I'll just pick up that gun and shoot myself.* He puffed the cigarette and thought about all those debutantes he used to screw back in New York City. He remembered the parties, the balls, Saturday afternoons at the Metropolitan Museum of Art. *If it weren't for this fucking war, I'd be all right,* he thought. *Goddamn stinking Japs.*

The cigarette shrank in size, its smoke curling toward the ceiling. A breeze blew in through the window, and Delane could hear traffic in the street outside. Back at the post, his buddies were running around in the woods. He wondered what they'd think when they found out he'd killed himself.

They'll probably think I was a coward, he thought, and then a chill passed over him. They wouldn't think he'd done anything romantic or poetic, and he cared more about what they'd think about him than the maids and room-service waiters who'd find him dead. His brow became ruffled with painful thoughts. Did he want to be remembered as the guy who killed himself because he was afraid to go to the front?

Delane didn't like that. But on the other hand, he didn't want to go back to the front. He couldn't stand any more of the constant tension of not knowing whether he'd be alive the next day, or even the next minute. The Japs were everywhere. They could slip into your foxhole at night and cut your throat.

79

On top of all that C rations were greasy and terrible, bugs were everywhere, and the filth was intolerable.

I can't handle it anymore, Delane thought, stubbing out his cigarette in the ashtray. He reached for the Colt .45 and picked it up, turning it around so that it pointed to his heart, and hooking his thumb around the trigger. *All I have to do now is pull the trigger. The war will be all over for me. They'll never be able to kill me.*

He wrinkled his nose and then burst into laughter. Killing himself so that the Japs wouldn't kill him struck him as funny. What did it matter either way? He was going to die no matter what happened. Even if the Japs didn't kill him and he didn't kill himself, he would still die one day.

This is silly, he realized. *I'm killing myself so that I won't be killed.* And then a bolt of terror passed through his body as he realized what Butsko would say after he was found dead in the Royal Hawaiian Hotel, a suicide note and a bottle of champagne nearby. Delane almost could hear Butsko's voice in the room with him.

"I always knew he was an asshole," Butsko would say. "I always knew the son of a bitch didn't have any guts."

Delane closed his eyes and placed the Colt .45 on the table. It was true: That was exactly what Butsko would say, and it was humiliating. *But I don't have to kill myself,* Delane thought. *I can return to the post and carry on as if nothing happened. If the Japs kill me, they'll kill me; but if I kill myself, everyone will think I'm an asshole.*

Delane imagined Frankie La Barbara howling with laughter when he heard the news that Delane had killed himself, and that settled the matter once and for all. *I'm not going to do it,* he thought. *Nobody's going to laugh at me after I'm dead and gone. I'm going back to the post right now.*

But first I think I'll finish off this champagne. He reached for the bottle and poured himself another glass, then raised the glass to his lips and sipped it down. *This is good stuff. I think I'll call down for another bottle.*

FIVE . . .

Lieutenant Dale Breckenridge approached regimental headquarters, which resembled the orderly room of Headquarters
Company except that it was four times as large. He climbed
the three steps, opened the door, and stepped into the orderly
room. Sergeant Koch sat behind his desk, and across the room
Pfc. Levinson banged the keys of his Underwood typewriter.

Sergeant Koch looked up. "Uh-oh," he said.

"What the matter?" asked Lieutenant Breckenridge.

"I guess you haven't spoken with Captain Spode lately."

"As a matter of fact, I haven't. What's going on?"

"You're in a whole lot of trouble, young Lieutenant."

"I am?"

"Yes, sir. Guess who was found drunk in downtown Honolulu this morning?"

"Who?"

"Corporal Lupe Gomez. He was AWOL, but guess how he
was carried on the Headquarters Company morning report this
morning?"

"I know," Lieutenant Breckenridge replied. "Has the morning report gone to Division yet?"

"What do you think?"

"It has?"

"You're fucking right it has. And do you wanna guess where the former Corporal Gomez is right now?"

"In the stockade?"

"You got it. And do you wanna guess where the former Sergeant Cameron is right now?"

Lieutenant Breckenridge groaned.

"Confined to quarters pending court-martial," Sergeant Koch said. "And do you wanna know where you're probably gonna be before the day is over?"

"Is Colonel Hutchins in?"

"Yeah, he's in."

"I want to have a talk with him."

"Are you sure?"

"Cut the bullshit, Koch. Just tell the old man I'm here and I want to talk to him."

"Yes, sir," Sergeant Koch said. He picked up the telephone receiver, pressed a button, and mumbled into the mouthpiece. He winced as Colonel Hutchins's voice boomed through both the earpiece and through Colonel Hutchins's door down the corridor.

"Send the son of a bitch in right now!"

Even Lieutenant Breckenridge heard Colonel Hutchins's voice. He turned around, pushed open the gate, and walked down the corridor, knocking on the door at the end.

"Come in!"

Lieutenant Breckenridge opened the door and saw Colonel Hutchins seated behind his desk, his face a beet-red color. Lieutenant Breckenridge marched to the desk, stopped, and saluted. "Good morning, sir!"

"You dumb fuck!" Colonel Hutchins said. "What have you done?"

"I can explain everything," Lieutenant Breckenridge said. "It was all a mistake."

Colonel Hutchins didn't invite Lieutenant Breckenridge to sit down. He picked up the stack of papers on his desk and let them drop. "I got plenty to do here and I don't need any problems, do you understand?"

"Yes, sir!"

"You've given me a big problem, and I don't like it!"

"I'm sorry, sir!"

"Being sorry don't make a fuck to me! It doesn't take any work off my back! It just makes me mad!"

"I was only trying to cover up for my men, sir. If I made a mistake, that was the reason. They're good men, sir. You know that as well as I do. They're just a little wild, but if they weren't a little wild, they wouldn't be the good fighters that they are."

Colonel Hutchins groaned and shook his head. He opened the drawer of his desk and took out his latest bottle of Old Taylor, raising it to his mouth and gulping some down. "Have a seat."

"Thank you, sir."

"Want a drink?"

"Yes, sir."

Colonel Hutchins tossed the bottle to Lieutenant Breckenridge, who unscrewed the cap and touched the mouth of the bottle to his lips, tilting his head back.

"Do you know what I have to do now because of you?" Colonel Hutchins asked. "I'll have to go up to Division and grovel in front of General Hawkins for about a half hour, and he's a pompous son of a bitch. He'll chew my ass out and call me every name in the book. I don't like that, Breckenridge. And it's all your fault."

"I had to give my men a chance, sir. Just blame everything on me. Put me in the stockade. Stand me before a firing squad. I don't give a fuck."

"Talk's cheap," Colonel Hutchins said. "I'm the one who'll have to go to Division and get down on my knees and beg."

"I'll go with you."

"That'll make it worse. I'll have to do it myself. You're confined to this post until further notice. Is that clear?"

"I know where two of the men are hiding in Honolulu, sir. I thought I might go get them and bring them back."

"Which two?"

"Pfc. La Barbara and Pfc. Shilansky."

"The worst of a bad bunch. Where are they?"

"In a whorehouse."

"They'll probably come back with the syph and the clap."

"I wouldn't be surprised."

"How do you know they're there?"

"Butsko told me. The madam told him. She's an old friend of his."

"Butsko knows every whorehouse in town. What did he have to say about all this?"

"He said I'm an asshole."

"You are."

The phone rang on Colonel Hutchins's desk and he picked it up. "Colonel Hutchins speaking. Yes. No. You did? Where was he? Oh, my God!" Colonel Hutchins groaned and hung up the phone. "Guess what?" he said to Lieutenant Breckenridge.

"What?"

"They just caught another one. Pfc. James O'Rourke. He was running around like a maniac on a banana plantation, of all places." Colonel Hutchins groaned as he held out his hands. "Throw me that bottle, willya, you goddamned dope?"

Jimmy O'Rourke had seen the Schofield Barracks post stockade from a distance many times since the division had been shipped to Hawaii, and it had always seemed ominous and foreboding to him. He'd heard all the stories about how it was the worst stockade in the whole US Army, and that the guards were a bunch of vicious sadists. It was a long distance from the main road, and consisted of barracks just like the barracks all over the post except that they were behind barbed wire and turrets with armed guards were at every corner.

The jeep stopped at the front gate of the stockade. Jimmy O'Rourke sat in the backseat, his wrists held by handcuffs. He still wore the fatigues they'd caught him with on the banana plantation. They'd sent bloodhounds after him, and the fucking mutts had tracked him down in no time at all.

"Out of the jeep," said one of the MPs.

Jimmy O'Rourke climbed down and looked at the barbed-wire gate. One guard was posted on either side of the gate, and inside was a small guardhouse.

"Here comes another one," a guard said with a fiendish grin.

One MP grabbed Jimmy O'Rourke by his shirt and pulled

him toward the gate. "I got a prisoner," he said, showing a sheaf of papers to the guard.

The guard looked at the papers. "Another AWOL, huh?" He glanced at Jimmy O'Rourke. "Afraid to go and fight for your country, prisoner?"

"I did more fighting for my country than you ever did, you fucking goldbrick," Jimmy said.

"Yeah?" the guard asked with a grin, showing a gold-capped tooth.

"Yeah," Jimmy replied.

"We'll see about that."

The other guard, who had a long lantern jaw, opened the gate. The MPs nudged Jimmy O'Rourke forward. Jimmy O'-Rourke walked into the stockade and fought the tide of fear rising inside him. The guards closed the gate, and the MPs pulled Jimmy O'Rourke toward the guardhouse. One of them opened the door and pushed Jimmy inside.

"What've we got here?" asked the stout sergeant sitting behind the desk, his head shaved smooth.

"An AWOL," said MP.

"No shit." The sergeant looked at Jimmy O'Rourke. "Miss your momma?" he asked. "Is that why you went over the hill?"

Jimmy O'Rourke didn't say anything. The sergeant frowned, stood up, and walked around his desk, stopping in front of Jimmy O'Rourke.

"I just asked you a question, prisoner."

"Fuck you," Jimmy O'Rourke said.

"Oh, yeah?" asked the sergeant.

"Yeah."

The sergeant looked at two other guards in the office. "You hear that, boys?"

They nodded.

The sergeant returned his attention to Jimmy O'Rourke. "Gee, you must be a real tough guy," he said. "Are you a tough guy?"

Jimmy O'Rourke refused to reply.

"I just asked you a question, prisoner."

Again Jimmy O'Rourke wouldn't answer.

"Gimme the papers," the guard said to the MPs. "I'll sign for the son of a bitch and take him off your hands."

The MP laid the papers on the desk and the sergeant signed them. The sergeant took two copies and returned two copies to the MPs.

"He's yours now," the MP said.

"Thanks a bunch," the sergeant replied.

The MPs gathered their papers, removed their cuffs from Jimmy O'Rourke's wrists, and marched out of the office, leaving Jimmy O'Rourke standing in the middle of the room with the three guards looking at him.

The sergeant sat on the edge of his desk and folded his arms. "This guy thinks he's a wise guy. How wise are you?" he asked Jimmy O'Rourke.

I'm not gonna answer him, Jimmy O'Rourke said to himself. *I'm not gonna play his fucking game.*

"I just asked you a question," the sergeant said.

Jimmy didn't reply. The two guards, each carrying a billy club, approached from either side. One poked his club into Jimmy's kidney.

"Stand at attention!" the guard said.

Jimmy pulled himself together and stood stiffly, his arms straight down his sides, stomach in and chest out.

"That's better," said the sergeant, standing and unfolding his arms. He stepped forward until his face was a few inches from Jimmy O'Rourke's. "Let me tell you something, Prisoner O'Rourke. We don't like AWOLs in this stockade, because an AWOL is a coward who's afraid to do his duty for his country."

Jimmy O'Rourke's eyes clouded over as he remembered the hell of the Guadalcanal beach, the bloody battle for Kokengolo Hill on New Georgia, and the deadly jungles of Bougainville. "I already did my duty for my country," he said. "When are you gonna do yours?"

A guard behind him poked his club into Jimmy's kidney again, and it hurt. "Keep your yap shut!" he said.

Jimmy spun around, drew back his arm, and punched the surprised guard in the mouth. The guard staggered backward, and Jimmy lashed out with his leg, kicking the second guard in the balls. That guard screamed and clutched his groin, bending over in pain, and Jimmy turned to the sergeant, who ran behind his desk.

"*Halp!*" hollered the sergeant. "*Halp!*"

Jimmy dived over the desk and grabbed the sergeant by the throat. He and the sergeant collided against the wall, but Jimmy didn't release his grip. The sergeant turned purple as he sagged to the floor. Then the door flew open and more guards rushed into the room, swinging their clubs.

A club hit Jimmy upside his head, and he saw stars. Another club whacked his head on the other side, and he was out like a light. He pitched forward onto his face as the sergeant screamed: *"Throw the son of a bitch into the hole!"*

Colonel Hutchins walked through the long winding corridors of division headquarters, a truculent expression on his face. He was half drunk as usual and angry because the word had come in on Pfc. Craig Delane just before he'd left his office. It seemed that Delane had got drunk on champagne in his hotel room and thought the Japs had come after him. He'd fired his Colt .45 wildly around the hotel room, and then the MPs showed up, charging him with being AWOL, impersonating an officer, stealing military property (the Colt .45), and reckless endangerment.

Colonel Hutchins knew it'd be in all the papers that afternoon and that the Army would be embarrassed. General Hawkins would chew his ass out, but trouble and pressure made Colonel Hutchins mad. He was spoiling for a fight. They could throw him into the stockade if they wanted to, but no generals were going to push him around no matter how many stars they wore on their collars.

"Hello, Bob," said a voice nearby.

Colonel Hutchins looked up and saw Colonel Jessup in the corridor. "Hi, Tim."

"I hear you're in trouble."

"I'm always in trouble."

"The old man's awfully mad."

"Well, I'm madder. Get out of my way."

Colonel Jessup stepped to the side, a worried expression on his face, and Colonel Hutchins proceeded to stomp down the corridor. He wore his belt low and his big belly hung over it. The corners of his mouth were turned down, and he looked like a bulldog. He turned left and right and left again, and found himself in front of General Hawkins's office. Sergeant

Somerall sat at a desk beside the door, and a clerk-typist sat at another desk on the other side of the door.

"I'm here for my appointment," Colonel Hutchins said, "and I'm a little early."

"Have a seat, sir."

"Have a seat yourself, soldier."

Colonel Hutchins walked toward General Hawkins's door.

Sergeant Somerall stood behind his desk. "You can't go in there!"

"The fuck I can't."

Colonel Hutchins twisted the knob and pushed the door open, storming into General Hawkins's office. The General sat behind his desk, and in front of him were three of his staff officers. A meeting was going on, and it looked like a serious one.

General Hawkins nearly turned green. "What the hell do you think you're doing, barging in here like this, Colonel!"

Colonel Hutchins realized that he'd fucked up again. "Sorry, sir."

"Get the hell out of here and wait until I call you in!"

"Yes, sir."

Colonel Hutchins turned around and walked out of the office, closing the door behind him. He tiptoed to a chair near Sergeant Somerall's desk and sat down. *Why do I do things like that?* he wondered. *What the hell gets into me?* He noticed Sergeant Somerall looking at him, a faint smile on his face.

"What's so funny, Sergeant?"

Sergeant Somerall wiped the smile off his face. "Nothing, sir!"

"Get the fuck to work!"

"Yes, sir."

Sergeant Somerall turned his attention to the papers on his desk and shuffled them around. Colonel Hutchins took out a cigarette and lit it up. *I've got to be real calm when I go in there to see the general,* he thought. *Otherwise I'm liable to wind up in the soup again.*

The MPs had to drag Pfc. Craig Delane into the guardhouse at the stockade because he was too drunk to navigate in a straight line by himself. The same sergeant sat behind his desk, purple marks on his throat from where Pfc. Jimmy O'Rourke had tried to strangle him.

"Now what?" asked the sergeant.

"Got a present for you," replied an MP.

"What's this one done?"

"You name it and he's done it."

The MPs threw the papers on the sergeant's desk, and the sergeant read them. "Holy shit," he said. "What a day this is turning out to be."

He signed the papers and the MPs took their copies.

"He can't walk too good," an MP said. "Somebody'll have to carry him to his quarters."

"Carry him my ass. He might haveta crawl, but he'll get there under his own steam."

Craig Delane stood unsteadily in front of the sergeant's desk, leaning first to one side and then the other. The two guards arose from their chairs and walked toward Delane, poking him with their billy clubs.

"Stand straight!" one of them said.

Delane tried, but he couldn't do it. He'd drunk three bottles of champagne before the Japs started coming at him out of the walls.

"I said stand straight!" the guard barked, slapping Craig Delane's biceps with his billy club.

Delane turned to him. "Who do you think you're hitting with that club, shitface!"

"What!"

The guard raised his billy club, and Craig Delane dived for his wrist, but his aim was off and wind whistled past his ears as he fell to his face on the floor. The guard clobbered him on the back of the head with his billy club, and blood appeared through Craig Delane's light-brown hair.

"Another wisenheimer," said the sergeant behind the desk. "Throw him in the hole."

The staff officers left General Hawkins's office, looking at Colonel Hutchins as if he'd just crawled out from underneath a toilet bowl. Colonel Hutchins glowered at them and snarled as he puffed a cigarette, and the phone on Sergeant Somerall's desk rang. Sergeant Somerall lifted the receiver and listened for a few seconds, then hung it up and said to Colonel Hutchins: "The general will see you now."

Colonel Hutchins stood and walked toward the door. He wore a fatigue uniform neatly ironed and carried his fatigue hat in his back pocket. Opening the door, he entered General Hawkins's office. General Hawkins was standing at the window, looking out.

"Sit down," General Hawkins said, his back to Colonel Hutchins.

Colonel Hutchins sat down and waited for General Hawkins to turn around, but General Hawkins didn't turn around. *He's trying to make me nervous and catch me off guard*, Colonel Hutchins thought. *Well, I can wait as long as he can.*

The room was silent, and bright sunlight streamed through the windows in two of the walls. Photographs of Franklin Roosevelt and General Douglas MacArthur were on the wall behind the desk, flanked by the American flag on the left and the division flag on the right.

"I ought to relieve you of command," General Hawkins said in a low voice barely under control. He still was looking out the window.

"If you did, where would you dig up somebody to take over my regiment in the two or three weeks between now and the time we land on New Guinea?"

General Hawkins turned around, his eyes goggling at Colonel Hutchins. "How did you find out about New Guinea?"

"It's all over the division. Everybody's talking about it. You can't keep a secret like that for long. You know the exact day we're moving out?"

General Hawkins scowled, clasped his hands behind his back, raised himself on his toes, and lowered himself. He wore his blond hair parted on the side, and he had a thick blond mustache. A graduate of West Point, he knew all the right people and was on his way to the top of the Army, if he didn't get killed first.

"I don't know what to do with you," he said to Colonel Hutchins.

"I think you're stuck with me until we get to New Guinea at least."

"You've made a big mess for me, you bastard!"

90

"I didn't do anything. There's a problem in my regiment and I'll take care of it, if you'll just get out of my road."

"All problems come from the top," General Hawkins said, raising himself on his toes again and looking down his nose at Colonel Hutchins. "A commander sets the tone of his unit. There's a problem in your regiment because there's a problem with you."

"Well," replied Colonel Hutchins, "my regiment is in your division, which means you've got a problem in your division. Is that your fault, since you're the commander and the commander sets the tone?"

"I've never liked you, Hutchins. You're a drunk and I wish I could get rid of you."

"You didn't talk that way when we were on Bougainville, sir. As I recall, my regiment saved your ass a few times."

General Hawkins wheezed and his shoulders slumped. He sat on the chair behind his desk and seemed to shrink inside his uniform. "This isn't Bougainville," he said weakly.

"I know where we are, and I know where we're going," Colonel Hutchins replied. "We'll be fighting the Japs in just a little while, and you're gonna need me because my regiment is lean and mean, and I'm the guy who keeps them that way. Did I ever let you down on Bougainville?"

"No."

"When the Japs pulled off their big counterattack on Bougainville, whose regiment was the only regiment that held its ground?"

"Yours."

"Do you remember Pat's Nose?" Colonel Hutchins asked, referring to Hill 700 on Bougainville.

"I do."

"Pat's Nose bore the brunt of the Jap counterattack, and do you know who stopped the Japs on Pat's Nose?"

"Who?"

"My recon platoon and Fox Company, and I was there too. I got shot on Pat's Nose, you may remember, sir, and I surely would've been killed. But my life was saved by the arrival of my men from the recon platoon, some of whom are in the stockade right now. I request your permission, sir, to go get them out!"

General Hawkins sat up in his chair. "But they're AWOL!"

"So fucking what!"

General Hawkins blinked his eyes in astonishment. *"Who in the hell do you think you're talking to!"*

"You!"

General Hawkins and Colonel Hutchins glowered at each other. General Hawkins wanted to bust Colonel Hutchins down to Private E-nothing and put him in the stockade, while Colonel Hutchins wanted to strangle General Hawkins on the spot. The room was silent except for snatches of conversation seeping through the door from the corridor outside.

Colonel Hutchins leaned forward and turned down the corners of his mouth. "In a few weeks, when the shit hits the fan on New Guinea, you're gonna wish you had more men like the ones from my recon platoon who're in the stockade right now."

"Maybe so," General Hawkins replied, "but they're AWOLs and I've got to throw the book at them."

"You don't have to throw anything at them."

"Oh, yes I do. The law is the law."

"You're the law around here, General. What you say goes. And your career is on the line here, too, sir. Let's not forget about that part. If the Japs kick our asses off New Guinea, you're gonna find yourself behind a desk in Washington so fast it'll make your head swim, if you're still alive that long; but you'll never get kicked off New Guinea with men like the ones in the stockade from my regiment."

General Hawkins put a cigarette in his mouth and lit it up. He blew smoke into the air and thought about what Colonel Hutchins had said. It was true: You couldn't have enough good soldiers in a tough fight, and a tough fight was looming for the Eighty-first Division.

"What can we do?" he asked Colonel Hutchins.

"You don't have to do anything. I'll take care of everything."

"What about the men in the stockade?"

"I'll get 'em outta the stockade."

"But they're AWOL!"

"They're not AWOL unless you say they're AWOL."

"But the MPs picked them up!"

"They made a mistake."

"Two of your men were on the front page of today's Honolulu *Daily News!* You can't cover up something like this!"

"Leave everything to me. If anybody asks you anything, refer them to me. The ones in the stockade I'll get outta the stockade, and the ones who're still on the loose will probably show up sometime today. The Honolulu *Daily News* will forget about the whole mess by tomorrow. As far as I'm concerned, all those men of mine were out on official business for the regiment. They were never AWOL in the first place. The MPs were overzealous in the performance of their duties. Feel better now, sir?"

General Hawkins pounded his fist down on his desk. "But one of them was found dead drunk in a gutter on one of the worst slum stretches in Honolulu!"

Colonel Hutchins smiled tolerantly. "He was on a reconnaissance mission, sir, because we're gonna have to fight in cities before this war is out, and it was part of his training."

"I don't want to hear anything more about this," General Hawkins said wearily. "Get out of my office."

Colonel Hutchins jumped to attention and threw a snappy salute. *"Yes, sir!"*

It was high noon in the whorehouse, and Frankie La Barbara was fucking his brains out. A whore named Barbara lay on her back with her legs wrapped around Frankie's waist, while Frankie lay on top and long-stroked her, cupping her ass in his hands.

"Oh, baby," Frankie murmured, "you've got the greatest cunt in the world."

"Fuck me, you big son of a bitch!" she replied passionately, although she didn't feel passionate at all. This was her job, and she customarily turned ten to twenty tricks a day, sometimes more.

On the next bed a whore named Flo was perched on her hands and knees, wagging her ass from side to side while Pfc. Morris Shilansky did it to her doggie-style.

"Ooooh!" Flo said. "It feels so good!"

Flo was acting, too, while thinking about the ranch in Texas that she hoped to buy someday, although the only ranch she'd ever own was the one in the painting that hung on the wall of her little room in the whorehouse.

Both beds creaked as they bounced up and down. The air was fragrant with perfume and sweat, and a horn blew down the street outside the window. Frankie huffed and puffed, because he was nearing his third orgasm of the day, and Shilansky's tongue hung out of the corner of his mouth, because he was on his fourth.

Suddenly, as if in a nightmare, the door to the room broke apart, and soldiers in green fatigues, carrying Thompson submachine guns, burst into the room. Frankie screamed, jumped into the air, and dived under his pillow, reaching for his Colt .45.

A hand clamped on his wrist. "Hold it right there, scumbag," said the nasal voice of Sergeant Cameron.

The whores screeched and held their fists to their cheeks. Shilansky's dick shriveled up and fell out of the well it had been drilling. He saw Pfc. Hotshot Stevenson pointing a Thompson submachine gun at him.

"Don't shoot!" said Shilansky, holding up his hand.

"Raise your hands over your head, you silly son of a bitch," said Hotshot Stevenson, who had been a professional pool shark and shoplifter before the war.

The girls covered themselves with sheets and wondered what the hell was going on. Sergeant Cameron yanked the Colt .45 out from underneath the pillow and tucked it into his belt. Frankie rolled over onto his back, sat up at the edge of the bed, and looked around, his face pale and his dick dripping a substance that looked like the white of a raw egg. He saw Lieutenant Breckenridge standing near the door, a big grin on his face.

"Having a little physical training?" Lieutenant Breckenridge asked. "Are these the new exercises we've been hearing about?"

Frankie didn't know what to say. He'd been caught with his pants down, and that's the worst thing that can happen to any man.

"Let's get our clothes on," Lieutenant Breckenridge said. "We're going home."

⬤ ⬤ ⬤

The MP sergeant looked up from the Spy Smasher comic book that he was reading. A tall, chubby man with his hands cuffed in front of him was pushed into the guardhouse by four MPs. The sergeant laid down his comic book.

"What the hell's going on here today? Every time I turn around, a new prisoner shows up! What's this one done?"

"He's an AWOL," one of the MPs told the sergeant. "He was hiding in a church."

"In a church?" The sergeant looked at the Reverend Billie Jones. "Why, you dirty son of a bitch."

The MP laid the papers on the desk, and the sergeant signed them. The Reverend Billie Jones thought he was like Christ being led before Pontius Pilate, and he was going to turn the other cheek, just as Christ had done.

The sergeant returned the papers to the MPs, who unfastened the cuffs on Billie Jones's wrists, turned around, and walked out of the guardhouse, closing the door behind them, leaving the Reverend Billie Jones with the sergeant and four guards, all armed with billy clubs.

The guards got up from their chairs and approached Billie Jones, hoping he'd do something wrong, because they were itching for a fight. Two of their buddies were in the hospital due to rowdy prisoners, and they weren't about to let that happen again.

The sergeant read the charges. "Another AWOL," he said. "Jesus Christ, they're running away like rats from a sinking ship today." He looked up at Billie Jones. "Are you a rat, prisoner?"

Billie Jones didn't answer.

"I just asked you a question, prisoner!"

Billie Jones didn't answer.

A guard poked his billy club into Billie Jones's kidney, and Billie Jones flinched.

"I asked you if you were a rat, prisoner!"

Billie Jones didn't rise to the provocation. He just stood at attention and thought of how great Christ must have been to put up with shit like this without blowing his top.

The sergeant got mad. He was having a bad day, and he wanted somebody to pay for it. He arose and walked around his desk, looking up into Billie Jones's face.

"You'd better answer me, prisoner!" he said.

Billie Jones didn't answer.

The sergeant spit in Billie Jones's face, and Billie Jones flinched. He got warm underneath his collar and felt his mind going weird. He wanted to beat the sergeant to death, but more than that, he wanted to be a good Christian and turn the other cheek. So he angled his head to the side and actually showed his other cheek to the sergeant.

The sergeant spat again, and some of the spittle flew onto Billie Jones's lips, making him nauseous. Billie Jones had turned both of his cheeks, and now he didn't have anything else to turn. The sergeant's face turned purple with rage.

"You'd better answer me, goddamnit!"

Billie still refused to answer, although his head was filling with steam.

A guard poked his billy club into Billie Jones's kidney. Another guard slapped him on the thigh. The third guard poked his billy club up Billie Jones's ass, and that did it.

Billie Jones jumped to the side and raised his fists.

"Get him!" the sergeant said.

The guards converged on Billie Jones, swinging their clubs. He deflected one blow with his left forearm and another blow with his right forearm, then clasped his hands together, swinging sideways at the head of a guard. He connected with the jaw of the guard, dislocating it. The guard was knocked cold and flopped onto his back, while the sergeant ran behind his desk and picked up the chair.

Another guard swung his club at Billie's head, and Billie ducked. The guard couldn't check his swing in time, and the club connected with the head of the guard who was charging Billie Jones from his blind side. The club caved in the side of the guard's skull and flung him to the floor.

Billie growled at the two guards and the sergeant advancing toward him with the chair held over his head.

"C'mon, you fucking bastards, I'll kill yez all!" Billie yelled.

The two guards attacked Billie, swinging their clubs. Billie caught a guard's wrist in his hands, but the other guard slammed him on the head. Everything went black in front of Billie's eyes, and he heard bells and birds. He staggered back, and the other guard clobbered him on the top of the head, but Billie was a big strong man and he wouldn't go down. The sergeant crashed his chair on Billie's head, and Billie's legs buckled slightly, but still he did not fall.

The door to the guardhouse was thrown open.

"What the hell's going on here?" hollered a voice as loud as thunder.

The guards and the sergeant turned around and saw a stout colonel with a beer belly charging into the guardhouse, followed by soldiers armed with machine guns.

"I said what the hell's going on here?"

The sergeant didn't know whether to shit or go blind. He decided the safest thing would be to come to attention and salute. Young Private Jilliam from the recon platoon recognized the Reverend Billie Jones underneath the blood covering Jones's face.

"It's Billie Jones!" he said.

Colonel Hutchins turned to Billie Jones and got mad. "Why, these sons of bitches have been beating up on him!"

"He tried to escape!" shouted the sergeant.

"I did not!" replied Billie Jones.

Colonel Hutchins didn't know whom to believe, but it didn't matter. "He's coming with me!" Colonel Hutchins shouted.

The Reverend Billie Jones smiled. "Blessed be the Lord," he said.

"But, sir . . ." protested the sergeant.

"But what, you son of a bitch?" replied Colonel Hutchins, waving his loaded Colt .45 around wildly.

"But he's a prisoner!"

"Not anymore he ain't!" Colonel Hutchins unbuttoned his shirt pocket and took out a sheet of paper, which he unfolded and handed to the sergeant. "I'm taking these men out of here too! Go get them for me!"

The sergeant read the names and realized every one of them had been thrown into the hole that day. "By whose authorization am I releasing these people, sir?"

"By my authorization!"

"Yes, sir!" The sergeant wasn't about to argue with a full bird colonel. He handed the paper to one of the guards. "Go get these men out of the hole!"

"Yo!"

The guard ran out of the door. The sergeant looked down the barrel of the Colt .45 in Colonel Hutchins's hand. The Reverend Billie Jones shook his head and tried to come to his senses.

"He spit in my face," Billie Jones said, "and then they beat the piss out of me, but they never knocked me down."

Colonel Hutchins smiled. Billie Jones was as tough as a block of steel, just the kind of soldier he'd need on New Guinea.

"Sir," said the sergeant, "how should I list these men on my daily report?"

"Just say they were released on my orders."

"But they're AWOLs!"

"They're not AWOLs. They've never been AWOLs. This is just an MP fuck-up. And you'd better hope I don't press charges against you for beating up my man."

"But he tried to escape!"

Just then the door opened and three men, covered with cuts and bruises, stumbled into the guardhouse. They were Corporal Lupe Gomez, Pfc. Craig Delane, and Pfc. Jimmy O'Rourke. Their eyes blinked and they appeared dazed because there was no light in the hole, and now the exposure to light was disorienting them.

"My God!" said Colonel Hutchins. "What happened to you?"

Craig Delane turned around and looked at Colonel Hutchins. "Is that you, sir?" he asked.

"It ain't nobody else."

"They beat me up, sir."

"Me too," said Pfc. Jimmy O'Rourke.

"Yo también," added Corporal Gomez, who was so punch-drunk he'd forgotten how to speak English.

Colonel Hutchins turned to the sergeant. "You son of a bitch, they *all* didn't try to escape!"

"But, sir . . ." cried the sergeant, holding up his hands.

"I oughtta kick the shit out of you myself!"

"But, sir . . ."

"Don't but me!"

"Yes, sir!"

Colonel Hutchins looked at his men. "Let's get back to the regiment!" Then he returned his malevolent glare to the sergeant. "I'm gonna press charges against you, you son of a

98

bitch! I'm gonna have you thrown into that hole where you threw my men!"

"Yes, sir!" said the sergeant, a catch in his voice.

Colonel Hutchins turned and stormed out of the guardhouse, and the rest of the recon platoon followed him.

The sergeant was left alone with his guards. He dragged his feet around his desk and collapsed into his chair.

"Damn!" said the sergeant, burying his face in his hands. "What am I gonna do now?"

"If I was you," replied one of the guards, "I think I'd go AWOL."

It was three o'clock in the afternoon, and Lieutenant Diane Latham's shift was coming to an end. She stepped out of the nurses' station, turned left, and nearly bumped into Lieutenant Dale Breckenridge, who was heading the other way at top speed.

"Oh!" she said, stopping and raising her hands to her face.

Lieutenant Breckenridge jumped backward as if he'd just seen a rattlesnake. "Excuse me, ma'am," he said, stepping to the side and walking around her, continuing on his way to the solarium.

He walked inside and saw Butsko seated in his wheelchair on one side of a big round table where the men were playing poker for chips.

Butsko looked up at Lieutenant Breckenridge. "Be with you in a moment."

Lieutenant Breckenridge walked to the window and looked at the parking lot below. His eyes came to rest on a yellow car that stood out among all the other cars, and he realized it was the Packard convertible belonging to the lovely Diane Latham.

If only I'd met her under different circumstances, Lieutenant Breckenridge thought. *Boy, would I love to get that girl into a bed.*

It occurred to him that he still didn't know what Bob Utsler had done to her, and he made up his mind to speak with Utsler as soon as he was finished with Butsko. Lieutenant Breckenridge took out his pack of cigarettes and lit one up, blowing smoke at the window. It rolled back at him and he saw a small figure in a white nurse's uniform enter the parking lot, heading toward the yellow Packard.

"It's her," he muttered.

She unlocked the door of the Packard, got inside, and put the top down. Lieutenant Breckenridge wished he could go for a ride with her, then remembered the last ride he'd taken with her and said "Ouch!"

"Talking to yourself these days?" Butsko asked, approaching in his wheelchair.

Lieutenant Breckenridge turned around. "I think I'm going nuts," he said.

"You've been going nuts ever since I met you," Butsko replied. "Have a seat. What's going on? By the way, who in the fuck beat you up?"

"You wouldn't believe it," Lieutenant Breckenridge said, sitting down.

"Was it one of the maniacs in the platoon?"

"It was a woman."

"A woman did that to you?"

"That's right."

"She must've been awfully strong."

"She kicked my ass off a cliff."

Butsko smiled. "Yeah?"

"Yeah. And you know who she is too."

"I do? Who is she?"

"Nurse Latham."

"No shit!"

"No shit."

"What'd you do to her?"

"I guess you could say that I lied to her."

"And she kicked your ass off a cliff?"

"That's right."

Butsko shivered. "Boy, I'd better be careful what I say to her. I wouldn't want to tell her a lie by mistake. I always thought she was a sweet kid."

"She's no sweet kid," Lieutenant Breckenridge said darkly.

"Did you fuck her?"

"No."

"That was your problem. You should have fucked her. That's all women really want."

"I'm not so sure about that. Anyway, I didn't have time to fuck her. As soon as we were alone, she kicked my ass off the cliff." Lieutenant Breckenridge sucked his cigarette and wrinkled his forehead, because he didn't want to talk about Nurse Latham anymore. "Never mind all that shit," he said to Butsko. "I came here to tell you what happened today."

"That's right too," Butsko replied. "What happened?"

"Everybody's back," Lieutenant Breckenridge said with a satisfied smile.

"No shit?"

"No shit."

"How'd they get back?"

"I took some of the men and got Frankie and Shilansky out of that whorehouse, and Colonel Hutchins somehow had the others released from the stockade."

"All the others got caught?" Butsko asked.

"The MPs picked up every one of them."

Butsko grimaced in disgust. "Dumb fucks. Can't even go AWOL right."

"Wait'll I tell you what your boy Pfc. Craig Delane did to the Royal Hawaiian Hotel," Lieutenant Breckenridge said, looking around and leaning closer so nobody could hear.

Lieutenant Breckenridge arrived at the officers' club shortly after five o'clock in the afternoon, and the first thing he did was check in at the bar. He ordered a whiskey and soda and sipped it, leaning against a wall because all the bar stools were taken.

It had been an exasperating day, but now it was over. All the AWOLs were back, and beginning tomorrow he'd start toughening up his men for the landing on New Guinea. He wished Butsko would be there to help him, but Butsko wouldn't be out of the wheelchair for another month. Lieutenant Breckenridge would have to go it alone.

The cocktail lounge was chock-full of the usual drunks. In the middle of the bar sat the middle-aged major with black hair who was always drunk and stole whatever money was left on the bar near him. His chest was covered with combat ribbons and he was a scandal all over the post, but no one ever made a harsh remark to him because one of the decorations on his chest was the Congressional Medal of Honor.

Officers arrived lively and smiling, anxious for a drink, and other officers staggered toward the doors, drunk out of their heads. Shortly before quarter to six, Lieutenant Breckenridge saw Lieutenant Jack Utsler enter the lounge and head for the bar, elbowing his way among the drunks, calling out his order to the bartender. Lieutenant Utsler got his drink and stepped back into a less-populated zone. Lieutenant Breckenridge was waiting for him.

"Hi," said Lieutenant Breckenridge.

"Hello, Dale," replied Utsler. "Heard you had a big problem in the regiment today."

"It was nothing," Lieutenant Breckenridge said with a wave of his hand. "It's all over now."

"Heard Colonel Hutchins and General Hawkins had a big set-to."

Lieutenant Breckenridge shrugged. "I don't know anything about it."

"They were really going at it, somebody told me."

Both men sipped their drinks. Lieutenant Breckenridge wondered why Utsler didn't say something about Nurse Latham. It seemed to him that Utsler should be mad at him, since Lieutenant Breckenridge had promised that Nurse Latham would fuck Utsler and it hadn't happened that way.

Or had it? Lieutenant Breckenridge's brow became furrowed. His curiosity was getting the best of him. He looked at Utsler, who calmly took out his pack of cigarettes and lit one up.

"Hey, Jack," Lieutenant Breckenridge said, "how'd everything go that night between you and that nurse I set you up with?"

"You mean the blonde?"

"Yeah."

Lieutenant Utsler smiled. "It went just like you said it would, Dale. She sucked my dick and then we screwed for a while."

"You get a hotel in town?"

"Naw, we did it in the woods. She was a real eager beaver, just like you said. Couldn't wait to get my clothes off. Thanks

102

a lot, by the way. Guess I forgot to thank you, huh?"

"That's okay, Jack." Lieutenant Breckenridge raised his glass and drained it dry. "I need another drink." he said. "Can I get you one?"

"Not yet."

Lieutenant Breckenridge pushed through the mob and made his way to the bar, ordering a double from the bartender and wondering whether Jack Utsler was lying. Lieutenant Breckenridge knew there were some jerks in the world who'd lie about screwing women, especially when the babe in question was supposed to be screwing everybody. No guy wanted to be the one she wouldn't screw.

Lieutenant Breckenridge waited while the bartender mixed drinks for the officers who'd ordered ahead of him. He glanced back at Utsler, who was talking with another officer. *Would he lie about something like that?* Lieutenant Breckenridge asked himself.

It's possible, he answered himself, because Utsler's response was extremely suspicious. First of all, he didn't think Nurse Latham was the slut he'd made her out to be when he'd described her to Utsler, although maybe she was; he couldn't say for sure. Second, if it had all gone as Utsler said it had, Utsler would have called sometime yesterday to thank him. But Utsler hadn't called. Why? Maybe because Nurse Latham had slapped his face or kicked him in the balls, and Utsler didn't want to talk about it if he didn't have to.

Third, if Nurse Latham had screwed Utsler and had such a good time, why would she kick Lieutenant Breckenridge off the cliff?

It didn't add up. Lieutenant Breckenridge decided that Utsler had lied, although it was impossible to say for sure. A man could never be sure about a woman. A man should never bet his life on his children being his children. Lieutenant Breckenridge had met numerous crazy females in his life, and knew they were capable of any weird thing. They could lie with a straight face and do the strangest things for no reason at all.

Lieutenant Breckenridge didn't want to return to Utsler and continue that conversation. The person he wanted to talk with was Nurse Latham. He thought he should apologize to her, and maybe while he had her on the phone, he could find out what had happened between her and Utsler.

Utsler was still having a conversation with another officer. Lieutenant Breckenridge paid the bartender for his drink and pushed to the side so he wouldn't encounter Utsler. He made his way through the throng of officers, who were trying to get drunk with the greatest possible speed, and finally broke loose, heading for the telephones in the basement lounge.

He descended the spiral staircase three steps at a time and saw the rows of telephone booths, about half of which were occupied by officers making calls. He jumped into an empty booth and dialed the residence where Diane Latham lived, hoping she was home.

"Lieutenant Diane Latham," he said to the person who picked up the phone.

"One moment, please."

He waited, taking out a cigarette and lighting it up. Then he heard her voice, and the cigarette nearly dropped out of his mouth.

"Hello," she said.

"Hi," he replied.

"Who's this?" she asked.

"Lieutenant Dale Breckenridge, and please don't hang up!"
Click!

The line went dead. Lieutenant Breckenridge shrugged and hung up the phone. *I guess she's still mad at me,* he said to himself. *I'll try again in a few days. Maybe she won't be so mad then.*

SIX . . .

On Monday of the next week the Eighty-first Division began serious training for the move to New Guinea. By then everybody knew they were returning to war, but not everybody knew where they were going. By Friday the word had got around that New Guinea would be the destination.

The infantry soldiers trained hard. They went on speed marches with full field packs up and down the mountains of Oahu. Men passed out in the heat and were revived with kicks in the ass or water poured on their faces out of canteens. Some didn't recover that easily and had to be taken to the post hospital, victims of heat exhaustion.

They went out into the boondocks and attacked hills, pillboxes, trench networks, and bunkers, practicing the principles of fire and maneuver, perfecting their tactical skills. It was grueling, tedious work, but they faced no real enemy. No one shot back at them. The combat veterans knew that textbook training exercises were one thing and real war was something else entirely. Yet, they had to get the basics down pat. Everybody had to learn to work together, the old combat veterans and the new replacements from the States.

Lieutenant Breckenridge trained his recon platoon hardest, because they always got the shittiest jobs. If other platoons speed-marched ten miles, the recon platoon speed-marched fifteen. If the other platoons did a half-hour of physical-training, the recon platoon did a whole hour. If the other platoons captured one hill a day, the recon platoon captured two.

Sometimes, when the recon platoon was in the boondocks, Lieutenant Breckenridge arranged it so that the chow truck wouldn't arrive for lunch and the men wouldn't get anything to eat. They'd train the entire afternoon and often a good portion of the evening on empty stomachs, so they'd get used to actual combat conditions, because chow trucks often couldn't make it to the front lines, and sometimes the men ran out of C rations.

If the chow truck did arrive, Lieutenant Breckenridge made each of his men do thirty push-ups before he could get into the chow line. If they happened to be back at the post during chow time, each man had to do twenty pull-ups, touching the back of his neck to the steel bar, before he could get into the mess hall.

Lieutenant Breckenridge took his men into the jungles of Oahu at night, when other soldiers were sleeping in their clean cots, with the roofs of barracks over their heads. Lieutenant Breckenridge led his men on complex reconnaissance patrols similar to the ones they'd gone on in actual combat on Bougainville and New Georgia. Sometimes they stayed out all night. Occasionally they stayed out three nights in a row, sleeping in the daytime in camouflaged holes with insects stinging them and furry little creatures crawling over them.

They laid mine fields in the middle of the night and picked them up before the sun came up in the morning. Each man became proficient in map reading and compass usage. One night Lieutenant Breckenridge blindfolded his men and they were driven to a remote region of Oahu on the back of a deuce-and-a-half truck. They debarked from the truck, which then drove away. The blindfolds were removed and they had to get back to the post on their own. They had no C rations with them, only one canteen each of water, plus water purification pills. It took them two days to return to the post, and they were more dead than alive, but the jungle they'd passed through had no Japs in it, and they knew it would be very different when they arrived on New Guinea, where Japs would be waiting to ambush them.

On Saturdays, after inspections, Lieutenant Breckenridge delivered his weekly troop-information-and-education lecture to his men, and he always spoke of the cruelty of the Japanese army, how they'd bayoneted babies and old ladies during the infamous Rape of Nanking, how they chopped off the heads of American pilots caught behind Japanese lines, how they tortured and maimed their prisoners and pulled out their fingernails for fun.

Under normal conditions the men would receive overnight passes after their Saturday inspections and troop-information-and-education lectures—and indeed, this is what occurred in most units of the Eighty-first Division, but not in the recon platoon. Lieutenant Breckenridge canceled all weekend passes and furloughs, and the men were confined to the post. They could go to movie theaters and beer halls on the post, but that was all. Lieutenant Breckenridge didn't want to take any more chances with AWOLs. He never got around to calling Nurse Latham again, because he was too busy.

It was worse than boot camp for the recon platoon. The days melted together into an agony of endless training, inspections, and chickenshit. Lieutenant Breckenridge was harsh with them, but they knew Sergeant Butsko would be even harsher if he were around. The men became angry, and Lieutenant Breckenridge skillfully directed their anger at the Japs. Day in and day out they trained, except for Saturday afternoons and Sundays; but on one weekend they continued to train, and that made them even angrier.

Lieutenant Breckenridge hammered them into tiptop physical condition, reacquainting them with basic military skills and forging their emotions into a white-hot molten edge of rage. After three weeks of training, the men were like time bombs waiting to go off. They knew they'd ship out soon, and everybody tried, through every nefarious method available, to determine the actual date of their departure; but that date was kept a secret from them, as was the exact location where they'd hit the beach on New Guinea.

• • •

Even General Clyde Hawkins didn't know when and where the Eighty-first Division was going, and he fretted like the rest of his men, trying to figure it out.

He spent hours poring over maps of New Guinea, trying to pick out likely places for the landing. He'd already been told it would be somewhere west of Hollandia, and he knew General MacArthur wanted airfields from which he could bomb the Philippines, in preparation for the big assault on that vast island complex. General MacArthur had vowed to return to the Philippines, and everybody, even the Japs, knew he was headed in that direction.

General Clyde Hawkins could pinpoint several likely objectives for his division, but he knew he might be completely wrong, because his mind didn't function the way General MacArthur's did. General MacArthur had originated a new form of warfare when he captured Hollandia and Aitape. He'd attacked unlikely objectives, lightly held, and taken them easily, at minimal cost in American lives. How could anyone guess where he'd go next? General Hawkins had a conventional military mind, and his tendency would be to attack the Japs where they were instead of where they weren't.

On his map of New Guinea he could see that the towns of Armopa and Sarmi would be important military objectives, but would they be important to General MacArthur? The Japs had major bases on Monokwari and Sorong on the Vogelkop Peninsula, and they'd have to be dealt with in some way. But perhaps General MacArthur would want to starve them out the way he was starving out the biggest Japanese base in the southwest Pacific: Rabaul, on the island of New Britain. Also, the islands of Wakde, Numfoor, and Biak would have strategic significance in the fight to take New Guinea.

On some days General Hawkins went out into the field with his men, but when he was in his office he studied his maps and tried to figure out where he and his men would be sent. Every passing day brought him closer to embarkation, and his nerves began to frazzle.

He read about the massive assault on Normandy, in France, by the armies of the United States, Great Britain, France, and Canada, and knew that a titanic struggle was being waged there for Europe, under the leadership of General Dwight D. Eisenhower, formerly one of General MacArthur's staff officers in Manila during the thirties. The eyes of the world were on Europe, and General Hawkins knew that the war in the Pacific was on the back burner, because the Joint Chiefs of Staff in Washington had decided that Europe was the most important objective of the war.

Then, on the tenth of June, a top-secret message arrived at General Hawkins's headquarters, for his eyes only. It was hand-delivered by a colonel named Drayton from the headquarters of Lieutenant General Walter Krueger, commander of the US Sixth Army, code-named the Alamo Force. Although he was tempted to tear the envelope apart to get at the news, General Hawkins opened it slowly and deliberately, because he didn't want to look like a fool to the colonel.

The message was simple and to the point: General Hawkins and his chief of staff were to report to General Krueger's headquarters on Hollandia on June 14 at 1400 hours. Reading between the lines, General Hawkins knew that he'd receive the orders for himself and his division from the horse's mouth at that time.

General Hawkins was poker-faced as he looked up from the document at Colonel Drayton. "I'll have one of my aides make a room available for you at the BOQ," he said.

"Thank you," replied Colonel Drayton.

General Hawkins picked up his phone and told Sergeant Somerall to send Lieutenant Utsler to his office immediately. Lieutenant Utsler knocked on the door approximately forty-five seconds after General Hawkins hung up the phone. General Hawkins told Lieutenant Utsler to take care of Colonel Drayton, and Colonel Drayton left with Lieutenant Utsler for the BOQ. General Hawkins then ordered General MacWhitter, his chief of staff, to come to his office. When General MacWhitter arrived, General Hawkins told him they were to report to General Krueger at Alamo Force headquarters on Hollandia on June 14.

General MacWhitter was tall and skinny, and his tan uniform fit him like pajamas. "I guess all our questions will be answered then, eh?" he said.

"I believe so," General Hawkins replied.

General MacWhitter returned to his office and told his aide, Lieutenant Racke, to make the necessary flight arrangements for him and General Hawkins. Lieutenant Racke in turn delegated the task to Technical Sergeant First Class Dumbrowski, and when Sergeant Dumbrowski called the Air Corps liaison to requisition the plane, his clerk, Pfc. Snelling, overheard every word of the conversation.

Within two hours everybody in the Eighty-first Division, from the generals and colonels in their headquarters to the buck privates on KP in the mess halls, knew that the move to New Guinea was imminent, and that General Hawkins and General MacWhitter were going to Hollandia on the fourteenth to get the final word.

General Hawkins and General MacWhitter departed from Clark Airfield on the morning of the thirteenth on an Army Air Corps transport plane, and stopped on Howland Island for refueling early in the afternoon. They resumed their flight and arrived at Henderson Field on Guadalcanal that evening, where they dined at the officers' mess and spent the night in a wooden shack.

The next morning at six o'clock their plane took off for Hollandia and arrived at noon. They went first to the officers' mess for lunch, then made their way to the building where General Krueger's office was located.

All the buildings in the area had been recently constructed by Army Engineers from shingle and prefabricated beaverboard components. General MacArthur had designated Hollandia as the site of his new forward headquarters, and the largest structure, made of three prefabricated buildings joined together, would be his residence.

It was in a spectacular spot, on the slope of mountain that overlooked the sparkling blue waters of Lake Sentani. Tiny islands with houses on stilts were sprinkled across the lake, and the entire area was surrounded by mountains and jungles. General MacArthur's bungalow was being painted white, and the soldiers were already referring to it as "Dugout Doug's White House."

Major General Hawkins and General MacWhitter presented

themselves at Lieutenant General Krueger's office at a few minutes before 1400 hours, and were ushered inside. As they marched to the desk in order to salute and report formally, they saw Lieutenant General Robert L. Eichelberger seated on a chair to the side of the desk. Although General Eichelberger held the same rank as General Krueger, the former was subordinate to the latter. General Eichelberger was in command of the US I Corps, code-named the Reckless Task Force.

General Hawkins and General MacWhitter saluted and reported, and although they were generals themselves, they were small potatoes compared to General Krueger and General Eichelberger, who were the ranking officers in the US Army in the South Pacific, under General MacArthur.

General Krueger was fifty-three years old, slender, with gray hair. He had been born in Flatow, West Prussia, and had a distinct Germanic appearance, although his manner was one hundred percent American. He and his family had emigrated when he was eight years old. He was reputed to be an expert on discipline and training.

General Eichelberger was also of a Germanic background, but he'd been born in Ohio and had attended Ohio State University before transferring to West Point. Like General Krueger, he was lean and gray, but he was shorter than General Krueger and five years younger. He had large ears and a big hooked nose that made him look like a buzzard.

General MacArthur planned overall strategy in the South Pacific, while General Krueger and General Eichelberger worked out the specifics. Their responsibilities and achievements were equal to those of General Omar Bradley, General Courtney Hodges, and General George S. Patton in the European Theater, but the American people barely knew of General Krueger and General Eichelberger.

The reason was that all news information about the US Army in the South Pacific emanated from the headquarters of General MacArthur, and the names of General Krueger and General Eichelberger were seldom mentioned prominently in communiqués, in contrast to the headquarters of General Eisenhower, who gave credit where credit was due.

"Have a seat," said General Krueger.

General Hawkins and General MacWhitter sat. Through the

window behind General Krueger's head they could see a waterfall near the crest of a mountain in the distance.

"How was your trip?" asked General Krueger in a genial tone of voice.

"Uneventful," replied General Hawkins.

"Those are the best kind."

"Indeed they are."

"I imagine you're a little tired."

"A little."

"Care for some iced tea?"

"If you please."

General Krueger picked up his telephone and mumbled into it, then hung up. "How's the fighting Eighty-first Division these days?" he asked with a smile.

"Ready to go," replied General Hawkins.

"Where do you think you're going to go?"

"I'd guess someplace on the Vogelkop Peninsula."

"That would've been a good guess six weeks or even a month ago," General Krueger said, "but the situation has changed somewhat since then. The Eighty-first won't be landing west of here at all. You'll be landing *east* of here."

This news took General Hawkins completely by surprise, and he glanced at General MacWhitter, because all their conjecture had been about possible beachheads west of Hollandia, which would be possible jump-off spots for landings in the Philippines.

General Eichelberger chuckled. "You look surprised."

"I *am* surprised," General Hawkins replied. "I thought all the ground east of here was pretty well secured."

"Well," said General Eichelberger, "in a way it is, and in another way it isn't. When we leapfrogged ahead to Aitape and Hollandia, we left a lot of Japs behind us, as you're probably aware."

"Yes, sir," replied General Hawkins. "I believe the entire Japanese Eighteenth Army is somewhere between Aitape and the Huon Peninsula."

"That's right," said General Eichelberger. "To be more specific, the Jap Twentieth Division and Fortieth Division is at Madang, and their Fifty-first Division is believed to be in the vicinity of Wewak."

112

"Uh-oh," said General Hawkins.

"I think you're starting to get the picture," General Eichelberger replied with a smile.

"They're moving west toward Aitape?" asked General Hawkins.

"You got it," replied General Eichelberger. "We might have bypassed the Jap Eighteenth Army, but that doesn't mean they're not there anymore and that they're not still looking for trouble."

There was a knock on the door.

"Come in," said General Krueger.

A soldier entered the office, carrying a tray with four tall, frosty glasses of iced tea. He served them and departed, closing the door softly behind him. The generals paused in their discussion and sipped the tea, which had a bright leafy taste, was sweetened with sugar, and was stacked with ice cubes. The office was hot, and the glasses became covered with tiny drops of condensation that grew and merged, dripping onto the hands of the generals. General Hawkins's mind was processing the information General Krueger and General Eichelberger had just given him. He deduced that the Eighty-first Division would land somewhere east of Aitape, to stop the attack that was coming from the direction of Wewak.

"Let's go to the map," said General Krueger.

The men arose and carried their glasses to the immense map hung on the wall to the left of General Krueger's desk. New Guinea was shaped something like a hot dog on the map, with its west end somewhat higher than its east end, about two feet long. General Hawkins located Hollandia on the northern coast of New Guinea, approximately midway between the end of the Vogelkop Peninsula to the west and Milne Bay to the east. Aitape was 125 miles east of Hollandia, and Wewak, where the Japanese Fifty-first Division was believed to be located, was 100 miles east of Aitape.

"Just tell me one thing," General Hawkins asked. "Do we know whether or not the Jap Fifty-first Division is already on its way to Aitape?"

"Light contact has already been made with patrols of Japs believed to be from the Fifty-first Division," General Krueger replied.

General Hawkins frowned. The situation wasn't very good.

The Japs might attack before he had time to deploy his men adequately. It could be a very difficult and costly battle.

"One more question before you begin," General Hawkins said. "Do we know whether the two Jap divisions in Madang are on the move yet?"

"We believe that they are," General Eichelberger replied. He was standing to the left of the map, and General Krueger stood to the right.

"Let me begin at the beginning," General Krueger said. He placed his long forefinger on the map near Madang and said: "The Jap Eighteenth Army is headquartered here under the command of Lieutenant General Hatazo Adachi. He moved his headquarters to New Guinea in March; previously he was in Rabaul. His Fifty-first Division arrived the same month. His Forty-first Division came here from China about the same time. His Twentieth Division has been here for quite some time. All three divisions were badly battered on the Huon Peninsula, but they still have a lot of fight in them. We estimate their total strength at around twenty thousand combat effectives, but only their Twentieth Division, consisting of perhaps six or seven thousand men, presents an immediate threat to Aitape.

"For our part," General Krueger continued, "we have two regimental combat teams, the 163rd and 127th, at Aitape, commanded by General Hall. Their combined total is ten thousand men, and at first we believed they would be sufficient to defend Aitape against the Japs. But we've decided to be safe, because for all we know, the rest of the Jap army might be right behind their Twentieth Division, and we don't know for sure what Japs might be west or south of Aitape. It has been decided that General Hall's men will basically defend Aitape, while the Eighty-first Division will land here"—General Krueger pointed to a spot on the map east of Aitape—"and act as a block against any Japanese attack from Wewak." General Krueger lowered his hand and turned toward General Hawkins. "Any questions so far?"

"It seems to me," General Hawkins said, "that if the Japs do attack from the east, my division will bear the brunt of that attack. Is that correct?"

"It is."

"How much time will we have to dig in?"

"Depends on when the Japs attack."

"How soon will we leave for Aitape?" General Hawkins asked.

"Friday morning."

General Hawkins blinked. That was only three days away. "That doesn't give us much time."

"You don't need much time," General Krueger replied. "Your transport ships are already in Pearl Harbor, waiting for you. Your supplies will be loaded tomorrow, and you will load the next day. The sooner you get to Aitape, the better off you'll be—don't you agree?"

"Yes, sir," replied General Hawkins, because there was nothing else to say.

"You should be ready to leave anyway. You received your preliminary notice more than three weeks ago."

"We are ready, sir, but we expected more than three days to get loaded."

"You can't always get what you expect," General Krueger said. "The Japs aren't going to wait for you. They're going to attack as soon as they can."

General Eichelberger cleared his throat. "That's right, and they're getting into position right now, while we're talking."

"Any more questions?" General Krueger asked General Hawkins.

"Not just now, sir."

General Krueger turned to the map again. "Then I'll continue," he said.

General Hawkins and General MacWhitter returned to Clark Field the next evening at ten o'clock, exhausted and cranky as the result of the long flight. They were met by a contingent of staff officers from division headquarters, and General Hawkins told them there would be a meeting in his office at 0800 hours the next morning for all staff officers, regimental commanders, and battalion commanders. Then General Hawkins got into the backseat of an OD green Chevrolet sedan and fell asleep. General MacWhitter got into the back of another Chevrolet, but he didn't fall asleep because of the huge quantities of coffee that he'd been drinking.

Both officers were driven home to their wives, who took

them in tow and put them to bed. Mrs. Hawkins wanted to get laid, but the general couldn't cut the mustard, and she didn't press the issue. Mrs. MacWhitter didn't want to get laid because she'd got laid that afternoon with a certain major in the Transportation Corps. She fell asleep, a smile on her face, while General MacWhitter stared at the dark ceiling of his bedroom, pondering all the imponderables of the battle that would take place to the east of Aitape, waiting for the caffeine to work its way through his system.

The next morning, at eight o'clock, the big meeting was held in General Hawkins's office. He told the assembly of officers where and when they were going, giving them all the details that General Krueger and General Eichelberger had given him. He pulled no punches. He told them they were going into a tough battle and they wouldn't have much time to prepare.

They'd have the remainder of that day and the next day to get ready to leave, and on Thursday they'd begin loading onto trucks for the move to the transport ships at Pearl Harbor. All men would be confined to the post. The officers could tell their subordinates when they were leaving but not where they were going.

The meeting dragged on, for there was much information to impart. A lengthy question-and-answer period followed. Finally, at 1230 hours, everybody seemed to understand what they were supposed to do. General Hawkins dismissed everybody and then fled to the officers' club for a few martinis and some lunch.

That afternoon all soldiers in the field were summoned back to their barracks and told that they were moving out the day after tomorrow. They were ordered to settle their affairs and pack all their personal belongings into their footlockers, which they would bring to the supply room the next morning for storage.

The soldiers didn't have many affairs to settle. They had no mortgage payments to worry about, no telephone or electricity to cut off, no magazine subscriptions to cancel. They just stuffed their civilian clothes into their footlockers, and a small percentage of the men had books to pack in with their civilian clothes. Some men tucked away photographs of their wives and girl friends, and others regretfully threw out

116

their photographs of Betty Grable and Rita Hayworth.

They fidgeted and sweated as they rolled their shelter halves and pushed gear into their full field packs. Old veterans and young replacements dreaded the thought of going to the front lines. They didn't know exactly where they'd disembark, but they'd been told they'd be in the thick of a brutal battle and they'd better get ready for it.

They hoped they were ready as they stuffed their field packs or sat on their footlockers, writing to loved ones back in the States, saying they were shipping in two days and telling their wives, girl friends, mothers, and fathers not to worry, that everything would be all right, although the GIs didn't believe that themselves. Each one wondered if he'd be alive two or three weeks from then, when the Eighty-first was on New Guinea and the bullets were coming thick and fast.

SEVEN . . .

It was the next night, and Butsko sat on an upholstered chair in the solarium, gazing out the window at stars twinkling in the sky. He knew that his men in the recon platoon were confined to their barracks, making final preparations for the move to the transport ships the following day. He had mixed feelings, because on one hand he wished he could be with them, but on the other hand he was glad he didn't have to go into the meat grinder again.

He was worried about his men the way a father would worry about his sons. He was afraid they'd be lost without him and Lieutenant Breckenridge wouldn't be able to bring them through. Lieutenant Breckenridge was smart, but he didn't have the experience Butsko had, and experience is as important in war as it is in any other field.

"Hello, Sergeant," said a familiar voice behind him.

Butsko turned around in his wheelchair and saw Lieutenant Breckenridge standing there in his fatigues. "I was just thinking about you," Butsko said.

"Here I am," Lieutenant Breckenridge replied. "I thought

I'd take some time out to come over and say good-bye."

"Well, have a seat, for Chrissakes," Butsko said, pointing to a chair. "You're not gonna run right out the door, are you?"

"I can stay a few minutes, but I've got to get back to the company pretty quick because we're pulling out in the morning, you know."

"I know. In a way I wish I was going with you."

"In a way I wish my leg was in a cast so I wouldn't have to go."

Lieutenant Breckenridge pulled the chair over and sat facing Butsko. He took out a pack of cigarettes and offered them to Butsko. Butsko picked one out with his stubby fingers. Lieutenant Breckenridge took one for himself and Butsko snapped his Zippo to flame, lighting both cigarettes.

Lieutenant Breckenridge inhaled deeply and blew the smoke out his nostrils. He was still smoking his customary pack and a half a day; he'd been unsuccessful in his efforts to stop or even cut down.

"I sure wish you were coming with us," Lieutenant Breckenridge admitted. "I'm going to have a helluva hard time without you."

"Bullshit," Butsko said, trying to give Lieutenant Breckenridge some confidence. "You know what you're doing. You don't need me."

"That's what you think."

"That's what I know. Just don't take any dumb chances and don't volunteer for anything. Stay calm, especially when the shit hits the fan, and you know it's gonna hit the fan. Don't ever be afraid to retreat, if that's what you gotta do. It's better to be a live coward than a dead hero. And whenever you stop someplace, dig in. Even if you don't feel like it, dig in. If the men give you any shit, and you know they're gonna give you shit as soon as they go ashore, just kick ass. That's the only way to treat them. It's the only thing they understand. You can't reason with them because they're too fucking stupid, and the ones who aren't stupid are crazy. If you can keep them in line, they'll come through for you; and if you can't, you won't last long."

Lieutenant Breckenridge thought for a few seconds about

what Butsko had told him. "I'll do whatever I have to do to get through this goddamned war."

"Now you're talking," Butsko said, a tone of approval in his voice.

Together the men sat in silence a few moments, thinking about the battles they'd been in and the battles that were to come. Butsko wished he had some more good concrete advice to give Lieutenant Breckenridge, but there was nothing else to say. If Lieutenant Breckenridge didn't know what to do by now, he'd never know.

Lieutenant Breckenridge glanced at his watch. "I'd better get back to the platoon," he said. "I'd like to stay longer, but I can't."

"I understand," Butsko said.

Lieutenant Breckenridge stood and held his hand down to Butsko. "Wish me luck, buddy."

Butsko raised his hairy right arm and shook hands with Lieutenant Breckenridge. "Good luck, kid. Keep your head down and kill a Jap for me."

"I'll do my best, Butsko."

"I'm sure you will."

They released each other's hand, and Lieutenant Breckenridge took a step backward. He looked down at Butsko, and Butsko looked up at him. A few seconds passed, then Lieutenant Breckenridge shrugged and winked to break the tension.

"Well, so long, Sergeant," he said.

"Take care of yourself, Lieutenant."

Lieutenant Breckenridge turned and walked toward the door. A figure in white emerged from the dimness of the hallway and entered the solarium. Lieutenant Breckenridge's jaw dropped a half-inch at the sight of the figure in white, because she was none other than Lieutenant Diane Latham, who'd pushed him off a cliff.

They looked at each other, and neither could think of anything to say. They passed each other warily, like two tractor-trailer trucks on a winding two-lane back road in Georgia. Lieutenant Breckenridge entered the corridor, making his way stolidly to the elevator, and Lieutenant Latham carried her tray of medication to the soldiers sitting at the usual ongoing nonstop poker game. She distributed medication to them and then worked her way around the room, finally stopping before Butsko.

"Time for your medication, Butsko."

He held out his hand. She put the tiny paper cup of pills into it. He tossed the pills into his mouth, and she gave him a cup of water to wash them down.

"I see you just had a visitor," she said. "He didn't look too happy."

Butsko held the cup of water to his lips. "You wouldn't be too happy, either, if you were a soldier and you were going back to the front tomorrow."

Butsko drank the water, and Diane Latham looked at him but didn't really see him. In her mind she saw Lieutenant Breckenridge running through the jungle, bullets flying around him and explosions going off everywhere.

"Where's he going?" she asked.

"If he knew, he wouldn't tell me; and if I knew, I wouldn't tell you." Butsko handed her back the cup. "I got a funny feeling that he ain't gonna come back."

She widened her eyes. "What makes you say that?"

"Because he was wounded on New Georgia, and then he got wounded again on Bougainville right after we got there. I think he's one of them hard-luck cases, and the next time the Japs won't miss."

"My goodness," she said, "that's an awfully pessimistic point of view."

"It's just a feeling I got. Might not be anything to it. I hope I'm wrong."

Diane didn't want to say it, but she had the same negative feeling too. Something told her that Lieutenant Breckenridge might not come back alive from wherever he was going. This made her feel bad, because she thought she'd been very cruel to him. It was possible that he'd die young, and she'd done nothing to make his life happier. In fact, she made his life unhappier because she'd pushed him off a cliff.

Diane Latham was a decent person, and she'd more or less forgotten about what Lieutenant Breckenridge had done to her. It didn't seem to weigh as much as what she'd done to him. She couldn't be responsible for his behavior, but she could be responsible for her own. She felt a powerful desire to apologize to him and wish him luck before he shipped out.

"Where is Lieutenant Breckenridge now?" she asked.

Butsko had been eyeing her slyly, and he figured she was thinking about Lieutenant Breckenridge out of more than idle curiosity. He knew enough about women to know that the ones like Nurse Latham didn't hold grudges for long and felt guilty whenever they'd been mean to somebody.

"He's back with his platoon," Butsko replied.

"Where's that?"

"What do you wanna know for?"

She looked away from Butsko. "I want to say good-bye to him."

"He's with Headquarters Company of the Twenty-third Regiment, Eighty-first Division." Butsko told her where that unit was located on the post.

"Thank you very much, Sergeant Butsko," she said, and she walked off with her tray of pills, passing them out to the other men in the solarium.

When the tray was empty, she returned to the nurses' station. She still had a half-hour before she went off duty, and she occupied her time with paperwork, glancing at her watch every few minutes, anxious to see Lieutenant Breckenridge and make everything right between them so she wouldn't have a guilty conscience anymore. Somehow her entire relationship with him seemed changed, now that he was leaving for the front and might never come back.

Finally it was time for her to go off duty, but her replacement hadn't arrived yet and she couldn't leave until her replacement arrived. She called the nurses' residence and found out that her replacement wasn't there. As she hung up the phone her replacement appeared in front of the nurses' station, only three minutes late.

Diane took the elevator down to the ground floor and walked quickly to her yellow Packard, putting down the roof and sliding behind the wheel, starting the engine and flicking on the headlights. She drove out of the parking lot and headed in the direction of the address Butsko had given her, aware it would be considered odd for a nurse to appear in male territory, asking for a young lieutenant. The men probably would think the worst possible thoughts about her, because men tend to think that way about women, but she wanted to see Lieutenant Breckenridge and apologize for kicking him off the cliff.

She drove on streets lined with barracks occupied by soldiers from the Eighty-first Division, and could see feverish activity through the windows and on the grounds surrounding the barracks as men packed and repacked, carried footlockers to their supply rooms, and tried to keep busy so they wouldn't worry too much about getting killed when they arrived at the front.

She found Headquarters Company of the Twenty-third Regiment and parked the Packard in the lot with the jeeps and Army OD Chevrolets. Nearby, a group of soldiers loaded crates onto a deuce-and-a-half truck, and they all turned around to look as she stepped out of the Packard, showing a bit of leg. One of them whistled; of course he was Frankie La Barbara, who never could behave himself when attractive females were around.

Diane ignored the whistle and crossed the street, looking both ways, heading for the orderly room. Men rushed around her carrying full field packs, wall lockers, footlockers, and crates of various sizes. They all stopped whatever they were doing to look at her, but she held her head high and climbed the steps to the orderly room. She pulled open the screen door and stepped inside.

Master Sergeant Gerald Kurkin looked up from his desk and couldn't believe his eyes. Pfc. Lawrence Nagle, who was stacking bound volumes of Army regulations in a crate, dropped a volume on the floor.

Sergeant Kurkin spotted the lieutenant's bars on Diane Latham's collar and responded like a true soldier. He leaped to his feet and screamed: *"Ten-*hut!"

Pfc. Lawrence Nagle jumped to his feet and held his hands stiffly down at his sides. The door to Captain Spode's office opened and that stalwart military commander poked his head out to see what the commotion was about. When his eyes fell on the voluptuous Diane Latham, he puffed out his chest and smiled suavely, stepping into the orderly room.

"Can I help you, Lieutenant?" he asked.

"I'm looking for Lieutenant Breckenridge," she replied.

"I believe he's with his platoon." Captain Spode looked at Pfc. Nagle. "Escort this officer to Lieutenant Breckenridge."

"Yes, sir!"

Captain Spode returned his gaze to Diane Latham. "If I can help you with anything else, please don't hesitate to ask," he said, a mischievous twinkle in his eye, even though he was shipping out in the morning and wouldn't have time to help her with anything; but men can't stop themselves from trying whenever there's a pretty woman in their vicinity.

"Thank you, Captain," she replied.

Pfc. Nagle sprang forward and approached Diane Latham. "This way, sir—I mean ma'am—I mean Lieutenant...."

Diane followed him out of the orderly room and down the steps to the ground and into the pandemonium of men rushing about.

"His platoon's in that barracks over there," Nagle said, pointing to the building next to the mess hall. "You'll have to wait outside while I go get him."

"Very well."

"I hope you'll be safe out here."

"Why wouldn't I be safe out here?"

"We got some crazy people in this company, sir—I mean ma'am—I mean Lieutenant."

"Yes, Sergeant Butsko told me all about them."

"You know Sergeant Butsko?"

"He's assigned to my ward."

"No kidding? Well, him calling the men in this company crazy is like the stove calling the frying pan black."

Diane smiled.

"You wait here," Pfc. Nagle told her. "I'll be right back. Don't take any guff from any of the guys around here."

Pfc. Nagle climbed the steps and entered the barracks. Diane stood beside the banister, her hands clasped behind her back, aware that all eyes were on her and that those eyes were filled with insane, animalistic lust. Instead of being frightened, it turned her on a little bit. She sometimes had weird, disgusting sex fantasies of many men screwing her, going down on her, having a big orgy, etc., but she was not the kind of person

125

who would let herself be carried away by mere sex fantasies.

Craig Delane turned the barracks corner and came into view, carrying a bazooka under his arm. He took one look at Diane Latham and said: "Hello, there. Can I help you, sir?"

"I'm being helped, thank you."

"You're certainly very lovely," Craig Delane said with a smile, taking off his fatigue hat, hoping she'd appreciate his aristocratic features. "Why, you're like a vision, standing here in front of the barracks—a vision of beauty and grace. Do you think we could get together for a drink a little later?"

"Aren't you shipping out in the morning?" she asked.

He blushed. "That's right too."

At that moment Pfc. Nagle and Lieutenant Breckenridge appeared, and Lieutenant Breckenridge saw Craig Delane making an obvious pass at Diane Latham.

"Get lost, Delane!" he said.

"Yes, sir!"

Delane turned around and walked away swiftly, carrying his bazooka. Pfc. Nagle smiled at Diane Latham as he passed her and headed back to the orderly room. Lieutenant Breckenridge descended the barracks stairs cautiously, looking at Diane Latham. He was amazed that she was there to see him.

"Hi," he said.

"Hello," she replied.

He stepped to the ground and looked down at her face, while she looked up at him. Soldiers ran all around them, but it was as though the young lieutenant and the beautiful nurse were in the calm eye of a hurricane.

"I'm surprised to see you here," he said.

"Sergeant Butsko told me you were shipping out in the morning, and I thought I'd come to say good-bye and to apologize. Is there anyplace we can be alone?"

"I don't think there's anyplace around here."

"My car's over there," she said, pointing toward the parking area. "We can go for a ride."

"I remember what happened last time we went for a ride."

"I'm sorry about what I did, but I was very angry at the time."

He nodded. "I guess I shouldn't have done what I did, either, but sometimes I use people, I suppose, and that's not nice."

"No, it isn't."

"I take it that Lieutenant Utsler didn't behave like a gentleman."

"He certainly didn't."

"I guess I'd better not ask what he did."

"No, you'd better not."

He looked at his watch. "I don't think I can go for a ride. I've got a lot to do here. Let's go over by the mess hall. There's less going on there. Jesus, these guys are looking at you like you're something to eat."

He placed his arm over her shoulder and they walked together toward the mess hall, while everybody in the vicinity wondered how Lieutenant Breckenridge, with his old acne scars and thick features, could get such an attractive girl friend. Lieutenant Breckenridge and Diane Latham left the tumult behind them and made their way to the rear of the mess hall, next to one of the less important roads in the area.

"This okay?" he asked.

"It's fine."

He took out his pack of cigarettes, offered her one, and lit both with his Zippo. He leaned his broad shoulders against the side of the mess hall, and she stood with her back to the streetlight on the corner, which made a halo around her golden hair.

"I wish," she said, "that we didn't get off to such a bad start with each other. I think that we might have been friends or—who knows—maybe even something more."

"It was my fault," Lieutenant Breckenridge admitted. "I just used you to get some information out of Jack Utsler."

She smiled dourly. "You told him I was a bad girl, didn't you?"

"Afraid I did."

"That was very cruel."

"Yup."

"But I suppose that doesn't excuse me from nearly killing you."

"It does seem like rather excessive punishment."

She laughed, and then he laughed too. It wasn't loud, bois-

127

terous laughter, but the laughter of amusement and relief. They felt as if they had more rapport, now that their initial encounters were placed into a comical perspective. But then, almost immediately, they thought of the war again.

"I wish you weren't shipping out tomorrow," she said.

"Me too."

She looked at his face but saw no fear on it, only concern and a bit of worry. "The damned war!" she said. "The damned Japs! They've turned the whole world upside down!"

"There's nothing we can do about it," he said, resignation in his voice. "We have to do our duty. The war is a big steamroller, and people like us can't stop it."

A salty mist covered her eyes. "Please be careful out there, Dale."

He laughed bitterly. "It doesn't matter how careful a soldier is. A bomb can fall on him when he least expects it. Or a stray bullet can knock him out of the ball game forever."

"Be careful anyway, would you, please?"

"I'll do my best."

"Promise?"

"I promise." He looked at his watch. "I think I'd better get back to my men. I'll walk you to your car, okay?"

"Okay."

He placed his arm around her shoulders and they walked slowly toward her Packard, wishing they could spend more time together. Lieutenant Breckenridge wondered whether he could take a short drive with her and throw a fast fuck into her someplace, but somehow it didn't seem like such a good idea. The time would drag on, and he couldn't be away for long. There was still so much to do.

The passed the mess hall and came to the company area again, turning right in the direction of her Packard which gleamed in the light of the street lamp.

"Do you have a girl friend back in the States?" she asked.

"Yes," he admitted. "I do."

"Where is she?"

"In New York City."

"What does she do there?"

"She's a model."

128

"Where did you meet her?"

"We went to college together."

"I see. Do you love her?"

"I suppose I do."

"What does that mean?"

"Well, I haven't seen her for a long time."

"Oh."

They crossed the street and approached her car. She knew how he felt, because she had a few boyfriends that she was supposed to be in love with. But they were far away, and love grows cool without regular fuel. She opened the door beside the steering wheel and turned to face him.

"Well, I guess this is good-bye," she said.

"Yep," he replied. "I wish we could spend more time together."

"I do too."

They looked at each other and felt the powerful, invisible pull.

"Kiss me, Dale," she said.

He took a step forward and clasped her in his arms. Their lips met and pushed against each other as she touched the back of his neck with her hands, moaning softly. He backed off slightly and kissed her more tenderly, feeling her firm breasts against his chest, becoming intoxicated by her rosebud fragrance. Their lips touched softly and their tongues entwined. An erection grew in his fatigue pants, and she pressed her belly against it.

Their private, blissful little paradise was shattered by the clapping of hands, whistles, and whoopees. Lieutenant Breckenridge tore his lips from Diane's and saw a group of his men standing beside the mess hall, grinning and applauding, leering in his direction.

Lieutenant Breckenridge blew his top. He turned away from Diane Latham and charged toward his men, who scattered in all directions. Frankie La Barbara ran to the left of the mess hall, and Corporal Lopez took off to the right. Craig Delane sped toward the orderly room, because he didn't believe that Lieutenant Breckenridge would murder him in front of Captain Spode; and the Reverend Billie Jones headed toward the barracks where he lived. Morris Shilansky dived underneath the mess hall, hoping Lieutenant Breckenridge wouldn't come after him there.

Diane Latham burst into laughter, because it was all so ridiculous. Lieutenant Breckenridge heard her and came back to his senses. He stopped, turned around, and trudged back to her.

"I don't know what I'm going to do with those guys," he said wearily.

"I think they're funny."

"You wouldn't think they were so funny if you had to deal with them day in and day out. They're driving me crazy."

"I think they like you," she said.

"What makes you think they like me?" he asked.

"Because they wouldn't have dared do that if they didn't like you."

"In that case, I wish they didn't like me."

"You don't mean that."

He shrugged. "Maybe I don't."

He looked at her and realized that their magic moment had passed. He had to get back to work. Maybe some other time.

"I've got to get going," he said.

"I know."

"I wish I didn't have to go."

She nodded. They gazed into each other's eyes and thought of all the fun they could have together, but the war came first. He placed his hands on her shoulders, bent forward, and touched his lips to hers. The kiss was short and sweet. He pulled back.

"I hope I see you again, Diane," he said.

"I hope I see you, too, Dale. Please be careful."

"I apologize for all the shitty things I did."

"So do I."

He pinched his lips together and took a step backward, raising his hands in despair. Then he let them fall to his sides as he turned around and walked back to the barracks area, stuffing his hands in his pockets and looking down at the ground, thinking about lost opportunities and dreadful possibilities.

She watched him go, a tall, broad-shouldered man who wasn't particularly attractive at first sight but who had a lot of charm, perhaps because he was from the South. She watched as he walked up the steps to the barracks building where his men lived and stopped in front of the door, then turned back toward her. He waved, and she stood on her tiptoes, waving back. Then he lowered his hand and entered the barracks. Lieutenant Diane Latham opened the door of her car and sat behind the wheel, brushing the tears from underneath her eyes. She started up the engine, backed out of the parking spot, and drove off into the night.

EIGHT . . .

The Eighty-first Division loaded onto four transport ships the next day and spent the next night in the holds of the ships, sweating in the dim light of electric light bulbs and stacked in narrow cots six high. The following morning they departed Pearl Harbor with an escort of destroyers, light cruisers, heavy cruisers, and an aircraft carrier.

The convoy hit a tropical storm southeast of the Marshall Islands, and the urinals became filled with vomit. Men puked everywhere, even in their cots, and the vomit dripped down to the men on the cots below them, and then those men puked too.

There was puke on the banisters of the ladderwells and puke on the deck. A man could eat dinner out of a metal tray and have the man sitting next to him puke all over the table. It was absolutely disgusting. All the transport ships smelled like puke, and the sailors sneered contemptuously at the soldiers who couldn't handle a little rough weather.

The storm lasted nearly twenty-four hours, the ships plowing through waves as tall as three-story buildings. Then the storm stopped, and a few hours later the sun came out. The sea flattened and the soldiers, pale and gaunt, climbed up to the deck for some fresh air.

The convoy passed through the Solomon Islands, and the old combat soldiers could see Guadalcanal on the far horizon, the green island evoking terrible memories of violence and pain. The convoy turned in a northwesterly direction after leaving the Solomons behind and cruised up the northern coast of New Guinea, passing the Huon Peninsula, where so much Japanese and American blood had been spilled already, staying beyond the reach of any shore batteries the Japanese might have at Madang.

The convoy arrived at its destination on the night of June 28 and dropped its anchors in the waters off Aitape, not far from the Driniumor River. The next morning the men went ashore in boats and landed in an area designated as blue beach, which was well within the American defense perimeter. They unloaded their equipment, regrouped, and futzed around while General Hawkins and his staff reported to Major General Charles P. Hall, commander of all US troops at Aitape, code-named the Persecution Task Force. General Hall told them that natives had reported considerable Japanese activity in the vicinity of the Driniumor River, where the Eighty-first's positions would be.

The men had C rations for lunch and then moved through the thick, tangled jungle toward the positions they were expected to hold. There was great confusion and much consultation with maps and compasses, not to mention radio calls back and forth across the jungle; but by nightfall most units were more or less where they were supposed to be, having replaced a screen of soldiers from the 127th Regimental Combat Team, which had been holding the area and praying the Japs wouldn't start some shit.

The Japs hadn't started any shit, except for an occasional skirmish here and there. But Japs were definitely in the area, in small numbers so far, with their main units approaching from the direction of Madang. Japs, in fact, were high in the trees on the east side of the Driniumor, observing through binoculars the new American unit moving into the region. The information was relayed back from headquarters to headquarters until it reached the command post of the Japanese Eighteenth Regiment, located in the hilly, heavily forested terrain along the southern branches of Niumen Creek.

The commander of the Eighteenth Regiment was Colonel Yukio Katsumata, and he lived in a tent on the top of a hill. Part of the tent was his bedroom, and the other part was his office. He was short, barely over five feet tall, with a moon face and a crew cut, thirty-eight years old, and he was sitting at his desk when Lieutenant Shoichi Hozumi, his aide, entered with a document in his hand.

"Message from Captain Unuma," Lieutenant Hozumi said, not bothering to salute, because Colonel Katsumata was easygoing about unimportant military protocol at the front.

"What does it say?"

"A large American unit is moving into the area, two regiments at least."

"Ah, so," replied Colonel Katsumata, looking down at the map on his desk. This was not good news. The Japanese Eighteenth Army was planning a major offensive against the American defenders of Aitape, and it had appeared to be a not insuperable task. But now, if the Americans were being reinforced, the task would become much more difficult.

"Radio the information to General Adachi," Colonel Katsumata said. "We'll let him decide what to do."

"Yes, sir."

Lieutenant Hozumi turned and departed, the white sheet of paper in his hand. He marched underneath the camouflage netting to the radio shack, and directed a radio operator to transmit the message to Madang. This was accomplished, and Lieutenant Hozumi returned to his office to do his paperwork. Two hours later, as the sun was sinking behind the horizon, he was notified that a reply had been received from General Adachi. Lieutenant Hozumi rushed to the radio shack to get the message. He read it eagerly.

It consisted of only one word: *Attack!*

The recon platoon was digging in for the night. Although it was nominally part of Headquarters Company, from which it received its rations and supplies, its orders usually came from Colonel Hutchins or his operations officer, Major Cobb.

This meant the recon platoon was more or less on its own,

and Lieutenant Breckenridge wanted to make sure they'd be safe throughout the night. He ordered his men to dig deep holes six feet apart and set booby traps in front of the position. Farther forward, near the bank of the Driniumor, combat engineers laid mines and strung out concertina wire, operating under orders from General Hawkins.

General Hawkins had deployed his regiment in a semicircle around the captured airfields at Aitape. His Fifty-eighth Regiment was south of Aitape, his Thirty-sixth Regiment was southeast of Aitape, and the Twenty-third Regiment was on the west bank of the Driniumor River. He figured this would provide all-around protection for the air bases, because he couldn't be sure exactly of which sector the Japanese would attack.

After other units stopped digging, the recon platoon continued to shovel deeper. The men complained, cursed, and swore, but Lieutenant Breckenridge showed them no mercy. The deeper the holes, the safer his men would be. He didn't want any casualties that could be avoided.

Finally, shortly after 2030 hours, Lieutenant Breckenridge inspected the holes and fortifications and pronounced them suitable. He ordered Sergeant Cameron to post guards and then took a leak at the newly dug latrine. He washed his hands and face in his helmet, brushed his teeth with water from his canteen, and made his way through the darkness to his tent, which Craig Delane, his runner, had pitched for him.

He crawled into the tent and lay on his poncho, but it was damp and clammy, due to the high humidity. Lieutenant Breckenridge's uniform was soaked with sweat, and his armpits were stinking already. *Here I am, back in the fucking jungle*, he thought glumly.

Mosquitoes flew into his tent and ate him alive. So did other insects of species the bug scientists hadn't even identified yet. Birds and monkeys shrieked in the trees, their habitat disrupted by the arrival of the American soldiers. Wild dogs barked and wild cats shrieked. The jungle was full of sounds, and Lieutenant Breckenridge couldn't relax. Those sounds might be Japs sneaking through the thick, tangled vegetation to slit the throats of Americans while they slept.

Lieutenant Breckenridge felt the old fear and tense caution

return; it was like somebody you despised coming to visit. His feelings were foreign and strange, because he'd been away from the war for so long. He realized he'd have to get adjusted all over again and hoped he'd be able to remain alive until he was one hundred percent efficient.

He knew that his men were having the same adjustment problems. The new replacements were probably scared to death. Lieutenant Breckenridge wished he had Butsko there with him to help out, but he'd have to go it alone. All the men were looking to him for leadership, and he'd have to provide it. They could show fear or confusion if they wanted to, but he couldn't. He had to be a superman. They had to respect him and obey instantly, without question, because of who he was and the fact that he was their platoon leader, an officer in the United States Army.

The heat and humidity were almost unbearable. He felt as though he were in a steambath. There was no breeze, and it was impossible for him to get comfortable. A mosquito bit him on the back of the neck, and he squashed it with the palm of his hand, then wiped away the goo. He lay back and closed his eyes, but little wheels kept turning inside his head, and he could feel the pressure of his blood in his arteries, pumping away. He rolled over onto his side, his immense weight on his hip and shoulder; they ached, because he had no mattress underneath him.

He recalled that he used to sleep well on the ground of Bougainville and New Georgia, but it had taken him awhile to get used to it. He'd probably have a few sleepless nights before he got used to it again. *This fucking war,* he thought. *Those goddamned Japs.*

His mind flashed back to Lieutenant Diane Latham. He remembered how sweet her lips had been when he kissed her on the night before he shipped out. He also remembered how wonderful her body had felt, those firm breasts and her slim waist. *I should've fucked her,* he thought, *even if I had to go AWOL for a few hours. For all I know, I'm going to get killed out here, and it would've been nice to have one last great piece of ass before I died.*

Then he became angry with himself, because he didn't like to think about getting killed. He ordinarily wasn't superstitious, but he was superstitious about death. He'd seen so much of it already. He'd come close to getting killed himself. He wasn't terrified of getting killed, but he didn't like the idea very much. He believed that if he imagined himself getting killed, he'd get killed, even though he knew the belief was irrational.

He heard a rifle shot, then another, then a burst of machine-gun fire, all close by. Grabbing his carbine, he bounded out of the tent and looked around, licking his lips nervously. The machine gun chattered again, and he saw the flashes of its muzzle blasts.

"Japs!" yelled Private Jilliam.

Adrenaline poured into Lieutenant Breckenridge's arteries like rocket fuel, and his heart pumped wildly. All around him men burst out of their tents, carrying their M 1 rifles, fixing their bayonets, and looking for Japs.

The machine gun fired again. Lieutenant Breckenridge ran toward it and saw Sergeant Cameron leaping through the bushes, heading in the same direction. Three more rifle shots punctuated the stillness of the night, but it seemed to Lieutenant Breckenridge that all the shots were coming from his platoon's position. His men jumped into their holes and peered into the night, holding their M 1 rifles ready, expecting a mass attack from the Japs, trying to swallow down their fear.

Lieutenant Breckenridge ran around the holes and saw the machine-gun bunker up ahead. Sergeant Cameron jumped into it, and a few moments later Lieutenant Breckenridge landed inside.

"What the hell's going on over here?" Lieutenant Breckenridge said.

"Japs, sir!" replied Private Jilliam.

"Where?"

"Over there."

Lieutenant Breckenridge looked in the direction in which Private Jilliam had pointed and saw moonlight glinting on the ripples and eddies of the Driniumor River. On the other side were trees and bushes jammed together, a thick wall of vegetation. Lieutenant Breckenridge blinked and examined the opposite shore, but couldn't see anything that resembled a Jap.

"I don't see any Japs," he said.

"Me neither," said Sergeant Cameron, who turned to Private Jilliam. "You sure you saw Japs over there?"

Private Jilliam's freckled right cheek twitched. He was sixteen years old but had said he was eighteen in order to enlist, and the recruiting sergeant didn't check information like that very assiduously. "I saw *something* over there, Sarge."

"Something?" asked Sergeant Cameron. "I see something over there too. I see trees and other green shit, but I don't see no Japs."

"Something moved," Private Jilliam said, but his voice quavered as if he knew that maybe he'd fucked up. "Looked like a Jap to me."

Sergeant Cameron turned to Lieutenant Breckenridge, and Lieutenant Breckenridge knew that Private Jilliam was a green soldier, a kid scared shitless, and he might have fired at a wild pig or a monkey. It would be best not to rattle him further.

Private Jilliam sat behind the .30-caliber machine gun, his long legs splayed in a big *V*. Lieutenant Breckenridge knelt beside him and placed his hand on Private Jilliam's shoulder. "Don't fire unless you're sure of your target," he said gently. "Calm down. The Japs'll have to cross that river to get over here, and it won't be easy for them. You'll have plenty of time to see them and get ready. Okay?"

"Yes, sir."

Lieutenant Breckenridge glanced at Sergeant Cameron. "Let's go."

"Yes, sir."

Lieutenant Breckenridge climbed out of the hole and walked back toward his tent, and Sergeant Cameron hunched along at his side.

"Why did you put a green kid behind that machine gun on our first night here?" asked Lieutenant Breckenridge.

"He's gotta learn somehow," Sergeant Cameron replied. "The only way to learn to do it is to do it."

"I don't think that's the best way. The replacements like Jilliam have their hands full just trying to adjust to the combat zone. They don't need any extra responsibilities right off the bat. I want you to place the veterans on guard duty for the first few nights, then we'll work the replacements in, understand?"

"Yes, sir, but if you don't mind my saying so, Sergeant Butsko would've kicked that kid's ass all over the jungle for firing at nothing."

"What makes you think he fired at nothing?"

"I didn't see nothing."

"Just because you didn't see anything doesn't mean there wasn't anything there. At least the kid wasn't asleep. If he was asleep, I would've cut his fucking throat, but he was trying to do a good job, and I can't fault him for that."

"Do you want me to relieve him now?"

"Let him finish his shift, then don't assign him again for a few nights. If you relieve him now, it'll demoralize him and take away his self-confidence. He won't be very effective in that frame of mind."

Sergeant Cameron sniffed and wiped his nose with the back of his hand. "He ain't very effective right now, either, if you don't mind me saying so, sir. I think a good kick in the ass will straighten him right out."

"I don't. Change the guard roster."

"Yes, sir."

Sergeant Cameron stopped and took his note pad out of his shirt pocket, holding it up to the moonlight so he could read the names. Lieutenant Breckenridge returned to his tent, crawled inside, closed the flap, and lit up a cigarette. He took off his helmet, placed his carbine beside him, and lay down.

He puffed the cigarette, looking at the peaked top of the tent and wondering if Cameron was right about Breckenridge's having been too soft on Jilliam. It was difficult to know for sure about those things. Butsko always said that he was too soft, but Lieutenant Breckenridge couldn't believe that kicking the men around would produce good results. That system might work for Butsko, but Butsko was Butsko. Lieutenant Breckenridge didn't want to be somebody he wasn't. In the past it had been easy to let Butsko run the recon platoon the way he wanted to, because he had confidence in Butsko, but Sergeant Cameron was a different type. Sergeant Cameron wasn't as smart as Butsko, and actually was much harsher than Butsko. Butsko at least had a few soft spots and a human side to his nature, whereas Sergeant Cameron was so hard, he was brittle. Sergeant Cameron wasn't as flexible as Butsko, and that meant

Lieutenant Breckenridge would have to pay more attention to the day-to-day operation of the platoon.

"Aw, shit," Lieutenant Breckenridge muttered as he puffed his cigarette.

Private Jilliam's eyes had not been playing tricks on him. Neither had he been firing at shadows or a wild pig. Japanese reconnaissance patrols were out in force that night, sizing up the new American positions and probing for weak spots. The information was gathered and relayed back to Colonel Yukio Katsumata's headquarters.

Colonel Yukio Katsumata was sound asleep on his tatami mat, snoring peacefully underneath the protection of his mosquito netting; but his intelligence officer, Major Tadashi Honda, was wide awake, collating data long into the night, making evaluations, interviewing leaders of patrols, and chain-smoking like a maniac.

Finally, at three o'clock in the morning, Major Honda decided that he had a clear picture of where the Americans were and how many were gathered opposite the Fifteenth Regiment. He wrote a brief report, which he would deliver to Colonel Katsumata first thing in the morning, and then he prepared for bed, pausing several minutes to pray before his photograph of the Emperor, because Major Honda was a very religious man.

NINE . . .

Frankie La Barbara was sleeping lightly when he felt fingers on his knee. He awoke suddenly and lashed out with his left hand, slamming Morris Shilansky who was in the pup tent beside him.

"Get your fucking hands off me, you bastard!"

Morris Shilansky jumped up from a sound sleep. "Huh! What?"

"Keep your fucking hands off me, you bastard!"

"What hands?" Shilansky asked. "What're you talking about?"

"You were feeling me up, you bastard!"

"I was not!"

"You was too!"

"I was sound asleep—what're you talking about!"

"You was feeling me up, you bastard!"

"You're crazy! I was dead to the world!"

Frankie felt fingers on his thigh this time. He smacked Morris Shilansky in the chops. "I said cut it out!"

Morris Shilansky raised his hand to the spot Frankie had smacked. "What're you, fucking crazy?"

"You trying to say you just didn't do it again?"

"Do what again?"

"Feel me up!"

"What in the fuck would anybody want to feel *you* up for?"

"It wasn't you?"

"No, it wasn't me."

"Then who in the fuck was it?"

"I think you're dreaming."

"I ain't dreaming."

Frankie felt the fingers again, this time higher.

"Uh-oh," he said.

"Now what?" asked Shilansky.

"You just didn't do that?"

"I didn't just do what?"

"Uh-oh." Frankie pinched his lower lip with his teeth. "Something's on me," he said softly.

"Well, it ain't me!"

"Flick your lighter and see what's on me, but take it slow. Don't scare him."

"Don't scare who?"

"I don't know. Just don't scare whoever it is."

Shilansky slowly and easily took his lighter out of his fatigue pant pocket and flicked the wheel. Sparks flew and the wick burst into flame, revealing two tiny slanted eyes gleaming in the light above Frankie's lap. The eyes were set in a triangularly shaped head, and the head was connected to the twisting, coiled body of a red snake five feet long.

Frankie La Barbara's eyes rolled up into his head and he nearly fainted from terror. Shilansky wanted to run away, but if he wanted to get out of the tent, he'd have to pass the snake, which was bending its long neck from side to side, looking at the two GIs.

Frankie's teeth chattered in his head and his heart pounded like a tom-tom. "I think he's gonna bite me!"

"Stay calm. Don't scare him."

"Kill the son of a bitch!"

"How can I kill the son of a bitch?"

"I don't know."

Shilansky was scared to death, but he tried to think straight

144

anyway. He realized that he couldn't kill the snake with his bayonet, because the snake was probably faster than he was. The only thing to do was try to shoot it. He reached for his M 1 rifle.

"What're you gonna do?" Frankie asked, on the point of hysteria.

"I'm gonna shoot the snake. You hold the cigarette lighter."

"Well, don't shoot me by mistake."

"I'll be careful."

"What if you miss?"

"What if I do? You got any better ideas?"

Frankie searched his chaotic mind for an idea, but couldn't find one. "No."

Shilansky raised the M 1 slowly, then stopped. "This is no good," he said. "I might shoot somebody walking by."

"So what?" Frankie asked.

"I don't wanna shoot somebody by mistake."

"What about me?"

Just then the flame on Frankie's lighter went out, plunging the tent into darkness. The snake moved in Frankie's lap, and Frankie shivered like a dog shitting razor blades.

"Do something," Frankie said.

"Like what?"

"I don't know, but do something anyway."

"I can't even fucking see, so how can I do something?"

"That snake's gonna bite me any minute now."

"I know what I'll do," Shilansky replied. "I'll go for help. I'll cut a hole through the side of the tent here and ask Lieutenant Breckenridge what to do."

"Hurry up!"

Shilansky whipped out his bayonet, which he'd sharpened to a razor's edge on the transport ship, and slit open the side of the tent.

"I'll be right back," he said.

"You'd fucking better."

Shilansky inched toward the big slit in the side of the tent. He stuck out his arm, then his head, then his upper body. He hoped he wasn't scaring the snake and that the snake wouldn't bite his leg or his ass. Pushing forward, he ripped the hole in

145

the tent wider; his fear made him push harder. He pulled his knees and legs outside and he was free!

It was the first light of dawn, and the rising sun made a faint glow underneath the horizon. Shilansky jumped to his feet and ran toward Lieutenant Breckenridge's tent. *"Halp!"* he screamed. *"Halp!"*

Meanwhile, inside the tent, Frankie La Barbara looked at the snake, who was looking at him, eyeball to eyeball. Sweat dripped down Frankie's forehead and cheeks, because now he could see the snake clearly in the light passing through the hole that Shilansky had cut. The snake angled his head from side to side. Frankie didn't know it, but the snake was scared too. He'd just been crawling around, saw the tent, slithered inside, and found himself with two gigantic creatures who made strange sounds, moved in threatening ways, and could emit sparks and flames.

The big red snake saw the opening in the side of the tent and thought he should go for it. He only had one monster to deal with, and figured he could escape if he moved quickly. In point of fact, the red snake wasn't poisonous. He was a constrictor, but he wasn't big enough to do any harm to a human being.

The snake dived through the opening, twisting and squirming, and landed outside. Frankie La Barbara couldn't believe his sudden good fortune, and now all he wanted to do was get the fuck out of that tent, because he thought the snake might want to return.

He lunged toward the front flaps of the tent and burst outside, raising his head and seeing Lieutenant Breckenridge, Shilansky, and several other soldiers approaching the tent cautiously in the distance. Frankie ran toward them, waving his arms. They stopped and gazed at him curiously, because he looked like a raving maniac.

"Where's the snake?" asked Shilansky.

"He ran away!"

"Which way?"

"Through the hole you cut!"

Lieutenant Breckenridge took charge. "All right, men, spread out and look for the snake. It was red?" he asked Shilansky.

"Yes, sir."

"Look for a red snake!"

The men from the recon platoon made a skirmish line and stepped cautiously over the ground, looking down for the big red snake. They combed through the area, poking their rifles and bayonets into bushes, kicking over boulders, glancing up at the branches of trees to make sure the red snake wasn't getting ready to drop down on them.

"I see him!" said Corporal Gomez, who carried a machete in his right hand.

The red snake realized he'd been seen and that he was in trouble. His instincts told him to get above the monsters chasing him, so he sped toward the nearest tree and climbed the trunk.

Corporal Gomez caught up with the snake when he was about three feet up the tree. Raising the machete high over his head, Gomez swung with all his strength and chopped the snake in two.

The snake was killed instantly, but his nervous system kept going. He fell from the tree and his two halves coiled into knots. Gomez raised his machete and chopped again and again, but still the pieces twisted and arched.

Gomez's arm got tired, and he took a step back. "That snake ain't gonna hurt nobody now," he said.

Lieutenant Breckenridge looked at his watch. It was four o'clock in the morning. "Everybody back to your tents or whatever you were doing!" he said.

The men trudged off, leaving the red snake's severed sections twisting on the ground. Frankie La Barbara crawled into his torn-apart tent and Shilansky followed him.

"Shit," said Frankie, "what're we gonna do if it rains?"

"I guess we're gonna get wet," Shilansky replied, lying down on his stomach and closing his eyes.

"Did you haveta cut the fucking tent open?" Frankie asked.

"Shaddup, Frankie. Lemme sleep."

Frankie grumbled as he lay on his back. He closed his eyes but was too agitated to sleep. So was everybody else in the recon platoon. It was their first night back at the front, and they knew they had to get up at five o'clock anyway. Some smoked cigarettes. Others closed their eyes and lay still. The

147

guards watched the jungle and the Driniumor River surging past on its way to the sea.

The first copper sliver of the morning sun appeared on the horizon as a meeting began in the headquarters of Colonel Katsumata, with all his battalion commanders and staff officers, including Major Honda and Lieutenant Hozumi.

They were gathered around the map table, which showed the Driniumor River and adjacent real estate, with blocks of wood painted red, blue, or yellow indicating positions of various units.

Colonel Katsumata held a long pointer in his right hand and aimed it at a spot beside the Driniumor River. "The American unit we are concerned with is here, and Major Honda estimates that it is a regiment with artillery and heavy weapons but no tanks. Is that correct, Major Honda?"

"Correct, sir," replied Major Honda.

"We have received an order from General Adachi last night to attack these Americans, and this morning a new order arrived that clarified the tactical objectives of our attack." Colonel Katsumata smiled and looked up at his officers because they all were taller than he. "Our goal in this attack will not be to drive the Americans out of Aitape. Our regiment is not large enough to manage that great task. But we are large enough to inflict casualties and damage on our enemies, and render them weaker for the time when our main effort will come against Aitape.

"General Adachi believes that the Americans have committed a foolish and dangerous mistake by capturing Hollandia and Aitape, leaving so many of us behind. General Adachi contends that the Americans have violated one of the most important principles of modern warfare, because in modern warfare the objective is to destroy your enemy's means for waging war—in other words, his soldiers and equipment—and not just capture land, because what good is land? All by itself, it has no strategic value at all. You must defeat your enemy's army in the field; that is the way to win wars. But the foolish Americans have chosen to disregard that principle. They have decided to leave the Eighteenth Army behind them, and perhaps by leaving us behind them, they think we're gone.

But we're not gone, are we, gentlemen?"

The officers smiled and shook their heads. Colonel Katsumata was making sense to them, but he was only telling them what they wanted to believe. It was good for their morale to make them think that the Americans had made an important mistake, and Colonel Katsumata wanted to raise their morale, because they'd been taking a beating for the last year on the various bloody battlefields of the Huon Peninsula.

"The Americans are building up their strength in this area," Colonel Katsumata continued, "and General Adachi wants us to interrupt that buildup. He wants us to attack the new American troops opposite us on the other side of the Driniumor before they can establish permanent fortifications and become accustomed to the area. General Adachi thinks we can catch them off balance and unprepared, and inflict a heavy blow. We will attack this new American regiment at night, take them by surprise, kill as many as we can, steal as much of their supplies as possible, destroy the rest, and then withdraw to where we are now, to wait for the rest of the Eighteenth Army to arrive. At that time we will finish the job and drive the Americans first from Aitape and then from Hollandia. Are there any questions?"

Captain Masayoshi Mochizuki raised his hand.

"Yes?" said Colonel Katsumata.

"You said that we will attack the Americans at night," Captain Mochizuki said. "What night?"

Colonel Katsumata smiled faintly and narrowed his eyes. "This night," he replied.

It was after breakfast. Lieutenant Breckenridge was returning to the recon platoon after a meeting with Colonel Hutchins, who told him to cross the Driniumor River with some of his men and patrol the opposite side to see what the Japs had there.

Lieutenant Breckenridge found Sergeant Cameron supervising the construction of a trench in which the recon platoon's two mortars would be situated. Sergeant Cameron saw Lieutenant Breckenridge approach and climbed out of the trench to see what he wanted.

"What'd the colonel have to say?" Sergeant Cameron asked.

"He wants us to patrol the other side of the river. I'll take

149

two men with me, and you take as many men as you think you'll need. Leave as soon as you get ready, and if I'm not here when you get back, report to Major Cobb and tell him what you saw. Got it?"

"How far are we supposed to patrol?"

Lieutenant Breckenridge took his map out of his shirt pocket and unfolded it. "Go in about a half-mile, to this row of hills here." He pointed to a row of hills on the map. "About this far. The colonel wants to know what the Japs are doing over there, if anything."

Sergeant Cameron nodded, taking a bag of Beech-Nut chewing tobacco out of his shirt pocket. "Who're you taking with you?"

"You can have first choice."

"I'll take Lopez, Billie Jones, and Hotshot Stevenson."

"Good enough."

Sergeant Cameron pulled a clump of chewing tobacco out of the bag and stuffed the tobacco into his mouth as he walked away to gather up his men. Lieutenant Breckenridge lit a cigarette and wondered who to select for his patrol, since Sergeant Cameron already had selected the best point man in Gomez, one of the strongest and most obedient men in Billie Jones, and the best sniper, Hotshot Stevenson.

Lieutenant Breckenridge lined up the old veterans in his mind and wondered which to take on the patrol. He definitely didn't want Frankie La Barbara, because Frankie put up a big argument whenever he was asked to do something. Shilansky was okay when he wasn't with Frankie. Craig Delane had no initiative but could follow orders. Jimmy O'Rourke was probably the best point man after Gomez. Lieutenant Breckenridge went down the list and finally decided on O'Rourke and Shilansky.

He rounded them up and told them what they were going to do. They didn't appear too happy about it. Lieutenant Breckenridge didn't want to go on the patrol, either, but orders were orders.

"We'll leave from my tent in about fifteen minutes," Lieutenant Breckenridge said. "We'll travel light: Just bring a can of C rations and a full canteen of water. Make sure you got enough ammo. Any questions?"

Nobody said anything.

"Fall out," Lieutenant Breckenridge said.

The two patrols crossed the Driniumor at ten o'clock in the morning, and Japanese scouts watched them through binoculars high in the trees every step of the way. The water was chest-high and the current was strong. The GIs moved slowly, holding their rifles high over their heads, touching their feet down carefully so they wouldn't lose their balance and drop in over their heads.

They advanced into the jungle on the other side, and the Japanese scouts kept them under observation. The Japanese scouts had been ordered to leave the GIs alone, because Colonel Katsumata wanted the Americans to think there were no Japanese troops in that sector.

The Japanese scouts wished they could ambush the Americans and slit their throats, but orders were orders. They watched the American soldiers and followed them around, but made no contact. The two patrols found an elaborate network of trails and some Japanese footprints here and there, but nothing to indicate that major troop movements were taking place in the area.

The patrols recrossed the Driniumor and returned to Colonel Hutchins's headquarters late that afternoon. Lieutenant Breckenridge and Sergeant Cameron reported to Major Cobb that they'd seen few signs of Japs. Lieutenant Breckenridge recommended that the regiment cross the river and occupy the other side. Major Cobb said he'd take the matter up with Colonel Hutchins when the latter returned from a meeting with General Hawkins.

TEN . . .

It was two-fifteen in the morning, and a three-quarter moon shone brightly in the sky. Frankie La Barbara and Morris Shilansky were posted inside one of the machine-gun nests on the treeline near the Driniumor River, keeping watch on the other side. They'd come on duty at two in the morning and would be relieved at four by another team.

Shilansky sat behind the machine gun and Frankie knelt on the left side with the ammunition crates. They wore steel helmets and OD tank-top shirts. Bugs swarmed around them and bit them, although both GIs were drenched with citronella and stank horribly.

"There's nothing going on out here," Frankie said, lying on his side. "I think I'll get me some shut-eye."

"Come on, Frankie. I can't watch this whole fucking river all by myself."

"There ain't nothing to watch. What the fuck are you talking about?"

"What if a Jap sneaks up on me?"

"No Japs are gonna sneak up on you. If they come, you'll see them crossing the river."

"What if they cross farther down?"

"Other guys'll see them farther down."

"What if they don't?"

"*If* is like *maybe* and *but:* It don't mean a fucking thing. Shaddup and lemme sleep. You worry like a cunt, you bastard."

Frankie rolled over and closed his eyes. He ran his tongue over his teeth, swallowed, and snuggled into the muck at the bottom of the hole. Shilansky wanted to kick his ass and wake him up, but knew if he did that, he'd have to fight Frankie, and he didn't feel like fighting Frankie.

Something caught Shilansky's eye. He jerked his head in the direction of the opposite shore of the Driniumor, scanning the bushes and trees, but couldn't see anything. *My eyes are playing tricks on me,* he thought. *The moonlight can make you see things that aren't there.*

A cricket chirped nearby. Frankie La Barbara snored. Other insects buzzed, and in the distance a bird squawked. Shilansky sat cross-legged behind the .30-caliber machine gun and saw the moon glint along its barrel. Beyond was the oleaginous Driniumor. He thought he saw something move on the far side, but knew it was only his imagination.

Frankie La Barbara continued to snore. Shilansky's mind wandered back to Boston, where he was from. He was the son of a house painter, and he'd lived in the big Jewish neighborhood off Blue Hill Avenue, which the gentiles called Jew Hill Avenue. Boredom and a love of fancy blondes, fast cars, and zoot suits had propelled him into a life of crime. He started with burglaries, worked his way up to holdups of small businesses, and finally made it to the top, bank robbery; but he was never that good at it and had been arrested a few times. He'd done time at the Bridgewater House of Correction, and the warden said he could get out early if he joined the Army, so he joined the Army.

Often he thought he should have stayed in the Bridgewater House of Correction, because it was better than getting shot at on filthy, hot, bug-infested tropical islands, but at the time it had seemed like a good idea. He could wear a snappy uniform, hit on fancy blondes, and fight Hitler.

Instead he was sent to the South Pacific. He wasn't wearing a snappy uniform, there were no fancy blondes around, and he wasn't fighting Hitler. Things hadn't worked out the way he'd thought. Just then his reverie was interrupted by a particularly loud snore from Frankie La Barbara. It sounded like a circular saw hitting a two-by-four plank, and Shilansky was sure the snore could be heard all over the regimental area. He leaned to the side and shook Frankie's shoulder.

"Wake up!" he said.

Frankie opened his eyes and reached for his rifle. "Huh? What?"

"Wake the fuck up!"

Frankie blinked and looked around. "What's the matter?"

"You're snoring too loud, you bastard."

"I am?"

"Yes, you are."

Frankie rubbed his eyes and wondered what to do about his snoring. Actually, he suspected that he hadn't been snoring at all. He thought Shilansky had awakened him because he wanted some company.

"Somebody's coming," Shilansky said.

Frankie heard footsteps and turned around. It was Sergeant Cameron walking toward them through the shadows. Sergeant Cameron stood at the edge of the hole and looked down at the two GIs.

"What the hell's going on here?" he demanded, placing his hands on his hips.

"Nothing's going on, Sarge," said Frankie.

"Nothing at all," added Shilansky.

"Oh, yeah?" replied Sergeant Cameron. "I heard somebody snoring over this way."

"It wasn't me," said Frankie.

"Me neither," said Shilansky.

"Stay awake, you two," Sergeant Cameron told them. "Keep your eyes open. You fall asleep, you're liable to get your throats cut by a sneaky Jap."

Frankie La Barbara looked up at him. "Ain't no Japs around here," he said.

"How do you know?"

"Because there ain't. If there was, we woulda seen them by now."

155

"Oh, yeah?" said Cameron. "Well, sometimes when you don't see them or hear them, that's when you gotta be the most careful. Got it?"

"Got it, Sarge," Frankie said.

"How about you?" Cameron said to Shilansky.

"I got it, too, Sarge."

"Good. Make sure you remember it."

Sergeant Cameron turned and walked away. He was pretty sure Frankie La Barbara had been snoring, but he couldn't be one hundred percent sure. He'd have to come back and check later.

In the distance he heard *whump, whump, whump*. The sounds came from the Japanese side of the river, and he spun around, a cold chill coming over him despite the torrid, humid night atmosphere. He'd know those sounds anywhere. They were the sounds of mortars being fired not far away.

"Hit it!" he screamed. *"Hit it!"*

He held his steel helmet on his head and ran to the nearest trench, which was the one he'd just been in with Morris Shilansky and Frankie La Barbara. When he got close, he tucked in his head and dived. He soared through the air and saw Frankie and Shilansky clawing at the bottom of the hole, trying to get deeper. Sergeant Cameron landed to their left and lay still, both hands on his helmet.

Barrrrooooommmmmm! The first mortar shell exploded less than a hundred yards away, knocking over trees and sending clods of earth flying through the air. The second mortar shell landed closer, making the ground tremble as if an earthquake had struck. Then a slew of mortar shells landed simultaneously in one huge crescendo of destruction, blowing up the mess hall of Company F, landing on the headquarters tent of Company B, and wreaking havoc throughout the jungle. The next barrage blew up a section of the minefield and tore holes in the concertina-wire barricade.

The soldiers scrambled out of their tents and dashed toward their holes, diving in and covering up. The new replacements were scared to death, and some actually shit their pants as they huddled in their holes, while the old veterans thought it was like the return of a terrible nightmare.

156

Lieutenant Breckenridge had been awakened from a light sleep by the first *whump, whump*. Like Sergeant Cameron, he knew exactly what the sound signified. He slung his bandoliers of ammunition around his neck, grabbed his helmet and carbine, and charged out of his tent, heading toward his trench twenty yards away. He pumped his legs as fast as he could as the sounds and flashes of the first explosions spread across the regimental area. Nearing his hole, he jumped in feet first, flattening out on the bottom, and a few seconds later Pfc. Craig Delane landed on top of him.

"*Ouch!*" said Lieutenant Breckenridge.

"Sorry," replied Delane, rolling off him.

Barrrrooooommmmmm! A mortar shell smashed into the ground nearby and caved in the wall of the trench, covering Lieutenant Breckenridge and Craig Delane with dirt.

They coughed and sputtered as they clawed their way to the hot, dank air. Taking deep breaths, their heads sticking out of the ground, they saw shell bursts all around them, trees being blown to bits, and tons of earth exploding into the air.

Both were old veterans. They knew the mortar barrage was preparation for a ground attack. Digging their way out of the ground, they crawled toward the crater the shell had made and slid inside.

"Radio Colonel Hutchins," Lieutenant Breckenridge said. "Tell him we're receiving heavy mortar fire."

"Right," said Pfc. Craig Delane, raising the walkie-talkie to his dirt-streaked face.

Thirty yards away, Corporal Lupe Gomez and Pfc. Billie Jones lay in the bottom of their trench, waiting for the ground attack to begin. Corporal Gomez sharpened his bayonet on a bar of white washita stone from Arkansas, although it already was as keen as a razor's edge.

"Fucking Japs," Gomez muttered, stroking the bayonet blade back and forth on the washita stone. "I keel them all. I cut their throats. I tear out their hearts and stuff them down their throats. I cut off their balls."

The Reverend Billie Jones lay quietly, his circular wire-rimmed eyeglasses perched on the end of his button nose. The war had returned suddenly and he was trying to adjust to it. He knew the Japs would attack any minute now. The shit was about to hit the fan.

The Reverend Billie Jones had survived numerous attacks before, and he knew how bloody and ferocious they could be. It would be hand to hand and down and dirty until one side or the other won. Waiting for the attack to begin, Billie was plagued by religious and moral considerations. The Sixth Commandment said "Thou shalt not kill." Christ said to love your enemy and turn the other cheek. Billie believed he shouldn't have anything to do with the war, but on the other hand, he believed it had to be fought. He believed the Japs were evil wicked agents of the Devil. They had to be stopped. Hirohito was the Antichrist.

His conflicting unresolved beliefs frustrated him and made him angry. He thought of his old pal Homer Gladley, who'd been shot twice in the back on Bougainville and had died several days later. Billie Jones had sworn to avenge Homer's death, and the time to do that would come soon.

The Reverend Billie Jones gripped his rifle tightly and waited for the attack to begin. Beside him, Corporal Gomez slowly and methodically sharpened his bayonet.

"I cut them from their knees to their nose," Gomez said through clenched teeth. "I fuck up their faces. I skin them alive. I eat their livers for dinner."

Not far away, in another trench, Pfc. Jimmy O'Rourke, the former stuntman from Hollywood, lay beside Private Jilliam, who was from the Ozark Mountains of Missouri. Private Jilliam was so frightened, he trembled uncontrollably.

Pfc. Jimmy O'Rourke was aware of the sixteen-year-old's terror because he could hear his teeth chattering and feel him shaking next to him in the trench. Jimmy O'Rourke was scared, too, but not as much as Private Jilliam. Jimmy O'Rourke had been through this many times before. He knew what to expect, more or less. The most terrible fear is the fear of the unknown, and that was the fear that had Private Jilliam in its grip.

Private Jilliam whimpered. He wanted to turn around and run away, but he was too scared even to do that. He'd already shit his pants, and the hole stank badly. He was ashamed of having shit his pants. He wished he were dead.

Pfc. Jimmy O'Rourke had been in Hollywood so long, he tended to think that life was one big movie and that the war he was in was just another war movie, except that he, and not Clark Gable, was the star. In point of fact, although Jimmy O'Rourke appeared to be a fairly normal person, he really was as nutty as a fruitcake, and occasionally, when under pressure, he had psychotic episodes in which he couldn't separate fantasy from reality.

He was under pressure just then, and somehow, in his fucked-up mind, the jungle of New Guinea became a sound stage at Twentieth Century-Fox. He turned toward Private Jilliam and placed his hand on the lad's shoulder.

"Be strong," he said, the way he thought Clark Gable would say it. "We can lick 'em."

When his hand touched Private Jilliam, the young man nearly jumped out of his skin. He looked at Jimmy O'Rourke, and Jimmy O'Rourke had a confident, big-brotherly smile on his face.

"Stick with me," Jimmy O'Rourke said, "and you'll be okay."

Private Jilliam nodded his head in a staccato rhythm. "Okay, I'll stick with you, Pfc. O'Rourke," he stuttered.

"Good boy. And I'll stick with you."

"Thank you, Pfc. O'Rourke."

Pfc. Jimmy O'Rourke smiled broadly and squeezed the young man's shoulder. "Just remember, my boy, that the Japs out there are just as scared as you are. They don't wanna come over here, but they have to, and when they come, we'll be waiting for them. We'll kick them in their behinds and send them to hell, won't we, boy?"

"We will?" asked Private Jilliam.

"Sure we will," Jimmy O'Rourke replied, imagining the cameras zooming in on his profile. "There isn't anything to be afraid of. All we can do is our best, and when that bullet comes with your name on it, there isn't anything you can do about it anyway, so what the hell, right?" He grinned the way Clark Gable grinned, and he tugged his left ear the way Clark Gable tugged his left ear, while mortar rounds fell all around them, transforming the jungle into a holocaust of explosions and flames.

"This is all your fault!" Morris Shilansky screamed. "If I'd've gone AWOL alone, I would've made it. I'd be on the beach at Waikiki right now, cooling my head and heels."

"Shaddup!" said Frankie, gnashing his teeth. "I'm trying to think."

"You stupid son of a bitch!" Shilansky yelled. "You crazy fucking asshole! Why did I ever get mixed up with you in the first place!"

Sergeant Cameron lay to the left of both of them. "That'll be enough of that!" he said. "Calm the fuck down!"

Shilansky wanted to calm down, but he couldn't. His fear had become anger, and he'd focused his anger on Frankie La Barbara. He thought that Frankie was to blame for their lying underneath a mortar barrage.

"I hate your fucking guts!" Shilansky screamed.

"Up your ass with a ten-inch meathook!" Frankie snarled in reply.

Shilansky blew his cork and dived onto Frankie La Barbara, who was lying on his stomach on the ground. He tore off Frankie's helmet and punched him on the back of his head. Frankie saw stars, but he had a thick skull and didn't go unconscious. He jerked back his elbow with all his strength and it sank three inches into Shilansky's stomach.

Shilansky expelled air and doubled over, clutching his stomach. Frankie La Barbara rolled to the side and got out from underneath Frankie. Sergeant Cameron jumped in between them.

"Cut it out, you two!"

Frankie's right-fist haymaker was already en route, and he punched Sergeant Cameron on the jaw. It was a mistake— Frankie had intended to punch Shilansky—but Sergeant Cameron got in the way, and Sergeant Cameron fell back, his eyes rolling up into his head. Frankie pushed him out of the way and jumped on Shilansky, who still was clutching his stomach. Shilansky fell sideways to the muck at the bottom of the hole, and Frankie landed on top of him, swinging with both fists. A left cross made blood spurt out of Shilansky's nose. A right

160

uppercut connected with Shilansky's jaw and made his head snap back. Shilansky collapsed and Frankie jumped on top of him, ready to beat him to death, when suddenly the mortar barrage ended.

The onslaught of silence was eerie, and Frankie's ears still rang from the violence of the mortar barrage. He knew what was going to happen next and looked down at Shilansky, slapping him lightly on his cheeks.

"C'mon, wake up!" Frankie said. "The Japs're coming!"

Shilansky lay on his back, blood streaming from his nostrils, out cold.

"Wake up!"

Shilansky didn't move. Frankie crawled to Sergeant Cameron, grabbed him by the front of his shirt, and shook him.

"Wake up, Sarge!"

Sergeant Cameron was out cold too. Frankie then heard a blood-curdling sound coming from the other side of the river.

"Banzai! Tenno heika banzai!"

Frankie looked up and saw hordes of Japanese soldiers rush out of the jungle on the other side of the Driniumor River, and wade into the water, holding their rifles with bayonets affixed high in the air. Japanese machine guns and small-arms fire opened up from the treetops in an effort to keep the Americans pinned down.

Frankie knew that he and the others couldn't let themselves get pinned down. They had to fight back if they wanted to survive.

"Help me, you bastards!" he hollered at Shilansky and Sergeant Cameron, who were still knocked out.

They couldn't help him, so he had to help himself. He jumped behind the .30-caliber machine gun and dropped to his knees, working the bolt once, ramming a round in the chamber. He pushed the gun from side to side on its transverse mechanism, to make sure it was working properly, and then aimed at the center of the Japs advancing across the river, pulling the trigger.

The machine gun barked angrily and danced on its tripod legs. Hot lead spat out of its mouth and flew into the midst of the Japanese soldiers. The bullets cut into them, tearing apart

161

their guts, and the Japanese soldiers fell into the water. Other bullets zipped into the ripples and eddies as Frankie swung the machine gun from side to side, aiming at more Japs, baring his teeth and trying to discipline himself to fire in bursts of six, otherwise the barrel would melt down and he'd have nothing left to fight with.

He aimed a burst into a thick gaggle of Japs one-third of the way into the river, and the lead Jap's head shattered like an overripe watermelon, blood and brains spewing over the Jap's comrades; but still they moved forward, anxious to get on the dry land of the American side and really put their attack into gear.

Frankie chewed his lower lip as he fired his machine gun, and all across the Twenty-third Regiment's line, other GIs shot bullets at the advancing Japanese soldiers. Some of the Japanese soldiers fell back into the water, but the rest continued their charge, bouncing up and down as their feet touched the river bottom, screaming battle cries and shaking their rifles and bayonets, anxious to engage the Americans in hand-to-hand combat.

Shilansky opened his eyes; it sounded as if he were in the middle of a thunder storm. "What's going on?" he asked dazedly.

"Help me out, you fucking cocksucker!"

Shilansky turned toward the river, and his eyes goggled at the sight of the swarms of Japanese soldiers on the attack. Japanese machine-gun bullets raked across the front of the trench, and Shilansky ducked his head, but Frankie clicked his teeth nervously and continued to fire.

"I said help me out!"

Shilansky knew that the GIs had to fight back if they wanted to live through the day. Every GI had to take the chance, because it was the only chance they had. He raised himself and sat beside the machine gun, feeding the belt of ammunition into the slot, glancing nervously at the Japs, who now were halfway across the river and still advancing behind the cover of their machine-gun and small-arms fire. There were a great many of them, and Shilansky figured they'd concentrated their forces on that particular part of the line so they could achieve a breakthrough.

"Why us?" he muttered, guiding the belt of ammunition into

the machine gun and looking at Frankie La Barbara, whose face was covered with dirt and sweat and whose teeth were bared, sparks flying out of his eyes, as he swung the machine gun from side to side and shot Japs.

The end of the belt flew through Shilansky's hands, and the machine gun gobbled up the last bullets.

"Load me up!" screamed Frankie, unlatching the chamber plate.

Shilansky opened the next box of ammo and fed the belt into the chamber. Frankie slammed the plate down, took aim, and pulled the trigger. Nearby, Sergeant Cameron opened his eyes. He saw Frankie and Shilansky firing the machine gun and wondered what was going on. It was almost like a dream. He raised himself up and looked toward the river, seeing the Japs swarming across it.

"Holy shit!" he said.

Frankie and Shilansky ignored him. Sergeant Cameron picked up his rifle and rested it on the edge of the trench. He slammed a round into the chamber, clicked off the safety, and aimed at the lead Jap. He squeezed the trigger, and the butt of the M 1 rifle kicked into his shoulder.

In the river, a Japanese soldier clutched his chest, trying to stanch the flow of blood; but he couldn't, and a second later he collapsed into the river, letting his rifle go and floating away toward the sea.

"Where's the fucking artillery!" Colonel Hutchins screamed into his telephone.

"It's on the fucking way!" replied Colonel Jessup at division headquarters.

"What's the fucking holdup!"

"I said it's on the fucking way!"

"When?"

"When it gets there!"

Click!

The phone went dead in Colonel Hutchins's ear, and he turned to Major Cobb. "The cocksucker hung up on me!"

"Did he say it's coming?"

"Yeah, but he didn't say when."

Colonel Hutchins wiped his mouth with the back of his hand.

He'd received the reports from all his unit commanders and knew that his entire regiment was under attack. The Twenty-third would have to hold, because if it didn't, General Hawkins would blame him. Whenever something went wrong, General Hawkins always looked for somebody to blame, as if that did any good.

Colonel Hutchins strode across the office and took down his .45-caliber Thompson submachine gun from a peg.

"Where you going with that?" Major Cobb asked.

"Where the fuck you think I'm going?" Colonel Hutchins dropped four bandoliers of ammo clips around his neck.

"Sir, I don't think it's a good idea for you to go out there personally," Major Cobb said sternly.

"Well, I'm going anyway. You hold down the fort. If anything happens to me, take over the regiment."

"But, sir, you can lead the regiment better here!"

"That's your opinion."

Colonel Hutchins opened his desk drawer and took out a White Owl panatela. He lit it with his Ronson, dropped the Ronson into his pocket, and headed for the tent flap that led outside.

"Good luck, Cobb," he muttered over his shoulder.

The attacking Japanese soldiers were ten yards from the east bank of the Driniumor River, and Lieutenant Breckenridge fired his carbine as quickly as he could. He didn't waste time aiming carefully, because the Japs were bunched up and not far away and he couldn't miss. Again and again he squeezed his trigger, and then the first Jap reached shallow water, running through it toward the bank, screaming happily, shaking his rifle and bayonet.

Lieutenant Breckenridge shot at him and missed, but his bullet struck a Japanese soldier farther back, piercing his windpipe, and that Japanese soldier collapsed into the water, blood burbling out of his mouth. The first Jap jumped onto the beach, shouted victoriously, and then caught a burst from Frankie La Barbara's machine gun right in his breadbasket, mangling his guts; the Jap was thrown backward by the force of the bullets. He fell in the path of other charging Japanese soldiers, who pushed him out of the way, maintaining the momentum of their advance.

They ran up the riverbank and plunged into the jungle, where the American soldiers were deployed in foxholes. Lieutenant Breckenridge could see them jumping into the lead foxholes, their bayonets flashing in the moonlight. He knew from experience that it wasn't a good idea to wait for the Japs to come to you. It was better to counterattack and smash right into them, pushing them back or at least stopping them cold.

He stood in his foxhole and got ready to climb out, when he heard the whistle of artillery shells going over his head. The shells were headed from west to east, which meant they were friendly shells; sure enough, moments later the shells exploded in the river and on the far shore, blowing Japanese soldiers to bits, destroying their staging areas in the jungle, demolishing their mortar squads.

But still the main body of Japanese soldiers advanced, and Lieutenant Breckenridge knew they had to be stopped hand to hand and man to man. He climbed out of his foxhole; Pfc. Craig Delane watched his every move, wondering what he would do. Lieutenant Breckenridge held his carbine in his right hand and raised it high in the air.

"Forward!" he bellowed. *"Follow me!"*

He knew that many of his men couldn't hear his voice above the din of the artillery, but they could see him and realize what he was up to. That was the value of all the training they'd done on Oahu. They'd played this identical scenario through many times already, but this time it was for real.

"Up and at 'em!" Lieutenant Breckenridge yelled. *"Follow me!"*

Pfc. Craig Delane threw down his bazooka and walkie-talkie, because they'd only slow him down. It would be hand to hand and grim as hell from now on, and he didn't want to be encumbered. He climbed out of the foxhole and stood erect, fixing the bayonet on the end of his carbine and then lurching forward, following Lieutenant Breckenridge forward into the thick of the battle.

Forgotten was his father sitting behind his wide desk in New York City. Forgotten was his mother sipping tea in the afternoon with her elegant lady friends. Gone were all those charity balls at the fancy New York hotels, where he had tried to screw debutantes in broom closets. Now everything had boiled down to stab or be stabbed, kill or be killed.

"Follow me!" hollered Lieutenant Breckenridge.

"*Yyyaaaaahhhhhhhhhh!*" screamed Pfc. Delane, running in a hunch so that he wouldn't present too large a target to Japanese gunners.

Craig Delane saw movement in the corner of his eye. He turned toward it and saw a chubby figure of medium height, with a beer belly hanging over his belt and a cigar sticking out the corner of his mouth, carrying a submachine gun and running toward the Japs. *It's Colonel Hutchins!* Craig Delane thought. *Well, I'll be a son of a bitch!*

Colonel Hutchins chewed his cigar as he charged the horde of Japanese soldiers coming at him. The Japanese soldiers jumped over shell craters and dodged around trees, shouting at the tops of their lungs, crazed with the thought of victory.

Colonel Hutchins stopped, tucked the butt of the submachine gun underneath his arm, leveled the barrel at the advancing Japanese soldiers, and pulled the trigger, blowing a hole in their front rank. Japanese soldiers dropped to their knees or fell backward, huge .45-caliber bullets in their bodies. One Japanese soldier was hit in his head, which burst apart, and he collapsed onto the ground with only shreds of meat, bone, and brains above his shoulders.

Colonel Hutchins stepped forward, firing the submachine gun, and Japanese soldiers fell to pieces in front of him. In the confusion and tumult of the battle, the Japanese soldiers couldn't see exactly where the automatic-weapons fire was coming from, but a keen-eyed young Japanese lieutenant spotted the muzzle blasts and ordered the men near him to shoot in that direction.

The Japanese soldiers raised their rifles to their shoulders and prepared to fire, when suddenly a big black shadow passed in front of them. It was Pfc. Billie Jones, the former itinerant preacher from Georgia, with his rifle and bayonet, and he had murder and mayhem in his eyes.

"*Yaaarrrgggghhhhhh!*" he shouted, thrusting his rifle and bayonet forward, impaling a Japanese soldier in his chest. Jones heaved the Japanese soldier over his shoulder as if he were a pitchfork full of hay, and batted the next Japanese soldier in the mouth with his rifle butt, making the Jap eat his teeth and gums busting his jaw. The Jap sagged to his knees, blood foaming out of his mouth, and Billy Jones stepped over him, parrying a Jap bayonet out of the way, dodging a Japanese rifle butt, and then kicking a Japanese soldier in the balls with all his strength.

The Japanese soldier shrieked horribly and dropped to his knees, clutching his groin, but his balls were four inches into his stomach, and the pain was too much. He pitched forward onto his face and Billie Jones stepped on his head and pivoted. All he could see were Japanese soldiers rushing toward him. He raised his rifle and bayonet and parried a thrust from one Japanese soldier, slammed another Japanese soldier in the nose with his rifle butt, kicked another Japanese soldier in the balls, slashed wildly with his rifle and bayonet, and caught a charging Japanese soldier on the side of his neck, severing tendons and arteries, making blood gush forth all over the Japanese soldier's and Billie Jones's uniforms. Billie Jones turned his rifle and bayonet around and smacked another Japanese soldier sideways on the cheek with his rifle butt, splintering bones and caving in the side of the Japanese soldier's head. The soldier grunted and went flying through the air, crashing into a young Japanese lieutenant who had been advancing toward Billie with his samurai sword in his hands.

The Reverend Billie Jones was like a raging bull. He wanted to exact revenge for the death of his buddy, Private Homer Gladley, and kill the filthy pagan Antichrist Japanese who wanted to rape American girls and enslave all Americans everywhere. Snorting from both nostrils, he spotted the young Japanese lieutenant with the samurai sword in his hands.

The Japanese lieutenant stepped cautiously toward Billie Jones, holding the samurai sword over his head. He was waiting for Billie to come at him so he could split his head open with his samurai sword. The young Japanese officer had done that in the past, and was confident he could do it again. He figured he was an expert swordsman, and indeed he was, but Billie Jones was over six feet tall, weighed 260 pounds, and was an extremely powerful human being. On top of all that, Billie Jones was angry enough to eat the young Japanese lieutenant alive.

The Japanese lieutenant watched Billie Jones aim his rifle

and bayonet forward and charge. Coolheaded, poised on the balls of his feet, the Japanese lieutenant waited for Billie Jones to come within head-chopping range.

Billie Jones knew what the Japanese lieutenant was up to, because this wasn't the first Japanese officer he'd ever faced in close combat. Billie maintained his forward momentum and thrust his rifle and bayonet forward in a feint, then pulled it back quickly.

The Japanese lieutenant was faked out of position before he realized what Billie Jones was doing. Darting to the side like a matador, the Japanese lieutenant expected Billie Jones to rush past him, his side undefended; then the Japanese lieutenant could hack his skull open.

Instead, to his amazement and horror, he saw Billie Jones lunging directly at him, Billie Jones's rifle and bayonet aimed at the Japanese lieutenant's chest. The Japanese lieutenant jumped backward, swinging his samurai sword down and to the side. The blade of the sword struck Billie Jones's rifle, deflecting the bayonet away, and its point swished past the Japanese officer's right biceps.

Billie Jones's forward movement caused his chest and shoulders to collide with the Japanese lieutenant, who lost his footing and fell onto his ass. Billie Jones thrust his rifle and bayonet down to the ground, and the Japanese lieutenant twisted out of the way, rolling over, and getting to his feet.

Billie Jones jabbed again with his rifle and bayonet, and caught the Japanese lieutenant off balance. His bayonet stuck halfway into the Japanese lieutenant's stomach, and the Japanese lieutenant's eyes bugged open at the sudden, unexpected pain. The Japanese lieutenant was a fine swordsman, but he wasn't fine enough. Billie Jones pulled back on his rifle and bayonet, and blood poured out of the Japanese lieutenant's stomach, covering his pants, running down his leg. Dizziness, confusion, and pain overcame the young Japanese lieutenant. He knew he was going to die and became frightened. His knees sagged, and then Billie Jones slammed him in the face with his rifle butt. The Japanese officer was thrown to the ground by the force of the blow.

Billie Jones bent over and picked up the long, curved samurai sword gleaming in the moonlight. He knew from experience that samurai swords, machetes, and axes were excellent weapons in hand-to-hand combat, even better than rifles and bayonets. Billie Jones laid his rifle and bayonet on the ground and held the samurai sword in both his hands. It felt heavy enough to do damage and was perfectly balanced.

"Banzai!" screamed a Japanese soldier nearby.

Billie Jones turned and saw three Japanese soldiers rushing toward him, their rifles and bayonets aimed at his heart.

"You fucking bastards!" Billie Jones bellowed.

Billie Jones raised the samurai sword over his head and charged, his face a mask of ferocity and hatred. The Japanese soldiers lunged at the same time with their rifles and bayonets, and Billie Jones swung down, the blade of the samurai sword striking against the rifles and bayonets, knocking them toward the ground. The Japanese soldiers raised their rifles and bayonets for another try, but Billie Jones beat them to the punch.

He swung the samurai sword from the side and chopped off the head of the Japanese soldier on the left. The Japanese soldier's head went flying into the air, and blood gushed like a red geyser out of his neck. Billie Jones drew back the samurai sword and swung mightily again. He hit the next Japanese soldier on his right biceps, cracking through the bone, lopping off the Japanese soldier's arm. The arm fell to the ground, and blood poured out of the stump beneath the Japanese soldier's shoulder, while Billie Jones's samurai blade continued its forward movement, smashing into the Japanese soldier's rib cage, lodging between two bones.

Billie Jones tugged the handle of the samurai sword, but it wouldn't come loose. He pulled again, but the samurai sword was stuck inside those bones.

"Banzai!" shrieked the third Japanese soldier, thrusting his rifle and bayonet toward Billie Jones's gut.

Billie Jones let go of the samurai sword and pounced on the rifle, clamping his big hands around it and pulling hard, trying to yank it out of the Japanese soldier's grasp. But the Japanese soldier wouldn't let go. He gritted his teeth and held on tightly, trying to wrest it out of Billie's hands.

But Billie wouldn't let go, either. He snarled and tried to twist the rifle and bayonet loose, when out of the corner of his eye he saw a fourth Japanese soldier sneaking up on him from the side, hoping to stick him while he was preoccupied with the third Japanese soldier.

The fourth Japanese soldier tiptoed closer, thinking Billie Jones hadn't noticed him, but Billie was waiting for him to come within ball-kicking range. Meanwhile the third Japanese soldier, who was trying to twist his rifle and bayonet out of Billie Jones's big hands, had to admit to himself that Billie Jones was stronger than he and decided to try a bold dramatic move. Letting go his rifle and bayonet, he jabbed his fingers toward Billie Jones's eyes, intending to gouge them out and then take his rifle and bayonet back.

But Billie Jones had chosen that moment to attack the fourth Japanese soldier. Letting go of the third Japanese soldier's rifle and bayonet, Billie Jones leaped to the side and lashed out with his size eleven and one-half combat boot. It rose swiftly in the air as the third Japanese soldier's fingers scraped past his ear, and the toe of Billie's combat boot smacked into the groin of the fourth Japanese soldier, crushing his balls into two tiny pancakes and mangling his dick beyond all recognition.

The fourth Japanese soldier screamed horribly, dropping his rifle and clutching his scrotum with both hands. Billie Jones plucked the rifle out of the air, turned it around, and pivoted in time to see the third Japanese soldier thrusting his rifle and bayonet, which he'd just picked up, toward him. Billie darted to the side, and the third Japanese soldier's rifle and bayonet streaked past.

The third Japanese soldier quickly caught his balance as the fourth Japanese soldier clutched his battered balls and jumped up and down, screaming and shouting, in terrible pain, while in the immediately vicinity American GIs and Japanese soldiers were locked in close combat, trying to stab each other, bash each other with their rifle butts, kick each other in the shins, or do anything possible to kill their opponents so that they could stay alive themselves.

The third Japanese soldier aimed his rifle and bayonet at Billie Jones's chest and narrowed his eyes. Meanwhile, Billie Jones glowered back, seeing in this Japanese soldier all that was wicked in the world. For all Billie knew, that was the Japanese soldier who'd shot Private Homer Gladley in the back. Both men knew that one of them would be dead within the next minute or two. The Japanese soldier could see that Billie was stronger, but thought his superior speed would enable him to kill the huge American soldier. Billie Jones was enraged and wasn't thinking much. The smell of blood was in his nostrils, and all he knew was charge and kill.

The Japanese soldier feinted with his rifle and bayonet; at the same moment Billie Jones threw all of his 260 pounds behind his rifle and bayonet, propelling them forward. It was no feint. The Japanese soldier saw his mistake too late. He couldn't run and couldn't hide. He didn't have time to get out of the way, either. His speed was not the great advantage that he'd thought. Billie Jones's bayonet sliced easily into the Japanese soldier's soft belly, and the sudden onslaught of fiery pain caused the Japanese soldier to have one last brilliant insight into war: *It's all a matter of luck,* the Japanese soldier realized, as chaos and darkness overwhelmed his mind.

Billie Jones pulled back his rifle and bayonet, and blood oozed out of the Japanese soldier's stomach. The Japanese soldier dropped to his knees before Billie Jones, and Billie Jones looked down at him. It was as if the Japanese soldier were praying to Billie Jones, who felt triumphant and powerful.

Billie Jones kicked the Japanese soldier in the face and jumped over him, charging the Japanese soldiers attacking in waves from the direction of the river, wanting to massacre them all.

A horde of Japanese soldiers charged toward the machine-gun nest manned by Pfc. Frankie La Barbara, Pfc. Morris Shilansky, and Sergeant Luke Cameron. The Japanese soldiers were only twenty yards away, and Frankie La Barbara wasn't worried about the barrel melting down anymore, because it was too late for that. His forefinger held the trigger in its firing position, and the machine gun sputtered and wiggled, sending a nonstop spray of hot lead into the ranks of the Japanese soldiers, who maintained their headlong rush, although many were cut down like wheat before a scythe.

Sweat poured from Frankie's swarthy features, and his teeth were clenched so hard, his gums hurt. Japanese bullets were kicked up around the edge of the trench, but he didn't flinch. He knew that his only hope was to kill as many Japanese soldiers as he could and maybe then they'd stop their charge; but it didn't look as if they were stopping yet, and they were awfully close.

Next to Frankie, Morris Shilansky fed the belt of ammo into the chamber of the machine gun. The air was foggy with bullet smoke, which furled inside Shilansky's throat and made him cough. He knew that the Japs would be all over him in just about another minute, but his rifle and bayonet were lying nearby and he'd be able to defend himself.

Shilansky hated to fight hand to hand. The mere thought of it made his hair stand on end. But he would do it if he had to. He'd fight with every ounce of strength in his body, if that's what it would take to stay alive. More than anything else, Morris Shilansky wanted to stay alive. He wanted to stay alive so that he could go back to Boston someday and rob more banks.

Next to Shilansky, Sergeant Cameron rested his M 1 rifle on the edge of the trench and slowly squeezed off the rounds. Sergeant Cameron was a southerner with a cool head and a deliberate manner. He never got shook up about anything. Aiming at a Japanese soldier carrying an Arisaka rifle and bayonet, Sergeant Cameron squeezed off a round, and the Japanese soldier went tumbling asshole over teakettle, a bullet lodged in the center of his chest.

Sergeant Cameron moved his M 1 rifle an inch to the right and squeezed off another round. The Japanese soldier in his sights lost his footing and tripped over his feet, dropping to the ground and clutching his stomach, which had been torn apart by the bullet from Sergeant Cameron's M 1 rifle.

Sergeant Cameron moved the rifle two inches to the left and found a Japanese officer in his sights, waving his samurai sword over his head and screaming *"Banzai!"* Sergeant Cameron grinned as he squeezed his trigger. The Japanese officer stuck out his tongue and closed his eyes, dropping his samurai sword. His knees gave out underneath him and he collapsed onto the ground as his soldiers ran over him, closing in on the machine-gun nest.

Frankie La Barbara ground his teeth together and grimaced as he swung the machine gun from side to side on its transverse mechanism and mowed down howling Japanese soldiers, who

172

now were only five yards away. But every Japanese soldier who fell was replaced by another Japanese soldier behind him, and there was another Japanese soldier behind that one. They just kept on coming. Colonel Katsumata had concentrated his strength on that section of the American line, intending to make it the focal point of his breakthrough.

The Japanese soldiers were nearly in the trench, and the three GIs knew the time had come to fight it out at close range. Frankie La Barbara and Morris Shilansky scrambled for their M 1 rifles and raised them in the air, getting to their feet. Sergeant Cameron already had his M 1 rifle in his hand, and he jumped up suddenly, lunging forward with his rifle and bayonet at the same time, impaling a Japanese soldier who was leaping into the trench. Sergeant Cameron's bayonet sank up to its hilt in the Japanese soldier's stomach, and the Japanese soldier's velocity knocked Sergeant Cameron off balance. Sergeant Cameron fell onto his back, and the dead, bleeding Japanese soldier landed on top of him. A Japanese combat boot lowered itself toward Sergeant Cameron's face, and Sergeant Cameron twisted out of the way, shouldering the dead Japanese soldier off him and getting to his feet, carrying his M 1 rifle and bayonet with him.

Japanese soldiers were everywhere, surrounding him, but most were intent on moving onward, to strike deeply into the American rear. Some, however, knew that they had to finish off the American GIs in that trench. Sergeant Cameron, normally placid and somewhat slow-going, realized that his life was on the line and that a little extra effort was called for.

He pulled his rifle butt backward and slammed a Japanese soldier in the mouth, busting all his teeth, and thrust his rifle and bayonet forward, impaling a Japanese soldier in the neck, severing his windpipe and jugular. Blood spurted everywhere. Sergeant Cameron pulled his rifle and bayonet loose just as a Japanese bayonet sliced open his right arm and another Japanese bayonet nicked his side. The pain enlivened Sergeant Cameron, and he slashed to the side with his rifle and bayonet, cutting open a Japanese shoulder to the bone. He whacked another Japanese soldier on the nose with his rifle butt, kicked another Japanese soldier in the balls, and leaped out of the trench, landing in the midst of a swarm of other Japanese soldiers charging forward. Their momentum pushed him back into the trench again, where he landed on his ass.

He tried to get up, but a Japanese soldier, screaming victoriously, jumped with both feet onto Sergeant Cameron's belly, knocking the wind out of him. The Japanese soldier raised his right foot and brought it down with all his strength on Sergeant Cameron's nose, smashing it flat and knocking him unconscious. The Japanese soldier raised his foot again, to stomp Sergeant Cameron into oblivion, when suddenly an M 1 rifle butt appeared out of nowhere and slammed the Japanese soldier upside his head. The Japanese soldier was thrown into the air by the power of the blow, and Frankie La Barbara emerged from the press of battle, holding his M 1 rifle by its barrel and swinging the rifle like a baseball bat.

Two Japanese soldiers charged toward him, and he swung from the side, slamming the Japanese soldier to the right on the ear, caving in his skull. Blood and brains spattered in all directions, much of it covering the head and shoulders of the Japanese soldier on the left, who was knocked off balance by the stunned Japanese soldier stumbling into his path.

Frankie La Barbara caught the Japanese soldier on the left with his backswing, slamming him on the jaw, knocking it loose on its hinges. Blood welled up in the Japanese soldier's mouth as he sagged to the ground. Frankie looked around excitedly. No Japanese soldiers were attacking him at that moment, but he saw a group of them around Morris Shilansky, whose back was to the wall of the trench as he tried to fend them off.

"Yaaaaahhhhhhhhhh!" screamed Pfc. Frankie La Barbara as he charged the Japs, raising his M 1 high in the air. The Japanese soldiers couldn't hear his voice above the thunderous sounds of American artillery explosions on the other side of the river, and weren't aware that he was about to descend upon them like the angel of death.

Frankie swung straight down with all the power in his muscular arms, and the butt of his M 1 rifle whammed onto the top of a Japanese soldier's head, splitting his skull in two. The force of the blow caused the rifle butt to scrunch into the Japanese soldier's brains; they flew into the air in all directions, and some of the little pink bits landed on Frankie La Barbara's uniform, face, and even his lips, but he spit them out and swung backhandedly at the head of another Japanese soldier, connecting hard, flattening out the side of the Japanese soldier's head, and causing blood to spurt out of the Japanese soldier's ears, nose, and mouth. The Japanese soldier was flung to the ground by the force of the blow, and Frankie La Barbara swung again, connecting with the next Japanese soldier's head in a sickening *crump* sound, fracturing the Japanese soldier's skull, scattering his brains all over the landscape and all over Morris Shilansky, who was fighting for his life against the wall of the trench.

Shilansky had bayonet cuts on both of his arms and his face, and there was a gash in his side, but still he fought on, parrying and lunging, ducking and stabbing, always on the move, never presenting himself as a stationary target.

A Japanese soldier thrust his rifle and bayonet forward, and Shilansky parried it out of the way, coming around with the butt of his M 1 rifle, smashing the Jap in the chops. The Japanese soldier's lights went out and he fell to the side. Shilansky feinted with his bayonet at another Japanese soldier, but that Japanese soldier was a grizzled old combat veteran, and he didn't fall for it. Instead he feinted with his own rifle and bayonet, but Shilansky was too smart for that stuff. An obscure instinct deep in Shilansky's brain told him that the Japanese soldier would feint, so Shilansky followed up with a powerful lunge. The tip of his bayonet flashed in the moonlight as it flew forward, glancing off the Japanese soldier's breastbone and burying itself between two of the Japanese soldier's ribs and sinking into the Japanese soldier's heart, slicing it fatally.

The wound disgorged great gobs of blood. Shilansky pulled back on his rifle and bayonet, but it was stuck in the Japanese soldier's chest and wouldn't dislodge. The Japanese soldier fell to the ground, and Shilansky planted his foot on the Japanese soldier's ribs and tried to pull his bayonet out, but it wouldn't come loose. Shilansky was so intent on what he was doing, he didn't see the Japanese officer standing on the edge of the trench above him, his samurai sword poised to cleave Shilansky in twain.

Frankie La Barbara, parrying the lunge of a Japanese bayonet, happened to see the Japanese officer out of the corner of his eye.

"Watch out!" Frankie shouted.

Shilansky looked up. The Japanese officer began his swing. Shilansky didn't have time to get out of the way.

Blam!

A shot was fired and the Japanese officer faltered. He closed his eyes and the blade of his samurai sword dropped downward, losing its force. Shilansky bounded out of the way, and the Japanese officer fell into the trench, a bullet hole in his back. A few feet from where the Japanese officer had been standing, Lieutenant Breckenridge stepped forward, a wisp of smoke curling upward from the barrel of his M 1 carbine.

Lieutenant Breckenridge looked around and saw men locked in close combat all around him. They spat and grunted as they tried to stab, kick, and choke each other. A crescendo of violent explosions came to his ears from the other side of the river. Japanese soldiers were everywhere, swarming over the regiment's position like ants. Reinforcements were needed, but he didn't have time to call for them. An entire wall of Japanese soldiers, screaming at the tops of their lungs, charged toward him, aiming their bayonets at his chest. Lieutenant Breckenridge dropped to one knee, raised his carbine to his shoulder, lined up the sights, and pulled the trigger as fast as he could.

Blam-blam-blam-blam-blam! The Japanese soldiers fell to the ground one after the other, tiny red dots on the fronts of their shirts. Lieutenant Breckenridge aimed at the last soldier and pulled the trigger of his carbine.

Click!

The clip was empty. The last Japanese soldier was almost on top of him. Lieutenant Breckenridge didn't have time to reload. The Japanese soldier continued his charge, and Lieutenant Breckenridge jumped to his feet, charging back. The Japanese soldier realized that a giant of a man was coming at him, but the Japanese soldier was brave, and he thought it would be wonderful to die for his Emperor. He shrieked *"Banzai!"* and thrust his rifle and bayonet toward Lieutenant Breckenridge, who raised his carbine, parried the Japanese rifle and bayonet to the side, and kicked upward with his knee.

The Japanese soldier's forward motion caused him to crash

into Lieutenant Breckenridge, and then he got the knee. It lifted him a foot off the ground and mashed his testicles into hamburger. The pain was so terrific that the Japanese soldier lost consciousness for a few moments, and when he came to, he was lying on his back on the jungle floor. Lieutenant Breckenridge's bayonet streaked toward his stomach, and there was nothing he could do about it. The bayonet plunged into the Japanese soldier's stomach, and the pain was incredible, but still he did not die.

Lieutenant Breckenridge was going to stab him again, when he heard footsteps coming at him from his left side. He spun around and saw several Japanese soldiers charging toward him. Aware that his carbine was empty, he quickly pushed the button and pulled out the clip, letting it fall to the ground as he reached into a bandolier and plucked out a fresh clip. He tapped that one into the chamber and fired point-blank at the Japs.

Blam-blam-blam-blam-blam! The bullets blew the Japs away, but behind them were more. *Blam-blam-blam-blam!* Lieutenant Breckenridge shot them down and then shot at more Japs coming at him from the other side. Spinning around, he shot at Japs attacking him from behind.

Click!

Out of ammo again. He reached toward a bandolier and realized when he touched it that it was too light to have any more clips left in it. He groped toward his other bandoliers, realizing with terrible dismay that they were empty too. He was really out of ammo now. Three Japs rushed toward him and he thought, *Fuck it,* and leaped forward to engage them. One Jap thrust his rifle and bayonet at Lieutenant Breckenridge, and Lieutenant Breckenridge parried them out of the way, slamming the Japanese soldier in the mouth with the butt of his carbine, slashing the next soldier across the face, and kicking another one in the balls. Finally, in the crush of the fight, a Japanese soldier pushed his rifle and bayonet toward Lieutenant Breckenridge's heart.

Lieutenant Breckenridge saw the danger at the last moment and slammed the Japanese rifle downward with the bottom of his fist, but he was a split second too late, and the Japanese bayonet sliced open his thigh. The pain was so fierce, it blinded Lieutenant Breckenridge for a moment, but only for a moment.

"You son of a bitch!" he screamed, holding his carbine in his right hand and mashing it into the Japanese soldier's face.

The Japanese soldier staggered backward, blood spurting from his nostrils, and another Japanese soldier swung upward with his rifle butt, aiming for Lieutenant Breckenridge's jaw; but Lieutenant Breckenridge held out his carbine to block the blow, and the Japanese soldier managed to whack the carbine out of Lieutenant Breckenridge's hands.

Lieutenant Breckenridge responded by kicking the Jap in the balls, and the Japanese soldier shrieked in pain, dropping his rifle. Lieutenant Breckenridge caught the rifle in midair and smacked the butt into the mouth of another Japanese soldier, then spun around and slashed wildly with the Japanese rifle and bayonet. The bayonet tore a patch of scalp off the skull of a Japanese sergeant with a Nambu pistol in his hand. Lieutenant Breckenridge punched the Japanese sergeant in the mouth with the butt of his Arisaka rifle, and as the Japanese sergeant fell backward, Lieutenant Breckenridge yanked the Nambu pistol out of his grasp.

Lieutenant Breckenridge turned to the left and saw a Japanese soldier charging toward him. Lieutenant Breckenridge raised the Nambu pistol and pulled the trigger. The pistol fired, making Lieutenant Breckenridge's ears ring, and the Japanese soldier fell to the jungle floor. Another Japanese soldier rushed toward Lieutenant Breckenridge from the right, and Lieutenant Breckenridge turned in that direction, aimed, and pulled the trigger again. The Nambu fired and the bullet slammed into that Japanese soldier's mouth, not touching his teeth, but blowing the back of his throat into the air, snapping apart the spot where his spine was connected to his head. The Japanese soldier was killed instantly and collapsed onto the ground.

Lieutenant Breckenridge spun around and could see no more Japanese soldiers nearby at that moment, but ferocious hand-to-hand battles were taking place not far away, with bayonets clashing against each other and occasional shots being fired. Lieutenant Breckenridge's heart beat rapidly, and he looked down at blood oozing from the wound on his left thigh, a wound that felt as though a burning torch were being held against his flesh. His uniform was spattered with blood from Japanese soldiers he'd killed, and his hands were slippery with blood and gore. His veins and arteries were full of adrenaline, and he couldn't stand still any longer. He ran toward the spot where the fighting was the thickest, and his eyes spotted something shiny lying on the ground.

It was a samurai sword, long and curved, the handle covered with interwoven strips of leather. Lieutenant Breckenridge transferred the Nambu pistol to his left hand and picked up the samurai sword in his right hand. He raised the blade in the air and shouted a wild Rebel yell as he charged into the hottest point of the battle, limping slightly on his left leg because some of the tendons in his thigh had been severed.

He saw Japanese and American soldiers grunting and farting as they tried to kill each other. Swinging down the samurai sword, he cut a Japanese soldier's head in half as if it were a coconut. Raising the Nambu pistol, he shot another Japanese soldier in the face and blew his brains out onto other Japanese and American soldiers fighting nearby.

He swung the samurai sword from the side and lopped off the arm of a Japanese soldier. Backswinging sideways, he smacked the blade into the thigh of yet another Japanese soldier, cracking through the bone and slicing easily through the rest of the flesh. The Japanese soldier's leg fell off; it happened so suddenly he couldn't believe it. The Japanese soldier collapsed onto the ground, still wondering what had hit him, and Lieutenant Breckenridge jumped over his body, landing near three Japanese soldiers surrounding Pfc. Jimmy O'Rourke, whose rifle had just been knocked out of his hands.

Pfc. Jimmy O'Rourke believed that his number had come up. The three Japanese soldiers were going to kill him—he was sure of that—and he had nothing to fight with but his bare hands. All three of them lunged at him at the same time. Jimmy leaped onto the Japanese soldier in front of him, hoping somehow to snatch the rifle out of his hands.

Meanwhile, Lieutenant Breckenridge was in the middle of a powerful swing with his samurai sword. Its blade sliced through the neck of one Japanese soldier, and the Japanese soldier's head was thrown into the air like a foul ball off the bat of Jolting Joe DiMaggio. Then Lieutenant Breckenridge jumped in front of the next Japanese soldier, who had been so intent on stabbing Jimmy O'Rourke in the back that he hadn't even noticed Lieutenant Breckenridge.

Suddenly the Japanese soldier saw an American giant in front of him, and it scared the shit out of him. This Japanese soldier wasn't a typical Japanese soldier, because he wasn't very brave and didn't think he was strong enough to defeat the huge American officer in front of him, so he turned tail and prepared to run. But he wasn't fast enough.

Lieutenant Breckenridge was three-quarters of the way into a powerful downward swing before the Japanese soldier could step away, and the blade of the sword cracked the Japanese soldier's head in two, then cleaved down into the Japanese soldier's neck, snapped apart his collarbones, and hacked into his chest, splitting eight ribs apart from his sternum. The Japanese soldier was thrown to the ground.

Meanwhile, Jimmy O'Rourke's fingers closed around the Arisaka rifle belonging to the Japanese soldier in front of him. The Japanese soldier pulled on his rifle, trying to get it back, but Jimmy O'Rourke wasn't about to let it go. Both men tugged on the rifle, huffing and puffing, trying to gain possession of it. Neither wanted to be defenseless on the battlefield, because death surely would come to the man without a weapon. The Japanese soldier tried to kick Jimmy O'Rourke in the balls, but Jimmy O'Rourke twisted to the side in time and received the blow on his outer thigh. He tried to elbow the Japanese soldier in the eye, but the Japanese soldier pulled back in time. The Japanese soldier then tried to kick Jimmy in the shin of his right leg. Jimmy happened not to be looking down at that moment. The toe of the Japanese soldier's combat boot connected with Jimmy O'Rourke's right shin, and Jimmy screamed in pain, letting go of the Japanese soldier's rifle.

Jimmy jumped up and down on one leg, holding his hurt leg in both his hands, hollering at the top of his lungs, as the Japanese soldier got into position and harpooned his rifle and bayonet forward. Jimmy came to his senses at the final moment and leaped onto the Japanese soldier's rifle, taking it in his hands again and raising his knee swiftly, despite all the pain, to kick the Japanese soldier in the balls, but the Japanese soldier was a wily son of a bitch, and he pivoted to the side. Jimmy's knee struck his hip.

Jimmy O'Rourke was rip-roaring, piss-cutting mad, and that made him stronger than he usually was. He pulled on the Japanese soldier's rifle, and the Japanese soldier had difficulty hanging on to it. Jimmy pulled again, and the Japanese soldier nearly let it go.

The Japanese soldier knew he was in trouble. He realized that his American opponent had become stronger somehow, while he was becoming weaker. He decided that the time had come to throw some shit into the game. In a sudden, unsuspected move he turned his rifle loose and jabbed his fingers toward Jimmy O'Rourke's eyes.

Jimmy saw the fingers coming and ducked in time. The Japanese soldier's fingers crumpled against Jimmy O'Rourke's forehead. Now Jimmy was so mad, he didn't even give a damn about the rifle anymore; he let it go and grabbed the Japanese soldier by the throat, squeezing with all his strength.

The Japanese soldier coughed, clamped his fingers around Jimmy O'Rourke's wrists, and tried to break Jimmy O'Rourke's grip, but nothing would break Jimmy O'Rourke's grip at that point. The Japanese soldier knew something about jiujitsu, and hooked his right leg around Jimmy O'Rourke's calves, pulling in with his leg and pushing forward with his body, trying to trip Jimmy O'Rourke.

The ploy worked, and Jimmy O'Rourke fell backward; but the ex-movie stuntman knew basic acrobatics, and he spun around in the air so that the Japanese soldier was underneath him when they hit the ground.

Jimmy hadn't relaxed his grip one bit on the Japanese soldier's throat, and now that he was perched on top of the Japanese soldier, with all the leverage on his side, he squeezed harder. The Japanese soldier's eyes popped out of his head and his face became red as he grabbed Jimmy O'Rourke's wrists and tried to break his hold.

But Jimmy O'Rourke wouldn't let go, and his fingers tightened around the Japanese soldier's windpipe, threatening to cut off his air. The Japanese soldier dug his fingernails into Jimmy O'Rourke's flesh, hoping that would work, but it didn't.

The Japanese soldier pushed his fingernails in deeper, drawing blood from Jimmy O'Rourke's wrists; but that only made Jimmy O'Rourke madder, and he squeezed harder, pressing down on the Japanese soldier's Adam's apple with his thumbs.

The Japanese soldier coughed and sputtered. He wriggled and tried to break loose, to no avail. Jimmy O'Rourke clamped down on his windpipe and the Japanese soldier couldn't breathe. The Japanese soldier panicked, knowing he'd black out at any moment. He bucked like a wild mustang, but Jimmy had ridden wild mustangs during his stuntman days, and he stayed put.

The Japanese soldier choked. No air could reach his lungs now, and his mind spun around in circles. His grip on Jimmy O'Rourke's wrists weakened, and Jimmy O'Rourke gritted his teeth, putting all his strength into one last squeeze.

Snap. It was a soft, subtle sound, signifying that the Japanese soldier's neck had broken. The Japanese soldier was dead, and his arms flopped down to the ground. Jimmy released the Japanese soldier's neck and noticed the blood on his wrists where the Japanese soldier had jabbed him with his fingernails. Jimmy felt dirty, somehow. He wanted to be like Clark Gable or John Wayne, killing Japs with dash and bravura, but instead he'd just choked a man to death with his bare hands, and it had been kind of gruesome, like something that would happen in a Boris Karloff movie.

Jimmy heard shouts and battle cries all around him, but he was in a world of his own as he rested on his knees, gazing down at the dead Japanese soldier, who was a wiry little man with a Fu Manchu mustache who stank of perspiration and raw fish. American artillery shells blew apart real estate on the other side of the Driniumor River, and Jimmy O'Rourke couldn't help feeling revulsion for the dead Japanese soldier, because he looked so alien and almost inhuman with his yellow skin, high cheekbones, and peculiar slanted eyes. He thought the Japanese soldier had an evil, fiendish appearance, like a snake or an illustration of a dragon, because newspapers and magazines had convinced Jimmy that Japanese people were beastlike and inhuman, so it was a normal mental reflex for him to see the dead Japanese soldier within that framework.

Something compelled Jimmy O'Rourke to look up, and he

froze with fear at the sight of a Japanese soldier aiming an Arisaka rifle at him, about to pull the trigger. The Japanese soldier was too far away for Jimmy to attack, and Jimmy couldn't run away from a bullet. All he could do was remain on his knees, straddling the dead Japanese soldier underneath him, and wait for the bullet to come.

The Japanese soldier tightened his finger around the trigger. The dead man lying underneath Jimmy O'Rourke had been a close friend of his, and he wanted revenge. The trigger only had one-sixteenth of an inch to go, and Jimmy was wondering whether he'd open his eyes at Saint Peter's Gate or in the ovens of hell (most probably the latter, he thought), when suddenly the Japanese soldier closed his eyes and dropped to his knees.

Standing behind him, his teeth bared like a wildcat's, was Corporal Lupe Gomez, his sharpened, bloody bayonet held point up in his right hand and his entrenching tool, the blade locked into its L position, in his left hand, covered with the brains of the Japanese soldier.

The Japanese soldier pitched forward onto his face, and Corporal Gomez spun around, swinging the entrenching tool to the side, crashing the blade into the face of a nearby Japanese soldier. The blade sank into the Japanese soldier's head cavity, scrambling his brains. Corporal Gomez pulled the entrenching tool out just in time to parry to the side a lunging Japanese rifle and bayonet, and then Corporal Gomez stepped inside the Japanese soldier's guard, punching up with the bayonet in his right hand, burying the blade to the hilt in the stomach of the Japanese soldier, whose eyes rolled into his head, blood welling over his lips.

Corporal Gomez pulled the blade out, saw movement out of the corner of his eye, turned, and saw a Japanese rifle and bayonet streaking toward his chest. "*Aaaiiiiieeeee!*" he screamed, dodging to the side, then diving forward, stabbing his bayonet into the belly of that Japanese soldier, then pulling it out and leaping away before the Jap even hit the ground.

He landed in front of two Japanese soldiers, who were surprised to see him suddenly before them. They charged immediately, holding their rifles and bayonets level, aiming for his heart. Gomez swung wildly with his entrenching tool, slamming one Japanese soldier on his hands, breaking knuckles and mangling cartilage, and the Japanese soldier screamed as he dropped his rifle and bayonet.

"*Aaaaiiiiieeeee!*" replied Corporal Gomez as he swung his entrenching tool around and clobbered the other Jap on the head, busting into the Japanese soldier's skull cavity, splattering his blood and brains into the air. Then Corporal Gomez turned to the Japanese soldier with the broken, bleeding hands.

Corporal Gomez was surprised that the Japanese soldier hadn't run away, because he couldn't fight with broken hands. He wasn't anxious to kill an unarmed man with his hands hanging down at his sides, but war was war, and what else could he do? He raised the entrenching tool in the air. The Japanese soldier just stood there, apparently waiting to be killed, but then, as Corporal Gomez commenced his downward death stroke, the Japanese soldier's foot lashed out, and Corporal Gomez realized that he'd underestimated the Japanese soldier.

The Japanese soldier's foot connected with Corporal Gomez's balls, and the pain was so terrific that Corporal Gomez folded. He fell to the ground, writhing and groaning, cupping his groin in his hands, gritting his teeth. His consciousness, drowning amid all that pain, told him that he was about to die.

The Japanese soldier happened to be a karate expert, as deadly with his feet as with his hands, and he raised his foot with the intention of splitting Corporal Gomez's head open with one quick, powerful stomp of his heel, when suddenly the bloody tip of a bayonet appeared in the middle of his chest, and his raised foot fell to the ground, along with the rest of him.

Pfc. Frankie La Barbara was standing behind the Japanese soldier, and he pulled his rifle and bayonet out of the Japanese soldier's back. Frankie La Barbara's face and uniform were covered with blood and gore, and some of the blood was his own. He'd lost his helmet somewhere along the way, and had a three-inch gash on his scalp that oozed blood over his left ear.

He felt wild and crazy, even worse than usual. He looked around, but somehow there didn't seem to be as many Japs as before. No Japs attacked him; they were all engaged in fighting other American GIs. Frankie La Barbara stalked toward the closest Japanese soldier, whose back was to him, and harpooned him in the back with his rifle and bayonet. The Japanese soldier dropped to his knees, and Frankie La Barbara sidestepped to a position behind another Japanese soldier, took aim, and plunged his bayonet into that Japanese soldier's left kidney.

The Japanese soldier shrieked horribly and reached around to cover the wound with his hand, while Sergeant Cameron, who'd been standing in front of him, slammed him on the forehead with his rifle butt, splitting his skull. The Japanese soldier collapsed onto the ground.

Sergeant Cameron, whose nose was a lump of bloody, shattered flesh and cartilage, thought a second Jap was standing behind the Jap he'd just clobbered, so he thrust his rifle and bayonet forward; but Frankie La Barbara parried the blow and stepped so close to Sergeant Cameron that their noses almost touched.

"It's me, you asshole!" Frankie La Barbara shouted.

"Oh."

Frankie La Barbara turned around and saw scattered groups of men fighting, but in general the battlefield had quieted down considerably. The sun was just below the horizon, and the dawn illuminated heaps of bodies everywhere. Frankie La Barbara oriented himself and looked east, where he saw Japanese soldiers retreating, running toward the river. Remembering the colossal horde of Japanese that had attacked a couple of hours ago, he realized that the Japs had taken a lot of casualties.

Frankie La Barbara wanted the Japs to have more casualties. He spotted his machine-gun nest and trotted toward it so he could fire a few final bursts and kill more Japs. He carried his rifle and bayonet in his right hand and jogged lazily toward the machine-gun nest, because he was tired from all the fighting and in fact was too fatigued to feel the full elation of victory.

The ground surrounding the trench was littered with bodies, some Japanese and some American. Frankie didn't want to know yet which of his buddies were dead. He didn't even want to think about it. He approached the trench and saw that the machine gun had been righted and that somebody was lying behind the side of it closest to the river.

As Frankie drew closer he realized that the machine gun was pointed directly at him, and he stopped, a chill going up his spine. Squinting, he saw that the soldier lying behind the machine gun was Japanese. Frankie dived to the ground just as a burst of .30-caliber bullets flew over his head.

"Banzai!" cried the Jap behind the machine gun.

Frankie La Barbara yanked a grenade from his lapel and pulled the pin. Then he realized that a GI might be approaching the trench and might get blown up by mistake.

"Is anybody around?" Frankie shouted.

"Yeah, I'm around!" replied Pfc. Morris Shilansky, his voice coming from Frankie's right.

"There's a Jap behind our machine gun!" Frankie said.

"You think I don't know that?"

"I'm gonna throw a pineapple! Are you far enough away?"

"Yup!"

"Anybody else around?" Frankie asked.

"Around where?" asked the voice of Lieutenant Breckenridge, to the left of Frankie La Barbara.

"Around my machine-gun nest!"

"I'm not that close!"

"I'm gonna throw a pineapple!"

"Go ahead!"

Frankie turned loose the arming lever and began counting, because if he threw it too soon, the Jap might throw it back. He drew back his arm and chucked the grenade at the count of four. It sailed through the dawn light and landed with a *clump* inside the trench. Frankie stuck his fingers in his ears and lay flat on the ground, waiting for the grenade to explode; but then, a few seconds later, he saw it flying back at him.

Frankie didn't know whether to shit or go blind. If he stood up and tried to run away, the shrapnel would blow him to bits, but if he stayed where he was, it would demolish him. The grenade landed a few feet in front of him, rolled a few inches, and then stopped, gleaming evilly.

Sweat poured from Frankie La Barbara's forehead, washing away some of the blood. He stared at the grenade, waiting for it to blow, but nothing happened. The seconds passed, and he realized it was a dud!

"What happened?" Lieutenant Breckenridge asked.

"It was a dud!" Frankie replied.

"I'll throw one this time!" Lieutenant Breckenridge said.

Frankie stuck his fingers in his ears again and flattened himself against the ground. Mosquitoes and other flying bugs swarmed around his bloody head, diving in to suck up the red syrupy nourishment. He saw a grenade fly through the air and disappear inside the trench.

Baaaarrrooooooommmmmmmm!

The ground shook under Frankie La Barbara, and clods of earth rained down upon him. He leaped to his feet and ran to the trench, holding his rifle and bayonet angled downward so he could shoot the Japanese soldier who'd been lying behind the machine gun. Smoke and the smell of burnt gunpowder swirled around the trench, and Frankie La Barbara jumped inside and saw the machine gun lying on its side. The head of the Japanese soldier lay to the right of the machine gun, a leg to its left. The Japanese soldier's torso hung on the edge of the crater left by the grenade blast, knots of guts hanging down from his belly.

Lieutenant Breckenridge jumped into the trench beside Frankie, and Shilansky landed on his other side. Lieutenant Breckenridge waved his hand in an effort to make some of the smoke go away, and narrowed his eyes. He saw Japanese soldiers holding their rifles and bayonets high, wading across the Driniumor River, heading toward the far side as fast as they could.

"Get that machine gun going!" Lieutenant Breckenridge shouted.

Frankie La Barbara lifted the machine gun and set it down on its tripod. The weapon was pockmarked from shrapnel, but the barrel appeared straight. Frankie sat behind it and worked the bolt. It was sticky, but Frankie rammed it back and forth, and after a few strokes it worked smoothly.

"Load me up!" said Frankie.

"I don't see no ammunition!" Shilansky replied.

Shilansky looked around. The trench wasn't what it had been before. The grenade blast had widened it and covered up the boxes of ammunition. Shilansky got down on his knees and dug with his hands.

"Ouch!" he hollered, pulling his hand out of the dirt. Three

of his fingers bled, cut by a fragment of an ammunition box that had been blown apart by the grenade explosion.

"Use your rifles!" Lieutenant Breckenridge said, flopping down behind the edge of the foxhole and aiming the Japanese Arisaka rifle in his hands at the back of a Japanese soldier wading across the Driniumor River.

The Arisaka rifle was a bolt-action weapon based on the German Mauser; it was not semiautomatic, like American M 1s. Lieutenant Breckenridge pulled back the bolt, pushed it forward, and clamped it down. Then he lined up the sights and trained them on the back of the Japanese soldier. He squeezed the trigger, and *blam*—the Arisaka rifle fired, but the Japanese soldier kept wading across the river, bouncing up and down every time one of his feet touched bottom, trying to get away as fast as possible.

Lieutenant Breckenridge worked the bolt again, aimed, and squeezed the trigger. The rifle fired, but the Japanese soldier continued to make his way across the river. Lieutenant Breckenridge realized that something must have happened to the sights of the rifle; it wasn't worth a shit anymore.

Then the Japanese soldier fell into the water, as if by delayed action. Lieutenant Breckenridge raised his head slightly and realized that other GIs in the vicinity were firing at the retreating Japanese, and one of them had hit the Japanese soldier whom Lieutenant Breckenridge had been aiming at.

"*Keep firing!*" Lieutenant Breckenridge yelled. "*Shoot the bastards down!*"

Frankie La Barbara and Morris Shilansky pulled the triggers of their M 1s, and Japanese soldiers in the middle of the river lost their footing, their heads sinking beneath the surface of the fast-moving water. The battlefield crackled with the fire of American rifles, and then Lieutenant Breckenridge heard the chatter of a machine gun. He turned toward the river and saw the Japs falling like flies.

Lieutenant Breckenridge wanted to kill some of them too. He crawled out of the trench and looked around for a good M 1 rifle. He didn't have to go far. One lay nearby, its barrel underneath a slim American soldier who didn't have a mark on him that Lieutenant Breckenridge could see. Lieutenant Breckenridge pushed the GI off the rifle, then saw the blood and guts. It was Private Jilliam, the sixteen-year-old kid, his belly cut open by a Japanese bayonet. A splotch of dried blood covered the side of Private Jilliam's face that had been lying on the ground, but otherwise he was pale; his blood had soaked into the ground.

Lieutenant Breckenridge paused. It wasn't every day that he saw a teenager killed in such a brutal manner. He knew that Private Jilliam had been frightened ever since the regiment had arrived on New Guinea, and Pfc. O'Rourke was supposed to have been looking out for him, but there comes a point where a soldier has to stand on his own, and Private Jilliam hadn't been able to do it.

Lieutenant Breckenridge shook his head as volleys of rifle fire echoed across the regiment's front line. He could imagine very clearly what had happened to Private Jilliam. The kid had been caught up in the patriotic fervor back in the States. Recruiting posters had fired his imagination, and he'd seen John Wayne fight off entire Japanese armies on the silver screen. He thought he'd look wonderful in a uniform, and all the girls would adore him, so he had lied about his age and signed up. The recruiting sergeant didn't check out Private Jilliam's application too thoroughly because he wanted all the warm bodies he could get.

And now Private Jilliam's warm body was cold. He'd get shipped back to the States in a pine box and get a hero's funeral. Maybe they'd even name a town square after him. He'd be remembered for years, and all he'd ever been, really, was a dopey little kid with his head up his ass most of the time.

Lieutenant Breckenridge crawled back to the trench and slithered inside. Pfc. Frankie La Barbara and Pfc. Morris Shilansky hugged their M 1 rifles against their cheeks and shoulders, pulling their triggers. Lieutenant Breckenridge looked down at the river and saw the Japs drawing close to the far side. He dropped onto his belly, clicked the safety off, aimed at the Japanese soldier closest to the far bank of the river, and pulled the trigger.

Blam!

The Japanese soldier stopped suddenly and his knees bent as he threw out his arms, dropping his rifle. Then he fell backward into the rippling water, which closed over his head.

189

"That's for Private Jilliam," Lieutenant Breckenridge muttered, moving his rifle a few inches to the right and aiming at another Japanese soldier. He squeezed the trigger and *blam*, that soldier sagged into the water, dropping beneath the surface and then bobbing to the top again, arms outstretched and legs splayed as the water carried his corpse toward quieter regions of the thick, tangled jungle.

ELEVEN . . .

Colonel Hutchins staggered into his command post tent, his uniform torn, a gash over his left eye, and a bayonet cut on his chest. He'd lost his helmet and he was splattered with blood. In his right hand he carried a bloody Japanese samurai sword, and in his left hand was his Colt .45 pistol, empty and also sticky with blood, because he'd been using it as a blackjack ever since it ran out of bullets.

"What the fuck is going on here?" he shouted.

Master Sergeant Koch sat in his chair, wearing his helmet, his M 1 carbine lying on his desk in case the Japs got close. Pfc. Levinson sat on the other side of the office area, typing a letter, also wearing his helmet, with his M 1 carbine lying on his desk too.

Master Sergeant Koch leaped to his feet. *"Ten-hut!"*

Pfc. Levinson jumped up and stood at attention.

Colonel Hutchins frowned. "Knock that shit off," he said. "As you were."

Both men sat down. The flap of Colonel Hutchins's office was thrown to the side, and Major Cobb emerged, wearing his little wire-rimmed eyeglasses on his pug nose.

"My God!" he said at the sight of Colonel Hutchins. "What happened to you?"

"Never mind what happened to me," Colonel Hutchins replied, pushing Major Cobb to the side and limping into his office. Major Cobb followed him, and Colonel Hutchins collapsed into his chair. Opening the drawer in his portable desk, he withdrew his metal flask of bourbon, unscrewing the top and taking a long swig, his Adam's apple bobbing up and down.

"I don't think you should drink so much of that, sir," Major Cobb said softly.

"Who asked for your two cents?" Colonel Hutchins replied. He wiped his mouth with the back of his hand and screwed the cap back on. "What the fuck happened to my artillery out there?"

"I don't know, sir. What *did* happen to it?"

"It stopped—that's what happened to it."

Major Cobb was confused. "Didn't the bombardment last long enough, sir?"

"No."

"Are the Japs still attacking, sir?"

"No."

"Then why do you need more artillery?"

"Because *we*'re attacking this time. Pass along the word to all the units on this length of the river. We're going across when I give the word."

"On whose orders, sir?"

Colonel Hutchins slammed the heel of his fist onto the desk. "On my orders, goddamnit!"

"But, sir—"

"Don't 'but' me! Do as I say!"

"Yes, sir." Major Cobb reached for the phone.

"Not that phone! Use your own phone! I need to make a call myself!"

"Yes, sir!"

Major Cobb leaped to his feet and ran out of Colonel Hutchins's office. Colonel Hutchins shouted, "Get me General Hawkins on the phone!"

"Yes, sir!" replied Sergeant Koch from the other section of the tent.

Colonel Hutchins picked up his receiver and listened as

192

Sergeant Koch made the connections. Sergeant Koch talked with numerous clerks and aides, and finally Colonel Jessup's voice came on the wire. "General Hawkins is busy right now," he said.

"What happened to the artillery?" Colonel Hutchins thundered into the phone.

"Is that you, Hutchins?" Colonel Jessup asked.

"Well, it ain't my mother! Put the general on the phone! I've got to speak with him!"

"I just told you that he's busy right now."

"Doing what?"

"Beg your pardon?"

"I said what's he doing?"

"That's an impertinent question!"

"Fuck you, Jessup! Tell General Hawkins that the Japs have broken through my line and I need to talk with him right away!"

"What?"

"You heard me! And tell him that the Japs are headed his way right now as I'm talking to you!"

"They are?"

"Are you gonna let me talk to him or aren't you, you goddamned twirp!"

"Hang on a moment!"

Colonel Hutchins heard the muffled sounds of hysterical screaming, and he smiled, reaching for his flask. He unscrewed the cap with his teeth and enjoyed a few more swallows. Then General Hawkins's excited voice filled his ears.

"How many Japs are headed this way?"

"None. Relax. Calm down."

"None?"

"That's right."

"But Colonel Jessup just told me that you told him that the Japs had broken through your line!"

"I lied," Colonel Hutchins said.

"You lied?"

"What happened to my artillery?"

"How dare you lie to my operations officer!"

"If I didn't lie to your operations officer, you wouldn't have talked to me."

There was silence on the other end. Colonel Hutchins opened

his desk drawer and took out half a pack of Camel cigarettes. He flipped one into his mouth and lit it with his Ronson.

General Hawkins's voice spoke softly into his ear; the voice sounded as though it was barely under control. "What did you want to speak with me about, Colonel?"

"I want that artillery back, General."

"What for?"

"Because I'm going across the Driniumor."

"Oh, no you're not."

"Oh, yes I am."

"If you go across that river, I'll court-martial you," General Hawkins said.

"If you court-martial me, you'll become the laughingstock of the Eighth Army, because how can you court-martial an officer who wins an important strategic objective for you?"

There was another pause on the other end of the telephone connection. Colonel Hutchins puffed his cigarette. His chest hurt when he inhaled. He wondered if a few of his ribs might be fractured.

"You think you can take the east bank of the Driniumor?" General Hawkins asked.

"No question about it. I got the Japs on the run, and if you give me some artillery support, I'll be in like Flynn."

"What if the Japs counterattack?"

"We kicked their asses over here. They ain't got nothing to counterattack with; otherwise, they would've thrown them in by now."

"You don't know that for sure."

"You gotta take chances in war, General. If you don't know that by now, you oughtta turn in your stars."

"I'd better back you up with something."

"Not a bad idea."

"How much artillery will you need?"

"All you can give me until"—Colonel Hutchins looked at his watch—"oh-four-thirty hours."

"Okay, Colonel. Keep me advised of your progress."

"Will do, General. Over and out."

Colonel Hutchins hung up the phone and smiled with satisfaction. He puffed his cigarette and touched his ribs. They were tender, but the blood had dried. "Sergeant Koch!"

"Yes, sir!"

"Get in here!"

"Yes, sir!"

Seconds later Sergeant Koch burst into Colonel Hutchins's office.

"Two things," Colonel Hutchins said. "First of all, find Major Cobb and tell him I want to speak with him immediately. And second, get me a medic."

"Yes, sir."

Sergeant Koch spun around and ran out of the office. Colonel Hutchins leaned back in his chair and took a deep drag off his Camel cigarette. *Half the time I have to fight the Japs,* he mused, *and the other half I have to fight the people on my own side, the dumb sons of bitches*. He shook his head in despair and reached for his flask of bourbon.

The order was passed along that all units of the Twenty-third Infantry Regiment would cross the Driniumor River at 0430 hours, right after the artillery bombardment ended, except for the Third Battalion, which would be held in reserve.

The artillery bombardment began at approximately 0410 hours, blasting the shit out of the jungle on the other side. The GIs huddled in their foxholes as fresh ammunition was delivered to them and medics tied bandages around wounds. The seriously injured were evacuated, and the dead were carried off by Graves Registry squads.

Lieutenant Breckenridge went from foxhole to foxhole, checked his platoon, finding out who was alive and who was dead. His left leg had been bandaged by a medic and didn't hurt too badly, and his happiness at still being alive was matched by his chagrin over the orders that they had to assault the other side of the river.

He came to the foxhole where Frankie La Barbara and Morris Shilansky were situated with their machine gun, and slid inside.

"You two ready to go?" he asked.

"Yeah, we're ready to go," Frankie said, without much enthusiasm.

"Don't forget to take that machine gun with you. We might need it on the other side."

"What?" shouted Frankie. "Are you kidding?"

"No, I'm not kidding," Lieutenant Breckenridge replied. "What makes you think I'm kidding?"

"It's so fucking heavy!"

"When we get on the other side, you'll be glad you've got it."

Frankie La Barbara looked at Shilansky. "You can carry the gun. I'll take the boxes of ammo."

"Fuck you," Shilansky said. "You carry the gun."

"Not me," Frankie replied. "I carried it yesterday."

"I carried it this morning."

"I carried it longer yesterday than you did this morning."

Lieutenant Breckenridge groaned and reached into his pocket. "You two get on my nerves, arguing all the time. I'll flip a coin."

"I'll take heads!" Frankie declared.

"No, I want heads!" Shilansky said.

Lieutenant Breckenridge flipped the coin into the air with his thumbnail. "Frankie called it first," he said. The coin toppled into the air and then dropped, landing on the back of Lieutenant Breckenridge's left hand, and he covered it with the palm of his right hand. Then he lifted the palm away. "Tails," he said. "Shilansky wins."

Shilansky smiled as he turned to Frankie. "You carry the machine gun," he said. "I'll carry the ammo."

"Your mother's pussy," Frankie replied.

Lieutenant Breckenridge walked toward his foxhole, dragging his ass. He was exhausted, hungry, and in pain from the wound on his leg. But he couldn't relax and have something to eat. There was no time. The regiment was going to attack, and he knew why. In war you had to exploit your enemy's weakness, and the Japs on the other side of the Driniumor were weak just then. The ground over there could be taken more cheaply now than later, when the Japs had reorganized and regrouped.

He slid into his foxhole; Craig Delane was sitting there, looking at his face in a small tin mirror, frowning at a two-inch cut on his left cheek. "I'm scarred for life," he said.

Lieutenant Breckenridge ignored his remark. "Any calls?"

"No."

"No *what*?"

"No, *sir*."

"I'm gonna close my eyes for a few minutes. Wake me up if anything happens."

"Yes, sir."

Lieutenant Breckenridge sat on the moist earth at the bottom of the hole, leaned his back against a wall, and closed his eyes, but he couldn't stop the images of men sticking each other with bayonets and bashing each other with rifle butts. He went slack against the wall of the foxhole, falling asleep and dreaming about war.

Lieutenant Breckenridge's jaw fell open, and Craig Delane thought that his platoon leader looked even worse than he did. Lieutenant Breckenridge was covered with blood. He had cuts on his arms, face, and various parts of his body. His fatigue shirt was torn to shreds. The bandage on his leg was soaked with blood.

Craig Delane took another look at his own face. At least he wasn't disfigured. At least he still was alive. He put the mirror into his shirt pocket and thought of the battle he'd just been in. It had been so bloody and gruesome, he was amazed that he'd survived. At certain points he'd thought for sure that he'd be killed, but somehow he'd done the killing himself, perhaps out of the powerful insanity that comes from being pushed to extremes.

But would he get through the next one? Craig Delane put on his steel pot and raised his head above the edge of the trench. He gazed across the Driniumor River and saw explosions, smoke, and flames. *How could anything survive that shelling?* he wondered, but he recalled that on Guadalcanal he and the rest of the Twenty-third had been subjected to an incredible shelling that had gone on for hours, and the majority of the men had survived; they hadn't even been dug in that well.

Craig Delane was exhausted, but not so exhausted that he couldn't feel anxiety. His stomach felt as though it were filled with acid, and the back of his throat burned. Electrical currents shot back and forth inside his skull. He couldn't sit still but kept fidgeting with pebbles and the buttons of his uniform; he lit up a cigarette and puffed nervously.

He thought of his father and mother back in New York City,

197

and got mad. They'd never done a goddamn thing for him, even though they had lots of money. All they cared about was appearances. All they wanted was for other people to look up to them and admire them. If he were to be killed in battle, it would be the best thing that had ever happened to them. They could puff out their chests and brag that they'd given a son for their country. That would make it all right for them to be dirty, rotten, filthy, stinking rich.

Craig Delane smiled grimly, because his thoughts had caused him somehow to make a simple obvious connection in his mind. *Maybe I fight so hard to stay alive because I don't want to give my mother and father the satisfaction they'd derive from my death!* He reached into the pocket of his tattered fatigue shirt and took out a package of Chesterfields. Lighting one up, he inhaled and swore that he'd remain alive by any means available so that he wouldn't give his mother and father the honor of having lost a son in the war.

The sun rose in the sky but still could not be seen through the explosions and trees on the other side of the river. The illumination made the smoke silvery and cast an eerie glow on the tortured, heaving jungle under bombardment. GIs peered at the opposite side of the river and hoped the artillery shells would kill all the Japs. They didn't want to go through two hand-to-hand fights in the same day.

The shelling diminished and a minute later stopped entirely. Lieutenant Breckenridge opened his eyes and turned around, blinking, trying to wake up totally. He saw whirlpools of smoke and crackling flames on the other side of the river. The time had come for the attack, and already he could hear battle cries up and down the Twenty-third Regiment's lines.

With one mighty leap he landed on the ground above the foxhole. He raised his carbine above his head and screamed, *"Follow me!"*

Stretching out his left foot, he began his run toward the river, the straps of his helmet dancing in the air like crazy snakes. The air was filled with the odor of gunpowder and burning vegetation. The Driniumor River twinkled in the light of the sun, and the men from the recon platoon came up out of their foxholes, brandishing their rifles and shouting at the top of their lungs.

Sergeant Cameron let out a Rebel yell. Frankie La Barbara made a Bronx cheer. Craig Delane roared like a lion. Corporal Lupe Gomez called the Japs faggots in Spanish. The men from the recon platoon swept down to the river and jumped in, kicking through the water, raising their rifles and bayonets high over their heads, hoping the Japs were too stunned by the artillery bombardment to open fire.

Craig Delane was a few feet behind Lieutenant Breckenridge, carrying the platoon's walkie-talkie and bazooka, in addition to his own M 1 carbine. The water rose up to Craig Delane's chest, and his arms were tired already from holding all the weight in the air. Somebody was talking on the walkie-talkie, but he couldn't hold it to his ear and find out what was being said.

Lieutenant Breckenridge leaped through the water like a wild horse, far in front of the recon platoon, his finger on the trigger of his carbine, ready to fire. He knew that the sooner he and his men reached the other side and found shelter, the better off they'd be. *"Let's fucking go!"* he yelled. *"Charge!"*

The water was up to his chest, and the current was strong. He bounded forward and noticed that the water was moving down toward his waist. This made him realize that he'd passed the midway point in the river.

"Faster!" he screamed. *"Hit that fucking beach!"*

Still there was no Japanese fire. The jungle ahead looked like nightmare alley. The water was down to Lieutenant Breckenridge's thighs, and he could make greater speed. Stretching out his long legs, he kicked water in all directions. Dead Japanese soldiers and mangled, blown-up portions of Japanese soldiers were sprawled all over the bank straight ahead. Lieutenant Breckenridge dashed forward; the water was down to his ankles now. He charged up the muddy bank and plunged into the jungle full of shattered trees and deep shell craters.

"Let's go!" he hollered. *"Hit it!"*

The men from the recon platoon, soaking wet, followed him out of the river and into the jungle. They ran around splintered tree trunks and hopped over holes in the ground, holding their rifles and bayonets ready to kill Japs.

Lieutenant Breckenridge slowed down, because he didn't want to lead his men into a trap. He stepped forward, peering into the devastated vegetation for signs of Japs. His orders were to move into the jungle about fifty yards, dig in, and await further instructions. He figured he was nearly fifty yards in then, but he advanced another ten yards to be sure, then turned around and ordered, *"Take cover!"*

The men from the recon platoon dived into shell craters or huddled behind logs and the stumps of trees. Lieutenant Breckenridge jumped into a hole and got down low. Craig Delane joined him a few seconds later, landing on his knees, still carrying all his equipment.

Lieutenant Breckenridge turned to Craig Delane. "Call Major Cobb and tell him we've reached our objective."

"Yes, sir."

Craig Delane raised the walkie-talkie to his face, pressed the button, and spoke the code words assigned to Major Cobb. Lieutenant Breckenridge listened to Craig Delane's report as he gazed at the jungle ahead. He realized now that the Japs had retreated beyond that area and were off in the jungle someplace, regrouping and preparing for the next round.

But the GIs from the Twenty-third had won the first round. Lieutenant Breckenridge turned toward his men and cupped his hands around his mouth. *"All right, you guys!"* he yelled. *"Dig in where you are, and dig in deep!"*

Look for

GO FOR BROKE

next novel in THE RAT BASTARDS series
from Jove

coming in May!